REASONABLE SIN

A CARSON BRAND NOVEL #2

CRAIG RAINEY

Craig Rainey Creative, LLC
AUSTIN, TEXAS

Craig Rainey/Craig Rainey Creative, LLC
Austin, TX 78660
https://craigrainey.com

Reasonable Sin/ Craig Rainey -- 1st ed.
ISBN 978-1-7371820-0-9

OTHER CARSON BRAND NOVELS

STOLEN VALOR

DARK MOTIVE

SOVEREIGN RULE

NATIONS LAW

ALSO BY CRAIG RAINEY

MASSACRE AT AGUA CALIENTE

THE ART OF PROFESSIONAL SALES

HOODOO WAR

For David, A True Reader and Friend

When you can no longer believe what you see, look away.

CRAIG RAINEY

PROLOGUE

TRAFFIC WAS HEAVY ON THE PASEO DE LA REFORMA. Mexico City glowed silver and alabaster as the thin air filtered the rising Sun, cool breezes flowing in thin streams like an unpredictable thermocline in tropical waters.

Dr. Carlos Ricardo Cantu, PHD of Anthropology sat behind the wheel of his small sedan, tapping his fingers nervously to the barely audible tune on the radio. He brought the car to an awkward halt at a busy intersection near the crowded Avenue Juarez. He surveyed with an eager eye an American coffee shop teeming with patrons.

The previous night's end-of-semester celebration had stretched until early morning, leaving its mark on him in a throbbing head and weakened body chemistry. He would happily trade his overworked liver for a strong double shot latte right now. He had much to do. A late start and his weakened constitution caused him doubt that he would catch up.

If it hadn't been for that morning's urgent phone call demanding he attend an unscheduled meeting in the crowded heart of Mexico City, he might have called in anyway.

Traffic moved with a languid apathy as the signal light changed. He kept a measured following interval from the dirty pink taxi ahead of him.

In the distance, over the slow moving, heavy traffic, he could see red and blue spinning lights, and the dark blue uniforms of the *Policia Federal*, as they directed impatient drivers around the damaged road where a giant sink hole had swallowed several autos the night before.

Gradually, he reached the cordoned off disaster site where he presented his identification and a copy of the emailed credentials he was instructed to present to the authorities to gain access to the disaster area.

A stern-faced police officer scrutinized his paperwork before directing him to park his car behind a white portable building near the large, gaping maw which used to be the lined pavement of the *Paseo de la Reforma*.

He left his car, glancing at the large crowd of curious onlookers pressed against the temporary fencing surrounding the sink hole. Cantu fastened his aching eyes on the ground before him as he approached the front door of the corrugated metal container which served as the command post.

His shoes rang with a metal hollowness as he climbed the narrow steel stairs and entered the noisy interior of a clammy air-conditioned office.

The narrow room was filled with serious men and women engrossed in equally serious hushed conversations. He scanned the room until he recognized Dr. Ibanez, one of his colleagues from the *Universidad Iberoamericana*.

Dr. Ibanez was among a tightly packed group consisting of two city politicians in expensive suits, and several police officials in highly decorated uniforms.

Ibanez acknowledged Cantu with a smile and nodded his apologies to the group as he moved towards his colleague.

"You look like the dead warmed in a microwave, Dr. Cantu," he said in a low but amused tone.

Cantu nodded crossly, making a rolling gesture with his right hand, prompting Ibanez to get to the point.

"You have, of course, heard the reports of the sink hole appearing in one of the oldest roadways in Mexico City, but there is more."

Cantu nodded impatiently and Ibanez looked about the room as if to root out eavesdroppers.

"The event has unearthed a find of profound significance."

Dr. Cantu watched Ibanez with a steady gaze. He chose to exhibit a calm which would appear both reserved and considering while causing minimal anguish to his throbbing head.

Ibanez paused a moment as he measured Dr. Cantu's reaction to his intentionally vague preface to his exciting news. His posture sagged slightly at Cantu's stoic demeanor. He leaned in closer as he continued in a low and singularly urgent tone.

"This find is historic in its apparent age and what it says about the indigenous people who lived here more than twenty-thousand years ago."

Dr. Cantu rubbed his temples tenderly.

"I presume I am here to see and evaluate the find. Can we take a look now?" he asked wearily.

"Dr. Cantu," Ibanez barked in frustration. "The find is deteriorating as we speak."

Cantu fixed the other with a confused look.

"I don't understand," Cantu stammered slowly. "Why are we talking about this? I am needed elsewhere today."

"Put on those overgarments and we will make our way to the site."

Ibanez pointed at four yellow plastic bins containing clothes and heavy boots.

Dressed in the heavy boots and protective gear, Dr. Cantu, Dr. Ibanez, and two unimpressed guides, left the portable building, making their way towards the ragged edge of the sink hole.

With practiced efficiency the guides fitted Cantu and Ibanez with Swiss Seats and rigged them with self-belaying rappelling rigs. After a brief explanation of the equipment's workings the four men stepped to the rim of the sink hole. Turning their backs to the dark chasm, they leaned over the edge, descending into the abyss.

Awkwardly, Cantu struggled to remember the guides' instructions as he struggled to manipulate the self-belay mechanism, descending slowly into the deep hole. As his descent into the darkness smoothed, he looked fearfully below him. The chasm was deep enough that unfathomable shadows obscured his view of the bottom of the hole. The stoutness and seemingly ample strength of the self-belaying lowering mechanism provided him scant comfort from his fear as he descended steadily into what he perceived to be a dark bottomless pit.

He recalled from radio reports broadcast during his drive to the site that at least a dozen cars and trucks had fallen into the sinkhole during the collapse. Although he searched with dread at what he might see, he saw no vehicles nor debris. He guessed that the autos and maybe the victims remained at the bottom, within the impenetrable darkness.

As they dropped beyond the reach of the climbing Sun, Cantu's helmet light clicked on automatically. He guessed that the light was rigged with a photoelectric sensor.

As they continued their slow journey the LED light revealed the compacted dirt and jagged stones of a roughly formed wall which gradually curved away, leaving him dangling above a dark sea of emptiness.

Cantu realized they dropped into the large chamber of an expansive cavern. With a glance above, he estimated the streets and buildings sat atop a cavern roof no more than 15 to 20 meters thick. He grew worried that the sinkhole might have further weakened the strata above to the point that he might fall in danger of being buried in a larger collapse.

His heart pounded in his chest as the group descended for several more minutes until Cantu's feet finally rested on the floor of the cavern. He looked high above him to the surface, allowing a moment for his heart to slow its trip hammer tempo. They were easily 100 meters below street level, maybe more.

With deep calming breaths Cantu looked around him. Visible in the narrow beam of his helmet lamp, he counted 20 cars and trucks piled atop, and partially buried within the loose earth and stone that had collapsed beneath them. He saw no human remains. He saw only discarded plastic bags and other debris left behind by the rescue team who had apparently removed the bodies before their arrival.

The guides disengaged his harness and released the self-belay mechanism from the heavy rappelling rope. With only a glance confirming they were moving, the guides led the way from the center of the cavern towards the dark perimeter edge of the cavern chamber.

As the small group approached the edge of the broad cavern, darkness engulfed them, pierced only by the narrow beams from their helmet lights and the broader reach of the high-powered flashlights the guides wielded. Without the aid of their LED lights and the guides' handheld Q beams, they would have been blind in the pitch.

Travelling some thirty meters further, Cantu felt the cavern floor change from hard packed soil to a soft and sticky slime. His heavy boots squished and sucked at his feet as the floor grew increasingly more saturated. His nose was assailed by a combination of ancient sodden soil and the dankness of pungent mildew.

Their lights reflected off standing water before them. The guides altered their course slightly left then through a smooth entryway which fed into a smaller chamber. Cantu observed the arched entryway with interest. It was unquestionably man made as was the low room in which they moved.

The water was ankle deep in the narrow chamber. Cantu's waterproof boots protected his feet as he sloshed forward. He spotted four low openings ahead in the moist, glistening wall which he guessed led to other chambers within the cavern complex.

The guides handed Cantu one of their Q beams and gestured towards the nearest opening.

Cantu's glance moved from the guides to the dark entrances before him. Without a word he trained the light on the nearest opening and moved towards the passageway.

Ibanez followed closely.

The dirt ceiling of the passage beyond the narrow opening was lower than the entry chamber, forcing Cantu to stoop as he followed the narrow corridor beyond the entrance into a tight narrow room, hardly large enough for he and Ibanez to occupy together.

Cantu froze at what he saw, drawing a long breath once again to calm himself. On the walls around them were intricate cave paintings. These drawings, however, were unlike any Cantu had studied in his career. The hieroglyphs and images were foreign to those he had beheld and written about over the years. What he saw at first glance convinced him that much of the hypothesis written and accepted as fact about the peoples - and the accepted theories of the sociology of those peoples - were at risk of, and likely would be completely disproven.

Cantu leaned closer to the wall to examine the intricacies of the cave drawings. The detail was incredible. Most cave paintings he had studied were simplistic and organic to the landscape and nature of the artist's surroundings.

These were more technically detailed – more intellectually advanced.

He turned to his companion, blinding him with the Q beam.

"Are there more?" he asked Ibanez.

The junior professor shielded his eyes from the bright beam as he squinted at Cantu.

"I have seen only grainy photos taken by the rescue team who found them. They told me that each chamber here contains similar cave drawings."

Cantu grasped Ibanez's shoulders drawing him nearer.

"Each is as detailed and advanced as this one?" he asked with renewed excitement.

Ibanez nodded mutely.

Cantu looked at Ibanez only briefly as his interest faded in favor of this new find. The possibilities and importance of the find crowded out any other consideration.

He looked once more to the ancient drawings on the wall.

"What are these images here?" he asked of Ibanez, pointing to geometric shapes and unfamiliar winged creatures.

Ibanez made no reply. He knew of Cantu's knowledge and experience in the area. The question was rhetorical.

Cantu moved the Q beam from image to image methodically, slowly, and deliberately. Finally, he turned to Ibanez. Cantu considered his companion absently as his mind whirled with the mysteries of the find.

"You mentioned that the find was deteriorating as we speak," Cantu asked almost as an aside. "What did you mean?"

Ibanez smiled with genuine sorrow as he looked around him in a manner that conveyed to his colleague that the answer was self-evident.

"The water all around us is rising measurably. The collapse destroyed a containment barrier to a branch of the Mexico City Aquifer. The aquifer is flooding the cavern slowly although the flow is increasing steadily. It is believed that this breach may completely reconfigure the aquifer, placing our water supply and the city's population at serious risk."

"My god," Cantu muttered. He reached out a protective hand towards the cave drawings, the realization that he and Ibanez would likely be the only people ever to see these unique drawings in person heavy on his mind.

The wall was soft and moist. He quickly withdrew his hand as if stung by a bee. His palm came away with a small part of the cave drawings.

"No!" he cried.

He rotated his wrist as he looked at his hand in the light of the helmet LED. The ancient earthen tones used to create the colors of the drawing covered his hand. He had never seen the Sienna's and Ochres used by those ancients in a wet state. It was as if he was one of the ancient artists leaving his own message on the cave walls, the organic paints wet on his hands.

He rubbed his fingers together, the muddy yellows and oranges slick and cool to the touch. He detected the faint smell of a familiar earthy sweetness.

It may have been his hangover, but he submitted to a crazy whim. He touched his tongue to the mixture on his skin.

Ibanez watched in dismay.

What was the professor doing?

He watched as Cantu lifted his head, lowering his hand in a strange gesture of helpless supplication.

Cantu stared at Ibanez with a curiously blank stare. Suddenly a grin split Cantu's lips and his eyes widened in pleasure.

"I have never felt so happy," Dr. Cantu announced with a laugh. His voice was free of the hushed tones of awe and mystery they had held since their entering the sacred caves.

Ibanez smiled uncertainly. His companion was acting strangely. He was unsure how to react.

"It is a tremendous find, Dr. Cantu," Ibanez agreed, trying to raise his tone slightly to match his companion's new energy level. "We have very little time to record this find."

"I feel like I am floating in the air," Cantu announced, lifting his muddied hand above him with a flourish of glee. "Like a fantastical sprite or fairy."

"Are you still drunk?" Ibanez asked of his colleague, his words heavy with condescension.

"No," Dr. Cantu said brightly. "My headache is gone. I feel great."

Cantu touched his tongue once more to the paint and mud on his palm. He ignored Ibanez as he examined the free spinning of his rising good feelings. A bright euphoria lifted him, lightening his heart and freeing his mind.

He faced his frowning colleague once more.

"There is something in the paint," he said tenderly. "There is something in the earth here. Try it."

With an eloquent gesture, Cantu smeared mud on Ibanez's face.

Ibanez shrunk from the gentle swipe, but not before he smelled and tasted the smeared mess. He immediately felt a giddy lightness behind his eyes.

When the guides finally entered the small chamber, impatient at their charges' long absence, they discovered the Doctors hugging, murmuring their mutual love and respect for one another.

By the time the guides managed to bring the helplessly distracted professors back to the surface, both exhibited alarming signs of giddiness, intoxication, and most puzzling, memory loss. Neither seemed to remember his name.

Once returned to the collapse site headquarters office, impatient officials put questions to the professors. The professors found no urgency in sharing their findings with the officials. Contrarily, neither of them seemed to remember where he had been nor how he had returned from the site.

He was three days in hospital before Ibanez was able to recall any of that day's events. When he was finally released from medical observation, he left the hospital on foot and found a phone two blocks away in a small grocery store. He placed a hurried call to his cousin Adrian.

That evening Dr. Damian Ibanez sat with his cousin Adrian Salado at a hotel bar near the sink hole site.

Ibanez downed a Tequila shot then looked around him impatiently. His cousin was frustrating him. How many times would he have to tell the story? He was afraid of someone overhearing and having him confined to a mental ward.

"He licked his hand," Ibanez repeated to his cousin. "And he suddenly became euphoric and giddy. I thought it was a hangover. He smeared it on my face, and I lost three days to whatever it was."

"All of this from licking his hand?" his cousin repeated for the third time.

"Yes. Yes. Yes."

Ibanez pointed at his empty shot glass. The bartender moved forward to refill the glass.

Adrian Salado sat silently as he watched the bartender work. He took a long moment, thinking about what he had heard. He knew the dangers of acting without thinking first. He valued his life and that made him cautious.

A glimmer of an idea flickered then grew from the general array of an idea into the more detailed shape of a distinct plan. As his understanding grew, his thoughts arranged themselves in precise order as he carefully constructed the presentation he could give to his boss, Don Fabian Aleman Castillo, head of the Pavoroso Cartel.

Adrian had to be certain he was accurate when he presented his idea to the powerful Cartel Don. He decided he would first act with caution. He would speak with his uncle, an older, wiser man of experience and intellect. He had ties deep within the Cartel. He also owned the largest excavation and earth moving company in Mexico.

1

CARSON BRAND LOOKED AROUND HIM FOR the hundredth time. The despair he felt was magnified by the hopelessness of escaping his prison cell. His first days there had seemed insupportable within the choking stench of death and human waste that permeated the stone walls and dirt floor of his prison cell. After generations of bearing silent witness to the suffering and hopelessness of those who had borne their final days there, the ancient cellar had become the embodiment of the hell housed within. Since those first days the wretched stink of the cell had long since faded into the background of his increased misery and pain.

For the first time in his life Brand felt a helplessness to affect the circumstances of his life's path. Even now, no more than a small spark of hope accompanied the daily hell that was his life. He despaired as every prisoner before him who had lived and died there.

Hours and days in thought-filled solitude had provided no insight towards finding the pattern that could be key to his escape. The longer he stayed, the more deranged his troubled imagination, the more remote his chances of finding the weakness in his prison that might yield his escape.

With the stolidness of the walls of this dungeon, his only chance for survival was hidden within the routine followed by his captors. To his retreating sensibilities that pattern combination seemed beyond his ability to solve.

Despite the irrational spark of hope that refused to leave him in peace, he knew he was beyond rescue or escape. His captors would kill him. It was a certainty.

He cursed as that small hopeful spark fired now. His chances were unimaginably poor. If he was to perish, better now than to abide in an insensate world of hellish torture and sickeningly torrid living conditions between those agonizing torture sessions. A clean death was preferable to being torn apart piece by piece until there was nothing left of him but those base elements that scarcely define a living creature.

He heard the guards shuffling around outside the thick plank wooden door of his cell. He looked blankly at the scratches in the rough wood where pervious occupants had clawed until their nails pulled free from their fingers.

As had been their habit every morning at this time, the guards left his cell unguarded to sneak off to the kitchen behind the main house where they loaded plates with breakfast food.

They chided him often knowing that the fragrance tortured him horribly. The irresistibly beckoning aromas incited an Amazonian-level rain forest deluge in his mouth, and a gnawing, grinding pain in his gut. Hunger even now knotted his stomach cruelly.

He pushed the grumblings of his stomach and the irresistible desire for food to the back of his troubled mind. The ever-present pain and soreness resulting from weeks of torture helped to distract him from his incessant hunger, but not much.

He groaned as he writhed to adjust his prone position on the cold floor. There was no bed, no chair, no bucket or pan for his waste. Tears burned his eyes as the memory of that day returned. Regret at trusting her was a palpable thing, flooding his mind in a wave of self-loathing. What was left of his manhood berated him for his ill-placed belief in her – or anyone who could hurt him as she did. He had risked his life for her. He had lost everything dear to him for her. He had mourned and plotted revenge for her when he presumed her dead. He had felt shame that at some level he had been relieved that she was gone from his life. That night had changed all of that.

Unwelcome, the events leading to his capture in the Rod Dog Saloon parking lot filled his world as it had so many times since the day she handed him over to the Cartel.

He frowned as the compounding pain of the memory rankled him. He had always trusted in his ability to react and overcome. An unaccustomed helplessness had consumed him that night. None of his training had helped.

2

(3 weeks earlier)

CHRISTINA WALKED WITH BRAND ARM IN arm as they left Rod Dog Saloon, leaning into him. Brand felt elated. Her curves pressed against him, reminding him of their nights together. The cool night air and having Christina with him gave him the most acute sense of satisfaction. He had believed her dead, placed back into the human trafficking hell from which she had narrowly escaped as a girl.

He led the way to his truck, parked in front of the strip center bar.

She pulled on his arm.

"I'm parked on the other side," she purred with what he could only feel was the promise of a wonderful night.

"I'll walk you to your car and you can follow me," he offered.

She nodded her agreement.

Brand looked into her eyes for a moment, unsure of the look she gave him. The cloud that had darkened her already dusky eyes passed as quickly as it had appeared.

He followed her to the opposite side of the building where several cars were parked in the alley between the bar and a large vacant lot.

"Here I am," she said, pointing to a black Mercedes coupe.

"Nice car," he observed as four large men appeared from out of the darkness.

Christina stepped away from Brand.

"Sorry, Brand," she said with real regret. "I had no choice."

Brand stared at her in disbelief.

As one, the men converged upon him, grabbing his arms. He struggled briefly. His resistance ceased when they pressed a gun into his back, leading him to a black SUV. Slip-tying his hands and rolling him into the back of the vehicle, they took him away.

Brand tried to trace their route, tracking their turns and stops with his knowledge of the city's streets and freeways. He was successful only for a few minutes before he lost track of right and left turns, stops at signal lights, and stop signs. From his bound position in the back of the dark SUV he saw only streetlights and the dim silhouettes of trees through the darkened windows.

He guessed that they headed south. He knew they were on a highway because of their increased speed and the grinding of the tires on grooved pavement. They travelled several hours until the SUV slowed, turning onto a rough dirt road.

As they drove, he listened to his captors as they spoke to one another in Spanish. He did not understand what they said. He picked up on single words and small phrases but was unable to follow their quiet conversations. He got the impression that he and his fate did not factor into their interests. He suspected that these grim men were accustomed to hellish deeds and gave the matter no more regard than a waiter did a meal delivered to a table in a restaurant.

Despite his predicament, Brand smiled without humor at the comparison. Who was he being delivered to? Was he the main course?

The SUV finally came to a halt. The driver killed the engine, leaving a strained moment filled only with the sounds of his captors exiting the truck with four slammed doors. The rear lift gate swung open. Brand remained in darkness because the dome lights had been disabled. They pulled him unceremoniously from the vehicle and placed him roughly on his feet. The pull ties were cut from his ankles, and he was dragged along into the gloom beyond the vehicle.

Brand ground his teeth. So, this was the end. He would die in the acrid dust, shot between the eyes. He felt no bravery, nor did he suffer regret. He felt only numbness and loss. His efforts against the cartel, even with the noblest of intentions, had been inconsequential. The idea that he had once believed his life had a purpose and that purpose was greater than himself seemed as ludicrous as it seemed vain. He decided to meet death as well as he could. These men demonstrated a disconnection learned from experience. To them he was just another task. Whether he died bravely or died as a crying blubbering coward, he knew they wouldn't care. Why would they judge the rat caught in a trap?

He was wrong. He was not killed that night. Two of the men donned night vision goggles, dragging him through a narrow tunnel entrance made of welded fifty-five-gallon drums. The narrow steel tunnel fed below ground into a larger subterranean chamber.

They moved easily through the absolute pitch of the tunnel, dragging Brand stumbling and bumping into unseen obstacles. He was certain they enjoyed his blind journey, watching him blunder along through their NVG's.

The descending angle of the dirt floor indicated they moved deeper into the earth. Brand knew they would soon reach a level plane before the tunnel rose once more to ground level. He had crossed into Mexico by a similar tunnel some time before. That tunnel had been flooded, and Christina had clung to him, terrified by the cold dark water. This tunnel was dry other than a thin sticky film of mud at the bottom.

Brand knew they were crossing beneath the Rio Grande River. His captors were taking him back to Mexico.

At the other end of the tunnel, they shoved him through another steel tube of barrels. He welcomed the light fresh breeze and a comparative clear vision after his blind journey through the tunnel.

They continued moving on for a few rods until they came to a caliche road where a car awaited them. They locked him in the trunk. The space was cramped, and the bumpy roads tossed him around roughly as they travelled for several more hours.

When the car finally slowed, ending its torturous motion, Brand believed they were deep within the Mexican interior. The trunk was opened, and he was dragged out and dropped onto a gravel roadbed. He looked around him, squinting in the mid-morning light. He was in the driveway of a large *'dobe* hacienda.

Shiny expensive sports cars were parked before the huge house. Verdant grounds with rich landscaping surrounded the house on all sides. Brand was lifted to his feet and led/dragged away from the car. Armed guards watched the prisoner escort with professional disinterest.

His captors led him around the side of the house and into the cellar of a small outbuilding beside the large hacienda. Stone stairs led to a basement door below the building. He was shoved through the door. At the end of a short hallway, he saw a rough-hewn wooden door with a large rusty padlock securing it by a rusty metal clasp.

With a rattle, one of the guards produced a ring of keys and struggled with the lock for a moment until it opened with a reluctant groan. The door swung open, and he was thrown to the dirt floor.

He twisted in the filth and dirt until he was able to balance upright on his knees. The cellar smelled of death, urine, feces, and dank earth.

He was uncertain how much of the human waste smell was the room and how much was in his pants. He had been trapped in the two vehicles for many hours.

3

FABIAN ALEMAN CASTILLO SMILED CONFIDENTLY as Michael Cervantes, his longtime lieutenant, informed him that Carson Brand was confined to the cellar below his guest house.

Castillo smiled at his private triumph. He took a moment to bask in his accomplishment. He looked away from Cervantes, unwilling to reveal the true joy that this news brought him.

Castillo's predecessor, Pablo Rojas, had prided himself in his attention to detail. He was a man who continually preached the superiority of the leader who attended to those details. He was often critical of Castillo's tendency to visit retribution upon those who failed him. The former boss had believed that if you want something done you should do it yourself. When it came to the men who served the Cartel, Rojas was the Edward Deming of the crime world. He rarely took a life for a lackluster performance.

When Rojas' subordinates failed, he had seen personally to the capture of Carson Brand, the American spy. His carefully detailed plans, however, failed to save him. Even the large force of handpicked men he had taken with him had failed to save him. And now Castillo was in charge. If Rojas had properly motivated his men and left the dirty work to those who feared failure, maybe Castillo would not be running the organization today.

In addition to assuming the role of head of the *Pavoroso* Cartel, he had successfully united all three major Cartels, creating the most powerful crime syndicate in the world.

Rojas had told him personally that the idea of uniting the Cartels was nothing more than "Blue Sky." Rojas was given to using Corporate American Terms. Rojas had considered himself more a CEO than a crime boss.

Castillo believed the vanity of Rojas did more to kill him than Carson Brand ever could. The Cartel was a criminal enterprise. Castillo was wise in that he never allowed himself to forget that. There is no C suite architecture in his deadly organization. There was no golden parachute for outgoing heads of the organization. This was a life of contrition. The ultimate survival of the fittest scenario.

Castillo took his seat behind his large desk. Despite his resolve to remain soberly composed, a smile brightened his cruel face. With a gesture he had summoned Brand before him. During his reign Rojas had access to the same people and resources as Castillo. Rojas had wielded the same authority as Castillo. Rojas, however, lacked the intellect and control of his organization that Castillo possessed.

"Does he stink of piss and shit," Castillo asked of Cervantes with a sneer of displeasure. This was not his first prisoner delivery.

"Si."

"Clean up the dog before you bring him into my house."

"Si, Patron."

Cervantes withdrew from the large room where Castillo controlled the operations of his organization. Castillo pointed at one of the large windows in his office. An armed sentry watched the boss intently.

Castillo beckoned him silently.

The man moved quickly to 10-foot-tall double doors leading to the wide covered porch beyond. The sentry entered, silently taking his place before Castillo's ornate wooden desk.

"Bring three guards to me. A prisoner is to be brought here and I want you and those men to secure him."

The sentry nodded, leaving with a rapid step once more by the large double doors. Closing them silently, he was immediately gone from view.

Within half an hour Brand stood wearily before the Cartel boss flanked by four armed guards. His newly provided damp, ill-fitting clothes, and disheveled wet hair hinted at the brutal cleansing he had received from the thugs with a high-pressure hose.

Cervantes stood to the side of the group, watching intently. He knew of this prisoner's killing of his old boss and the miraculous escape he had achieved afterwards. Cervantes' hatred for the man was obvious to all including the prisoner.

Cervantes relived a private fantasy he had nurtured since the day he had learned of the killing of his boss. It included, among many things, a slow and excruciating death for the American. He had loved Rojas like a brother. To the thug, the American's murdering him was a personal thing.

Cervantes glanced at his gloating boss. He was certain Castillo would not last as long as his predecessor. The man was too arrogant. He mistreated the men, punishing failure with openly displayed cruelty, making each an example for the others.

Cervantes doubted Castillo's inevitable death would elicit as strong an emotion within the cartel as the loss of the Don who had preceded him. He tolerated Castillo because his life depended upon it. That being said, no one retired from the job. All were removed feet first. Unless he missed his guess, Castillo would fade away more quickly than most.

"Mr. Brand."

Castillo addressed the prisoner from behind his desk.

"Your days of being a pain in the ass have come to an end. Although you are a nuisance, I want to thank you for helping me ascend to my current station."

Brand eyed the cartel boss critically but made no reply.

"You have nothing to say for yourself?"

"Thanks for the shower."

Castillo nodded to the guard.

The sentry Castillo had initially summoned to his office struck Brand in the midsection with an AR style weapon.

Brand doubled over but was held upright by the guards.

"It would be wise," Castillo spat angrily. "If you watch your mouth, asshole."

Brand inhaled painfully and straightened once more.

"Understood," he said in a faint voice.

"I have many questions for you," Castillo continued, his tone mild as he mastered his rage. "You will tell me who you work for and what your federal government has learned about our operation from you."

Brand nodded.

During his capture by Rojas, Brand had learned that the Cartel believed him an American government operative trying to infiltrate their organization. At the time, he had been a construction worker protecting a girl. Later he had been enlisted by the DEA as a private contractor. He had completed some training with the organization, but it had been made clear to him that he was not an agent nor even officially affiliated with any federal agency.

Castillo construed the nod as agreement with his description of the man's role within the American Federal Government.

"Good," he said with a triumphant smile. "The more easily you answer my questions, the less painfully you will die."

Brand looked at the rich hardwood flooring. He saw no way out of this. He saw no point in subterfuge. He knew his death would come no matter what he said or did from this moment forward.

"Answer the question and let's end this quickly."

Brand looked at the floor.

Castillo shook his head sadly. His appearance of regret belied the gratitude he felt at Brand's reticence. He wanted the man to suffer. He wanted him to linger in a region of anguish as long as he could be kept alive. His suffering would soothe the ache of humiliation he had caused him as the leader of a once feared and dreaded cartel. His remains would be hung in the public square so to speak. More accurately, he would be hung from under a bridge somewhere public. The agent would be a grisly warning against any other American interference in his operation.

He spoke with an almost tender regard to the damned captive.

"Your accommodations are significant in the history and the esteemed occupants they hosted before you arrived here. This dungeon was built by the Spanish for chieftains of the indigenous tribes who flourished here before the arrival of the Conquistadors. It is said that Atahualpa himself suffered under the ministering of Spanish inquisitors before he acquiesced to Spanish rule.

"More recently, rebellious Mexican politicians and, of course, rival cartel leaders have languished in our historic prison. Not all died, but many have. As you writhe in the remains of those before you, appreciate those others as they surely appreciated those who came before them.

"This is your last chance to speak willingly."

Brand looked only to the floor, his mind working at a way to get at the cartel boss, a last strike before his death. He saw no opportunity.

To Castillo it was clear that the prisoner would not talk immediately. The thought of what was to become of the stubborn prisoner pleased him, but Castillo cut the air with an impatient gesture and spoke to the guards as if he were annoyed.

"Take him back to the cellar," Castillo ordered in Spanish.

4

THAT INITIAL MEETING WITH CASTILLO SEEMED like it had been weeks before. It may have been more. It might be less. Brand had since lost track of time. His receding sensibilities told him that he could not survive much longer under the conditions to which he had been subjected.

He was still alive, and mostly lucid, so he deduced within the haze of his misery, that he had probably been imprisoned for less than a month.

During his confinement, he had been beaten and starved. The bright lights in the cellar had burned 24/7 for many days since his arrival. He could not sleep except in short moments when exhaustion dragged him into unconsciousness.

The beatings had started with his face and head. With the first beating his eyes had swollen shut, rendering him nearly blind. That had been a mixed blessing in that the lights no longer plagued him.

When the physical beatings failed to drag any information from him, his captors resorted to feeding him stale food tainted with some type of hidden filth or debilitating chemical that caused him to wretch and pass bloody diarrhea.

He had stopped eating after that. Following a week of self-imposed starvation, the guards had brought him a large meal free of whatever had been added to make him sick. Even with assurances from the guards that the food was untainted, he resisted until he finally gave in to irresistible hunger and the beckoning aroma from the filled plate.

Caution ignored for the moment, he had eaten the plate clean despite his misgivings. He was surprised when uncontrollable diarrhea and vomiting did not follow the meal.

Afterwards, he was as comfortable as he had been since his arrival. At least he was until the cellar door opened, and a large sweaty Mexican entered. He looked Brand over with open interest. He approached the prisoner with a boyish smile.

Brand relaxed reluctantly, wary of the unaccustomed friendly intent of the newcomer. This new man was the first of his captors to show any level of warm regard or pleasantness. He invested a few moments to getting acquainted with the prisoner, even sympathizing with his plight. He asked what he could do to help Brand to be more comfortable. He regretted with believable emotion that he could do nothing more for him.

In a flash, the stranger's face transformed into a mask of maniacal fury. He kicked Brand in the ribs as hard as he could. Brand suspected that he felt a rib break under the blow. He rolled away the short distance where the filthy wall stopped him. He covered his head and pulled his legs up to protect his midsection from the continuing kicks delivered by this new tormentor.

The new man spoke as he kicked Brand in the back and sides.

"I am Rabino," the sweaty man announced, his breath coming in gasps. "You will not leave here alive, but you will stay alive for a long time until I decide to allow you the relief of death."

With one last kick Rabino stepped back to survey his handiwork.

"Sleep well, *Volio*. We will begin your new journey of self-realization tomorrow morning."

The big man spat on Brand, turning on his heel. He stomped heavily from the cell, slamming the door with a terse word for the sentries outside.

Brand could not stifle the groans. Through his pain he heard Rabino's receding footsteps outside. Every breath was a knife sharp agony. Every move a white-hot poker.

The next chapter of his torture began the next morning. Brand had never experienced pain like Rabino was capable of ministering. Most of the injuries Rabino inflicted were internal, causing Brand to feel weak and sick all the time. His meals no longer contained foreign toxins but were limited to stale beans and rice and one metal cup of water each day.

Despite his faculties being diminished by the torture and poor food, he maintained a rough awareness of Rabino's and the sentries' schedules and habits.

Rabino's introductory threat of his tortured death convinced Brand that his only chance for survival was to find any gap in procedure or lapse in vigilance on the part of his captors.

Rabino limited his torture sessions to only a few hours in the middle of the day. Brand was certain that Rabino knew that the treatment he administered would kill him if it were plied for longer than a few hours each day. Rabino never lingered to appreciate his handiwork. It was almost as if he punched a time clock and was reluctant to stay one second longer than required.

It took only a few days of Rabino's torture sessions before there was a lag in the guards' vigilance towards him. Brand got the impression that they believed his will was being reduced to a sufficiently incapacitated condition where he was unable to resist or attempt to escape his incarceration.

Over the next few days, it required no acting skill to feign acquiescence or helplessness. He raged inside, beneath the agony, but he showed no resistance to the abuse nor to the sentries' discipline. He appeared a broken and lost vessel.

Whether intentional or not, the gamble worked. Eventually the guards rarely locked the stiff, rusty, padlock on the door to his cell anymore, confident in what they perceived to be a broken man with a broken spirit, crushed by the Sadist, Rabino.

This morning, as usual, the two guards moved away from the prisoner's door to receive their morning meal. Their voices receded into the distance as they left the outer corridor.

With a groan, Brand rose unsteadily and tested the door. As he hoped, it was unlocked and swung open stiffly on squeaky metal hinges. He peered around the edge of the door. The narrow hallway was empty. He stepped into the hall and closed the door behind him. He hobbled uncertainly along the short corridor, then up the few stairs to ground level. After his long time on the cold damp floor of the cellar, the effort caused his legs and ankles to cramp. His entire body screamed from his injuries, resisting his efforts to move.

At the top of the stairs, he peered around the grounds. He saw only the lush greenery of well-manicured and landscaped foliage, but no Cartel thugs. The back of the large house shone with large windows, but he saw no one looking through them. He moved his gaze towards the back of the property. A short distance from where he stood, the lush grounds surrendered their greenery for the rough sage and low trees of the semi-arid region beyond.

He felt certain that he would not get far in that rough country before he was recaptured or died from natural dangers.

Frustrated at the forces arrayed against him, including nature, he ruled out the desert as a direction of escape. Stepping carefully, he circled the small building with a limping pace. He kept the small building between himself and the main house.

Pausing at the corner, he surveyed the circular drive where he had arrived so long ago. The parking area was empty save for a shiny conversion van with a gaudy paint job parked at the nearest edge of the driveway.

Desperation guided his decisions. He saw the van as his only hope. If he could steal it, he might take his chances on the road.

Weakly, he pushed himself from the stucco wall and staggered with a lurching stride towards the vehicle. Through swollen eyelids he cast dim glances around him, alert for anyone who might notice his escape.

He arrived at the side of the van without hearing an alarm raised inside the house. He pulled weakly at the slide handle of the side door. He cast a thankful eye to the heavens when the handle moved in his hand. The side door slid open. Inside the van were stacked boxes with labels indicating they contained electronic equipment. An array of tools was racked on the driver side wall of the van.

Brand stepped in and pulled the door closed behind him. He stifled a painful groan as he crawled towards the front seat of the van. He spotted keys in the ignition. He moved to climb over the boxes between him and the driver seat when he heard a voice and footfalls approaching the van. He withdrew among the boxes as the back door opened. He was adequately concealed from whomever opened the back doors and was not discovered.

"*Volveré con las piezas lo antes posible*," the voice said to an unseen person.

Brand didn't speak the language, but he recognized a tone of good-natured humor. With distinct thuds, the man loaded additional boxes into the rear of the van. He closed the rear door with a violent slam. He heard crunching footfalls as the unseen man moved forward towards the driver side door.

Clenching his teeth against the pain, Brand moved as quietly and as rapidly as possible towards the back of the van, carefully moving boxes then replacing them behind him. As he attempted to move the two boxes the man had loaded into the back, he noticed that they were heavier than those up front with none of the colorful labeling.

Brand had hardly concealed himself behind the last box when the driver side door opened and a man with dark hair settled into the driver seat. He started the engine and mashed his foot on the accelerator. The tires spit gravel and the van pitched forward violently. Fighting to regain his balance, Brand strained against the pain raking his screaming nerves as the van swayed crazily, speeding away from the house.

The driver's cell phone rang, and he answered.

"*Hola.*"

There was a long pause as the driver listened to the caller on the other end of the call.

"*Si.*"

Brand waited breathlessly, certain that the driver was being recalled. His disappearance had been discovered.

"*No soy un servicio de entrega de alimentos.*"

Brand struggled to make sense of the conversation.

"*Si. Me llevaré comida a Pedro y a sus hombres, pero me debes.*"

The driver ended the call and laughed dramatically as he turned on the radio. Loud hip hop music filled the van as the vehicle careened along the dirt road.

Brand sighed with relief. His disappearance had not yet been noticed. He imagined the guards sitting outside the closed door of his cell, certain that the smells of their meal tortured their prisoner cruelly. They would expect no protest or acting out from their captive. Brand rarely protested or made any noises, so it would be some time before they grew suspicious of the silence within the cell.

The cramped conditions amongst the boxes taxed his weakened muscles and aching joints. Brand quietly and slowly repositioned the boxes around him, making more room for his tortured body in the cramped rear of the van.

Despite his discomfort, he grew curious about the recently added boxes. As before, he noticed that they seemed heavier than the others through which he had climbed over and around. Upon further inspection, he saw they were stout, unmarked corrugated cardboard boxes, the tops taped closed. He examined them in the dim light. As before, he noted they had no labels to identify their contents. They seemed constructed with a more utilitarian design than the others.

The weight was telling. He had his suspicions of what the boxes might contain. At first, he controlled his curiosity by giving his attention to the driver and the van's stilted progress. His chief concern was to escape his captors undetected. With an iron will he pushed his curiosity of the boxes' contents to the back of his mind and gave his attention to the erratic movement of the van, his suspicions of what the boxes contained worked on him.

Irresistibly, his attention returned to the boxes again and again. It occurred to him that only a few things could have the weight and the dense feel he felt from the boxes.

Finally, he gave in to his curiosity. He decided to learn what the boxes held. His remaining caution warned him that he should not risk the noise of breaking tape or ripping open one of the boxes. Despite the loud music, the driver might hear and be alerted to his presence.

Brand looked around him for a sharp object, perhaps a knife or screwdriver. He found a box cutter in a leather tool bag next to him. He carefully turned one of the boxes on its side and made a small rectangular incision in the side of the box. He turned the box at an angle where he could see through the slit. He saw the unmistakable color and texture of American currency packed tightly within.

He extended his incision and cut a three-sided square in the box about three inches tall and wide. He opened the square flap like a door, exposing stacks of money. He fished out a stack of hundreds, bound with a bank wrapper. The label read $10,000.00.

He pocketed the money and closed the little flap door. He searched the tool bags for tape but found none. He did find staples in one of the leather pockets, the type used to tack electrical wires to a wall. He pressed three of them into the box, binding the cut edges together on all three sides.

He shook his head, wondering why he had decided to steal Cartel money. He told himself that it was compensation for his imprisonment and torture. He experienced a twinge of guilt at the theft, which he pushed beneath a veneer of self-righteous entitlement. He considered taking more but resisted the urge.

He gave his complete attention to the movement of the van. There were no windows, and he could see little through the boxes towards the front and he had no view through the van's windshield. He had no idea how long the van would be on the road. The time was of concern. The longer he spent trapped in the van the more likely he would be trapped when the call finally came alerting the driver to check his payload. He did not know where the van would stop. Would he be met by a group of thugs?

Some fifteen minutes later the vehicle careened sharply to the left. With a lurch and a roar of grinding tires, the van skidded to a halt. The driver rolled down the window.

Brand peered between the boxes and watched as someone handed the driver several greasy bags. The smell of food tortured Brand to the point he debated climbing the box barrier and cutting the driver's throat with the box cutter. He clenched his teeth and closed his eyes, trying desperately to block out the aroma. The van lurched forward as the driver returned to the road, continuing upon his previous route.

They drove another ten minutes or more. With habitual disregard for the vehicle or his cargo, the driver stopped the van with a grinding slide of tires. He killed the engine and opened the driver door. He leaned in to collect the bags of food. He slammed the van door and Brand heard his footsteps as he walked away from the van.

Brand opened the rear door. He looked out carefully. He was in a large caliche parking lot filled with earth hauler tractor trailer rigs. Many of the tractors' engines idled while others were being started with a whining whir of high-powered ignition motors.

He knew that idling trucks and the sound of trucks being started indicated that the convoy would be moving out soon.

Brand slipped from the van, closing the door behind him. He approached one of the trailers squarely from the rear. If the driver happened to be looking, he wouldn't spot him in the mirrors. With an effort that left him breathless, he climbed the rear gate and slipped under the canvas cover. He burrowed under a thin layer of black sweet-smelling earth until only his nose and mouth were exposed.

Minutes passed, the delay seeming endless to Brand. Finally, the truck engine growled to life joining the sounds of other trucks mobilizing and leaving the large parking lot. Brand waited anxiously until the truck finally eased forward. He risked a look out the back from under the tarp. He saw no trucks following the one in which he hid. He guessed that his was the last truck in the convoy.

5

CAPTAIN RANDALL SURVEYED THE CORDON of green uniformed Border Patrol Officers, mixed with casually dressed DEA agents, and county uniforms. The information seemed legitimate. It was, in fact, the most credible piece of intelligence they had ever received about a Cartel drug shipment.

Reports from deeply placed infiltrators within the criminal organization insisted that the information came directly from Fabian Aleman Castillo, the new head of the cartel.

Randall glanced at his wristwatch. The time read 5:25PM, five minutes until the shipment was scheduled to enter the international crossing point at Del Rio, Texas.

He looked down the cordon of agents and officers lined across the bridge, blocking the entry lanes of the border crossing terminal. A small number of cars and pedestrians were being processed as they crossed into and out of Mexico.

Traffic was light for a weekday after five, he noted.

He heard the convoy before he saw it. *Ciudad Acuna* was clearly visible across the international bridge, crowding the southern bank of the *Rio Bravo*. The ramshackle buildings of the border town hid the heavy vehicles from sight.

As the low rumble of inbound tractor trailers grew louder, the officers on the line displayed nervous anticipation for what was to come.

During his twenty-four years with Customs and Border Patrol, Captain Randall had been party to numerous drug shipment seizures along the length of the border. He doubted the approaching trucks would carry the shipment they expected. The Cartel would never so openly display the presence of a drug shipment. The lengths drug traffickers went to disguise their transport, and the technology they used to do it was jaw dropping. The job had grown almost insurmountable for border officials already stretched thin with the red tape of the wave of illegals flooding the border.

CBP employed the timeless weapon against the drug runners, drug sniffing dogs - they had three Belgian Malinois brought in just for this event. They also employed an array of installed and portable electronic drug detecting apparatus.

Cartel traffickers were remarkably knowledgeable about the tech border officers used to apprehend drug shipments. Approaching the international crossing with large trucks at a specified time was not a consideration Randall was willing to believe. Still, the report was convincing enough that Randall mustered personnel from every LEA he could for the rendezvous.

He keyed his radio.

"Stay alert men," he muttered grimly into the handset.

This was potentially a distraction for the real shipment, he considered with apprehension.

Randall looked over the bridge rail. Dozens of green and white Border Patrol vehicles lined the river bank each way as far as he could see.

The first of the large trucks appeared at the Mexico end of the International Bridge. By the sound of the moving trucks, the officials on the other side were allowing the big vehicles through without inspection or the standard border crossing routine.

This troubled Randall. It was widely known that the Cartel controlled most of the Mexican government. Without official authorization, the Mexican border agents would not open their gates to a private shipping firm. Mexican border officers were not a part of a policing agency, but rather a public service organization, they followed guidelines mutually agreed upon by both countries. Opening the border in this way violated that agreement. The border was open at all points, but it was understood that protocol was maintained at the crossing points.

The first of the trucks came into view, obviously heavily laden, and slowly approaching the U.S. checkpoint. More trucks followed closely behind until the bridge was filled with single cab tractors pulling tarped open trailers. They appeared to be earth and gravel haulers.

Randall stopped counting at fifty trucks. He saw more mounting the narrow bridge. The first truck stopped at the American checkpoint with a whoosh of air brakes.

Officers surrounded the truck and began a standard vehicle search. The drug dogs eagerly pulled canine officers towards the truck.

As he watched the officers release the tarp securing the payload, three sedans with US government plates pulled into the reserved official parking spots near the CBP control building. Nearly a dozen men and women in suits quickly exited the vehicles and hurried towards Randall.

The first man to arrive produced a badge identifying him as Homeland Security.

"I am agent Dan Wilkerson. We need you to cease and desist, Captain Randall."

The next person, a woman in a dark pantsuit, produced a U.N. I.D. badge.

"I am Aadhya Maddukuri, envoy for the United Nations special council for International Border Divergence. You have no authority to detain these trucks."

"I am doing my job, Ms. Maddukuri. You have no authority to intervene."

Randall's reply elicited a smirk from the U.N. official.

"Prior to midnight last night you were correct. Apparently, you did not receive the memo from your higher up. The new president signed an executive order opening both U.S. continental borders as of midnight."

Maddukuri produced a stapled sheaf of papers from her slung attaché.

"Fortunately for you, Captain Randall, I have an extra copy."

She handed the paperwork to Randall.

The captain scanned the pages as one of his officers approached the group.

"Captain," the officer asked uncertainly, looking at the suited bureaucrats. "The first truck is clean. The dogs are finding nothing."

Captain Randall turned the stapled sheaf over and put the pages back in order. He crushed them as he looked at the officer.

"Call the men off. The trucks are cleared to enter United States of America Sovereign territory."

He glared at the U.N. official as he ended his order to the officer.

The officer hesitated as he considered what he had been ordered to do.

"Pass the word, Lieutenant."

The officer turned away with a growing expression of frustration and returned to his team.

Captain Randall stood with the suited visitors, watching each truck speed through the covered lanes of the border check station. He counted 165 in all. After the last had cleared his checkpoint, Randall turned to return to his office.

"Captain Randall," Maddukuri said to his back.

Randall turned on his heel.

"What else do you want?" he demanded tersely.

She produced a pocket constitution and held it up for the captain to see.

"The 100-mile border buffer zone is no longer lawful. I suggest you and your men learn the 4th amendment of your U.S. Constitution: The right of the people to be secure in their persons, houses, papers, and effects, against unreasonable searches and seizures, shall not be violated, and no warrants shall issue, but upon probable cause, supported by oath or affirmation, and particularly describing the place to be searched, and the persons or things to be seized."

She returned the book to her attaché.

"Your officer said it himself. There is no probable cause or evidence to support a further search of these vehicles."

Captain Randall considered the smug woman for a moment before he spoke.

"It was just reported that one of my officers was accosted inside our headquarters by a woman who matches your description. Get your asses off my border station before I have you detained, and strip searched."

6

CARSON BRAND AWAKENED SLOWLY. His thoughts came to him sluggishly, as if he were in a world of molasses. He had cottonmouth, assuring him he had drunk a lot of alcohol. He felt countless aches and pains throughout his body. Incredibly, he was experiencing a significant level of discomfort caused by nothing he could recall. Curiously, he felt a profound sense of well-being.

He looked around him. He was in a bed in what appeared to be a bedroom in a mobile home. Beside him he saw the lump of someone under the covers, but only long blonde hair showed over the top of the bed spread. He had no memory of how he had gotten there nor who the person next to him was.

He smiled as a warm glow relaxed him. He nestled back into the pillow. He was content. He felt a happiness that filled his heart. Neither the symptoms of his hangover, nor the deep throbbing pains in his body concerned him at all. He smiled at the water-stained ceiling. He was possessed with the feeling that he had everything to look forward to in life. He felt pleased with himself and all he observed.

A movement under the covers gave warning that his companion was awake. Lean tanned arms with tightly balled fists stretched above the covers. They were heavily tattooed with a multicolored, multi-subject mural. The outstretched arms lowered to the top of the blankets revealing the face of a blonde woman. She squinted at Brand and favored him with a broad grin.

"Good morning, pig pen," she greeted him with a laugh. "How'd you sleep?"

Brand smiled in return.

"Pig Pen?" he repeated blankly. "I feel great. I have to admit I don't remember much of last night."

"Not to worry, sugar. I have enough memories for the both of us."

She extended a hand and stroked his bare chest.

Brand interlaced his fingers behind his head, enjoying the caress.

"I'm starving," she announced, climbing out of the covers. She stood before him, naked and unembarrassed.

Brand's eyes appraised her lean body appreciatively. She was shapely, much of her tanned skin covered in tattoos. She bent and retrieved a long tee, pulling it over her head.

"Get up, lazy head," she prompted him.

He stood from the bed, naked. It was her turn to look him over. She seemed pleased.

Brand was around six feet tall. He was in decent shape for a regular guy who ate what he wanted and drank frequently. He was thick in the right places and his arms and legs were sturdy from a lifetime of outdoor labor.

He searched the floor until he located his jeans and tee shirt. He picked them up. They were covered in dirt and grime.

"I'll throw those in the wash for you," the blonde offered. "Wait here a sec."

She took his clothes and left the room. She was gone only a moment before returning, holding a pair of boxers and a tee shirt.

"Put these on."

Brand accepted the garments. As he put them on, she explained:

"Don't worry. These are my brother's."

Brand nodded. He would have felt horrible if she had cheated on someone with him.

"I'm hungry," she said once more as she left the room.

As he pulled on the boxers, he felt a twinge in his back. It was painful but it didn't really concern him nor hurt that much. It was more a noticeable discomfort than an injury. He slid the tee over his head. He felt as if the cartilage which bound his ribs to one another strained painfully with the movement. He dismissed the small discomfort as once again a keen sense of well-being washed over him. He grinned at the pleasurable sensation and left the room.

He moved slowly, with a limping stride down the long hallway of the mobile home, towards what he saw to be a living and dining area. He passed a bathroom, then a bedroom. The bathroom was unoccupied, a closely clumped mass of cosmetic jars, bottles and vials filled the vanity countertop. Towels and bras hung on the towel racks.

The bedroom was dark, but he could make out an unmade bed, clothes on the floor, and a desk with a computer screen and keyboard atop it surrounded by papers, with books strewn about.

Brand entered an open living, dining, kitchen area. As with the other rooms he had passed, the space was littered with clothing, debris, old food, dishes, and unidentifiable discarded personal items.

He saw the tattooed blonde at the stove and a man in his mid to late twenties at the kitchen sink, washing dishes.

"Hey, stud," the man said with a grin. "You are quite the Casanova; even better when you are cleaned up."

Brand smiled in return. Pig Pen? Cleaned up? He was confused.

"How about some eggs and bacon?" the blonde asked.

"That would be great," Brand replied.

He felt a sharp emptiness in the pit of his gut. Like the other discomforts, hunger bothered him none as his outlook on life grew more optimistic with every passing moment.

Brand cleared trash off a chair at the little dinette table and lowered himself slowly into the sticky wooden seat. Despite the pain failing to bother him as it might, the injuries causing the pain impeded his movements.

"Are you still sore?" the blonde asked as she flipped a pancake. "Your face is still a little swollen and I noticed a lot of tender spots all over you. How did you get all those injuries? The scar on your back looks like a bullet wound."

Brand shrugged.

He remembered nothing prior to this morning. The two paused a moment, expecting an explanation. When an explanation was not tendered, they returned to their individual tasks.

Brand watched them as they worked at breakfast and the dishes. It felt awkward that he couldn't remember either of their names.

"When did y'all get in last night?" the man asked of the blonde.

"After two," she replied.

They were silent for a moment, bent to their tasks.

"I love to do dishes," the man mused as he spun a glass in his hand, cleaning the rim. "It relaxes me."

"Leon," the blonde observed. "Everything relaxes you."

"I'm a chill dude, Dee."

Dee favored Leon with a sidelong glance as she dropped bacon into a pan.

"I like my bacon crispy, Pig Pen," she called over her shoulder to Brand. "I hope you do too."

Brand shook his head at the Pig Pen reference.

"I like it crispy too," he answered. "Why do you keep calling me Pig Pen?"

Dee glanced at him curiously.

"Seriously? You don't know why?"

Brand beamed an innocent smile in return.

"I have to admit," he said. "I don't remember much of last night."

"You were pretty loaded," she agreed. "What do you remember?"

Brand struggled once more to recall anything at all beyond waking that morning.

He shrugged impotently.

"Do you even remember my name," she asked, turning towards him, bacon grease dripping from a fork hanging limply in her hand.

"Dee," Brand replied brightly.

"Dehra," Leon hurriedly interjected as his sister's brow furrowed in anger. "She hates to be called Dee, bro."

"Sorry, Dehra," Brand apologized with genuine regret. "I heard Leon call you Dee and I thought I was being clever."

"So, you remember my brother's name but not mine?"

"No. I just heard you use his name too."

Leon grinned at Brand.

It occurred to Brand that Leon was enjoying the morning-after amnesia scenario. He wanted to be annoyed at Leon, but he felt only an overarching sense of happiness and wellbeing.

Dehra ignored the sizzling bacon as she glared at her guest. As much as she could feel humiliation after a one-night stand, she reddened at the shame that she had slept with a man who didn't even remember her name. With a final withering hard look at Brand, she returned her attention to the sizzling bacon.

The remainder of the breakfast preparation was conducted in silence. Dehra's anger was a palpable thing and weighed heavily in the room. Even Leon kept his comments to himself, although it was plain that the restraint was killing him.

Uncomfortable with Dehra's anger, Brand gave his attention to his surroundings. The strained silence continued as Leon rinsed and racked the last dish in the sink and drained the soapy water.

Dehra lifted three plates from the drying rack and filled them at the stove. She carried them to the table and set the first two before the empty chairs she and Leon would occupy. She dropped Brand's plate from a harrowing distance where it banged the tabletop, threatening to break the blue stoneware plate.

Brand unfolded a paper napkin and placed it in his lap then adjusted the plate and silverware before him. He waited for the others to sit and dig in before he raised his fork.

The plate held four strips of bacon, two pancakes with butter, and two eggs over-easy.

"I apologize to you both for my memory," Brand said. "I really don't remember much of anything past this morning. My memories are dim and sketchy beyond that."

Brand searched Dehra's face for some change in her stern visage. He spoke directly to her.

"Any help you can give me would be welcome."

Dehra broke a piece of bacon in half and ate one of the pieces. She did not look at Brand.

Leon watched Dehra from the corner of his eye, a hooded grin betraying his enjoyment of the drama before him.

Brand cut into the eggs.

The blonde was a tough customer. His discomfort grew as he weathered Dehra's ire.

He ate what he could under the growing angry silence. Finally, he wiped his mouth and rose from the table and his partially eaten breakfast.

Both Dehra and Leon looked at him curiously.

"I'm not sure how I can make this right," he admitted. "So, I am going to find my clothes and leave."

Brand pushed in his chair.

"Again, I am truly sorry that I offended you, Dehra."

He turned from them and returned slowly to the bedroom. He searched the messy floor for clothing that might look familiar – or at least fit him. With a groan, he remembered that Dehra had offered to wash his dirty clothes. He was stuck there in someone else's underwear.

Dehra entered the room where she saw him rising slowly from his hands and knees where he had been searching under the bed.

"Your clothes are in the wash," she said wearily. "They won't be done for another hour."

Brand nodded.

"Thank you," Brand said awkwardly. "Why were my clothes so dirty that they needed to be washed?"

"Are you serious," she asked with passion. "You really don't remember anything about last night?"

"Not a thing," Brand assured her. He felt a growing regret and embarrassment. "Tell me what happened."

Dehra sat on the bed, considering Brand as she decided how to begin. Finally, she mastered her temper with a sigh.

"We were at the Purple Cow – a downtown bar – when you walked in. You were covered with dirt from hair to heel. Your face was bruised, and you limped into the bar like you had just had your ass kicked. You looked like you had just climbed out of a grave."

She paused to evaluate Brand's reaction. She was still unconvinced that he was being truthful about his memory. His blank look encouraged her to continue.

"You sat at a stool a couple of seats down from where Leon and I were sitting. You ordered a drink – I mean that's what you said, 'Give me a drink.' I think the whole bar was silent as the bartender decided whether to give you the bum rush or the drink.

"Luckily for you it was Caleb, and he poured a shot of whiskey for you. You tossed it down and asked for another. Caleb told you that you would have to show some green if you wanted another. You pulled out a stack of hundreds and seemed surprised that it was there. You peeled off a C-note and the bar was open after that. You bought the bar rounds until closing, peeling off hundreds at regular intervals.

"You leaned towards me and asked me my name.

Dehra looked at him pointedly.

"I told you, and we started talking. You were very tight lipped about yourself, but you relaxed as the booze took hold. You said you were some kind of spy or something. You couldn't tell me why you were caked with dirt, but you were the most charming dirty guy I had ever met.

At the end of the night, Caleb sent everybody home. I asked you where you were staying, and you said you didn't know. Leon offered you the sofa and a shower.

"You asked me to wash your back for you and one thing led to another. I was drinking too, you know."

Brand processed the story silently. His gaze reverted from his memory loss to the blonde woman before him.

"I wish I could remember. You are a beautiful woman and I'm sure we had a great time."

Dehra grinned sheepishly.

"We put each other through our paces, for sure."

"Ahem," said a voice at the doorway. Leon leaned against the door jamb with a grin splitting his face.

"So, have we kissed and made up?" he asked.

Dehra frowned at him halfheartedly. Her mood was improving.

"Besides," she said to Brand. "I only know you as Pig Pen. You didn't give me your name."

Brand pursed his lips as he tried to remember his name.

"You probably won't believe it, but I don't remember."

"You couldn't find your wallet last night," Dehra said. "No cell phone either."

"We could name you," Leon said helpfully. "Like a puppy."

Brand favored him with a good-natured frown.

Dehra left the room for a moment. She returned with a large stack of hundred-dollar bills.

"These were in your pants pocket. I guess we can call you Ben," she said as she handed the money to Brand. "Or maybe we can call you Franklin."

Brand laughed at the joke as he looked at the large amount of money in his hand.

"Thanks," he said with sincere gratitude. It occurred to him that they could have taken advantage of his memory loss and gained a windfall. "Ben works for now."

Leon laughed as he left the room.

Dehra watched Brand closely as her curiosity got the better of her temper.

"I have never met anyone with amnesia before. I'm not sure what to do with you."

"The memory loss is strange," Brand agreed. "The fact that I feel so happy about it is what concerns me."

"You are happy about amnesia?" she asked incredulously.

"Since I woke up this morning," he explained. "I have felt extremely contented and pleased. It is like I don't have a care in the world."

"Walking around with a pocket full of money could be a contributing factor," she observed meaningfully.

Brand nodded.

"It helps. But I am concerned how I came into a stack of hundreds, especially since I am missing a wallet and I have no ID of any kind. I feel like I was hit by a truck and apparently, I was buried or something like that."

"I haven't heard of any banks being robbed, or liquor stores being held up lately. Where should we start if we are to find out who you are?"

"If it wasn't for the stack of cash, I would say we start with the cops. Maybe we should give it a couple of days until something changes. If I still have no idea who I am by then, we should go to a hospital."

"That sounds like a plan," Dehra agreed. "Maybe you can pal around with Leon until your memory returns. I have to work, or I would show you around."

Brand laughed with embarrassment.

"By the way, where am I?"

"You are in Uvalde, Texas."

"Why do I remember Uvalde, and know that I am from San Antonio, but I can't remember my name?"

Dehra shrugged and smiled sympathetically.

"San Antonio is close. Maybe we should start there."

"What do you mean?"

Dehra looked at him with an amused expression.

"Maybe familiar surroundings will jog your memory, silly."

"Right," he agreed sheepishly.

"I've got to get ready for work," she announced as she stood. "Leon will keep an eye on you until my shift is over."

"Thanks for understanding," Brand said.

She looked at him with a curious light in her eyes.

"You're welcome, Ben."

7

RICARDO SANCHEZ WAS A PROFESSIONAL site manager. He leaned back in his favorite chair, rocking ever so slightly, remembering the months of insults he had borne before that one day when he was finally recognized for his talent and regarded with the best job of his life.

He also was a gruff and authoritative man. He had managed men and facilities all his life. During his career, the employment fate of thousands of men and women had teetered at his whim. He also held no fear of managing millions of dollars' worth of property and equipment. In his view, the number of zeros behind the one was immaterial. He was not easily intimidated.

During his forty years of professional facilities management, he had grown his reputation to a level that he had never found it necessary to look for a job. Headhunters and even CEOs invested much time and money to lure him away from a lucrative position with an attractive company with the aim of hiring him to work in theirs.

The reputation, the acclaim, the need for his talents: all of that ended with the Pandemic. The Pandemic changed so much about the way business was done. Virtual offices and telecommuting reduced the on-site workforce to only those lowly few who maintained vacant and unused facilities. The new job requirements were basic and comparatively inconsequential. His experience and hard-acquired skillset no longer held the value they had when facilities were staffed and working. As the Pandemic spread and the death count rose, his unique skillset lost its value for company owners and heads of corporations.

He remembered that final call on the final day of his final job. His phone chortled on his desk. He glanced out the large plate glass window overlooking a million square foot warehouse facility. He lifted the phone on the second ring.

"Facilities," he answered with the proper authoritative inflection.

"Mr. Sanchez," the HR manager said without preamble. "Please check your inbox at your earliest convenience. You have a file to review."

"A file from HR?" he asked.

"Yes."

"Who do I need to release," he asked, feeling professional sorrow for the poor soul he would terminate today.

"Everything is in the file."

"The usual two weeks or is this an expedite?"

"Everything is in the file."

"This sounds serious," he noted with concern. "Is this a group termination?"

"Everything is in the file, Ricardo."

She called him Ricardo. She had never called him by other than his surname. He hung up the phone and hurried downstairs. He found a bright orange file in his inbox slot on the wall of the dispatch office. He returned to his office and opened the file on his desk.

He wasn't called to the H.R. office. He wasn't let down easy. He just answered the phone one day and he was released that afternoon. Technically he conducted his own exit interview.

He later learned that his position was spun off and ultimately filled with overrated security guards and professional baby-sitters.

For months, the phone didn't ring where once he had complained about the job offers. He posted his resume online, feeling genuine embarrassment from the action. There were no opportunities posted and he received no calls.

He ran through his severance package alarmingly quickly. As time passed and his finances became increasingly more fragile, he had to do what he hadn't done for years. He looked for a new job that did not involve facilities management.

Without exception, his experience and skillset left him overqualified for the positions for which he applied. Those rarely available facilities management positions for which he eagerly applied required none of his hard-earned experience nor his finely honed skill set. His worth was built upon quantifiable levels of competence and dedication, acquired over four decades of long hours and hard work. All of it accounted for nothing. He was the confederate currency of his time. Valued one day, worthless the next.

He nodded to no one as he rocked in his favorite chair and remembered the week prior when everything changed. He received an email for a job interview appointment. His wife had frowned knowingly when he broke the news of yet another potential employment opportunity. She had long before given up arguing with him about the necessity of employment over his principled and dogged adherence to settling for no less than the "required wage for the required task."

"Just take the job for now," she pleaded. "Things will return to normal and so will your job and salary."

She was wrong, Sanchez lamented silently. Corporate America found, by accident, that a lean, remote workforce, and an all but nonexistent overhead, increased profits exponentially.

Corporate downsizing through layoffs and furlough had always been unpopular. Cost reduction by eliminating bricks on the ground facilities, and the associated recurring expenses, and maintenance costs, became popular, lauded by enviro-activists as employee-centric and environmentally sensitive.

The corporate business model pivot was a win-win for everyone – except for Ricardo Sanchez. Unlike the hyperbolic new normal of a home bound work force, he couldn't do his job from a converted bedroom in his little frame house on the south side of San Antonio. He couldn't manage a million square foot facility with a *Zoom* conference, video app, or email.

Within weeks of him firing himself, industrial and office space went dark. Internal climate controls powered down with robotic ease to dormant settings day and night, monitored, and operated by computers.

He reflected upon the past few months. Each time he prepared for a job interview he repeated the same diatribe for his wife's benefit, until finally, she stopped trying to convince him to take any job he could find at a lower rate.

With his inevitable firmly set jaw, he refused to take a penny less than a thousand a week. He had invested a lifetime to reach his station and he would not waver from his standards. He was aware that his long drought of unemployment was easily avoidable if only he weren't a man of principles and courage. No matter, he argued, he would take no less than a thousand a week to apply his considerable skillset and experience-earned abilities to a job. He may be obsolete, he reasoned, but his honor was not.

Sure, the job market was saturated with willing workers. But none of them brought his experience to the position. Success in his vocation was often dependent upon nuance. The minutiae of his methods made the job look easy. His was the ease of the professional, derived from years of deliberate toil and perfect practice.

On the day of the interview Ricardo arrived early, as was his practice. He parked in one of the many available parking spots in the empty parking lot before a large warehouse facility. Tall concrete tilt wall construction and modern effects hinted at the newness of the facility. Ricardo guessed the building was no more than a year or two old. The owners were undoubtedly among those few investors who did not see the writing on the wall or were mid-build when the pandemic changed everything.

It wasn't just him, Ricardo mused with cruel pleasure, who had felt the rug jerked from under his feet.

He entered the steel and glass entry with a weary dread. As he approached the reception station his positive mood waned at the prospect of yet another job interview filled with withering looks and insulting practicality from an impersonal hiring manager.

As had become his practice, his response was planned, consistent, and reasonable. The dance was always the same. He attended these empty interviews for no other reason than to fulfill the requirements of his unemployment benefits. He knew his value. He also knew he was the only one who saw it in light of the new rules of the game. He would weather a friendly discussion about his impressive work experience. Compensation would be discussed – almost in passing – as if the money were only a pleasant side effect of the job.

The next phase was where he asked for more money than was offered, after which a less than pleasant conversation would begin about how the market did not support his requested wage and the position did not require his impressive qualifications.

Sanchez drove the dark clouds of impending disappointment from him. He was a principled man. Principle dictated that he comport himself pleasantly no matter the inevitable outcome of the meeting.

He approached a young, surprisingly lovely receptionist, seated demurely behind an opulent front desk.

She asked for his name with surprising pleasantness and genuine interest. Her courtesy was unexpected in a world where in-person interaction was rare and unwelcome. Manners were no longer required nor encouraged.

She rose from her leather chair, offered him a seat and a cold drink. He moved to the proffered chair uncertainly and stammered an acceptance of the drink. He managed to mumble that a bottled water would be nice.

After fulfilling his request for a bottle of water she returned to her seat with a promise that he would be seen soon.

Sanchez twisted the cap and sipped the cold water with a pleasant smile on his face.

No more than a minute passed before the pretty receptionist answered the silent signal of the phone. She spoke into the phone for a moment before again rising from her seat.

She asked that he follow her.

He followed her to an ornate entrance to what he assumed to be a conference room.

He attempted to avert his eyes from the receptionist's taut body moving enticingly beneath her smart business suit. He was only partially successful in that she turned in time to see him quickly focus his eyes on a spot on the floor, clumsily concealing the lengthy and direct gaze he had given to her shapely behind during their entire walk.

She smiled at him with nonplussed understanding before opening the door, gesturing that he should enter. She closed the heavy wooden door behind him and returned to her station.

Once inside, the interview was similar to the others. He took a seat in the lavish conference room where two men in pricy pinstriped suits and Rolex watches awaited him, seated at a rich dark-wood conference table surrounded by high-backed leather chairs.

As in previous interviews, his experience and job history were discussed and praised. After that Ricardo's forced happy talk reverted to a weary monotone as he broached the taboo of compensation.

He clearly made his demand for the requisite thousand a week. As before, the company representatives flatly refused the amount, stating that his wage was out of line for the job. That was where the similarities ended.

Before he could begin his anticipated and well-rehearsed response, they informed him in stern tones that they held firm at an offer of two-thousand dollars a week. They stressed that a lesser amount would not be adequate to ensure they placed the proper candidate in the proper position.

The stern men in the expensive suits assured him that he was correct in his belief that his vocation was an exacting one requiring the knowledge and acumen he possessed - a rare skillset which rated highly with their firm. They also assured him that they wanted to hire him precisely because of his no-nonsense reputation.

Sanchez stood from his chair with a smile, ignoring the early-morning news shows on network TV. He missed cable news. He hadn't been able to afford cable for months. His first check was due at the end of the week. After all those lean months, he knew he could afford it now.

He filled his thermos with coffee and left for the warehouse. He was expecting a large shipment today. The mystery surrounding it intrigued him. He was always early for work. The mystery shipment added to his enthusiasm.

Two hours later, as he stood in the huge empty warehouse, Ricardo smiled once more at the memory of the insulting offers he had weathered. He was where he should be, doing ehat he was meant to do.

He held his clipboard just below his eyeline as a lengthy line of tractor trailers filled with rich fragrant earth entered the brand-new warehouse building.

He counted the trucks while his staff directed the drivers as they backed their trailers near the rear wall of the large warehouse. As quickly as they placed the trailers, his crew uncoupled them, waving directions to the drivers in their departing tractors.

It was just after midnight when the last truck tractor left the building and the huge electric overhead doors uncoiled, securing the building. Ricardo's final count was 165: 165 trailers at nearly 100 cubic yards of soil each!

Ricardo wondered why trailers loaded with dirt were being stored inside an expensive brand-new building in a high-end industrial park in San Antonio.

His experience provided him a unique insight to the value of the floor-planning of inventory in a warehouse space. In his estimation, a warehouse full of old gravel trailers filled with dirt was not a cost-effective use of valuable infrastructure.

With a shrug he remembered his two-thousand-dollar weekly wage. The well-dressed businessmen didn't seem to place the same value on money that he did.

Ricardo made his way to his office and logged the receiving numbers into the laptop he had been instructed to use for the shipment. He completed his report then powered down the laptop, packing it into a cardboard shipping box.

He carried the box to the front office and handed it to a man in a suit who awaited him in the same chair he had occupied before his interview in the lavish meeting room.

The man rose, leaving the office without a word.

Ricardo shrugged once again. He locked up, arming the elaborate biometric alarm system.

8

CASTILLO WATCHED CERVANTES WITH A CRITICAL
stare. His lieutenant was one of the few holdovers from the
previous regime. His value was unquestioned, but his allegiance
sometimes caused the cartel boss concern.

Don Castillo relied heavily upon his ability to interpret the
intentions of others, almost as keenly as might a mind reader.
Cervantes troubled him. It was nothing Castillo could readily
identify. His instincts often caused him occasional chills and
frequent doubts. Around Cervantes, his Spidey senses tingled
like a high voltage wire in wet weather. He decided at that
moment that he would kill Cervantes before long.

Cervantes found it very difficult to avert his gaze from the
two severed heads on the floor before Castillo's desk. Cervantes
learned long ago the weight his boss placed upon his gut
instincts. Many men had been put to death for no more than a
twitching in Castillo's thumb. Castillo's habit of reading another
was a thing of fear amongst the men. Cervantes had witnessed
many deaths visited upon men he believed were innocent of
crimes for which Castillo declared them guilty. Cervantes now
expended great effort to conceal any tell-tale minutia, his
anxiety veiled behind a stoic mask.

"He didn't disappear into thin air," Castillo surmised,
breaking a long uncomfortable pause. "The heads of these two
guards prove that they had no part in his escape."

He pointed a stiff finger at the floor where lay the severed
heads of the two guards who had gone for breakfast.

Cervantes worked at the mystery of why severed heads exonerated the dead men with whom they were once attached. Add two more to the pile.

He glared at Cervantes, pointing a stiff finger in his direction.

"You have been unsuccessful in locating him or any trace of him," Castillo accused.

Cervantes remained motionless. Despite the accusatorial tone, he knew that the Boss was not expecting a reply. The lieutenant also knew with certainty that any word from him would weigh heavily against his already slim chances of surviving this meeting.

"I'll make you a once in a lifetime offer," Castillo said with a generous flourish of his left hand. "Your life for his. You pick any four men you want. You find Carson Brand and kill him. If you fail, you will die. If you succeed, you will live. As a bonus, if you succeed, I will let your mother in Mexico City live also."

Cervantes pursed his lips. His stoic demeanor was not quite adequate to conceal his fear at the threat against his dear mother.

Castillo saw that he had pierced his Lieutenant's hard shell. He did not smile or give the appearance that he enjoyed the victory. He left tells and tell-tale giveaways to his victims. He turned to the patio windows just in case.

He wanted results and believed he had offered a prize valuable enough to motivate, even one whose loyalty he doubted, to achieve remarkable things.

"Before he dies, however, find out who he works for and what they know. I think Rabino was too kind with him."

Castillo, his back to Cervantes, surveying the landscaped grounds through the huge windows, waited for Cervantes to leave. The meeting was over. He heard Cervantes shuffle on the rich wood floor.

"Take the heads with you," he commanded in a threatening voice which hinted at the precariously controlled ire he felt. "Let them serve as a reminder to you of your commitment to me and this task."

Cervantes moved towards the grizzly remains, lifting the heads by the hair. He avoided looking at the grinning death mask expressions of their dead faces. He set his teeth against the distasteful task and strode from the room, careful to drip as little blood and tissue on the floor as he could manage.

9

LEON DROVE AS HE LIVED HIS LIFE, at top speed and haphazardly, as if he hadn't a care in the world. He drove as if the laws of physics did not apply to him. Brand crouched fearfully in the passenger seat as the little pickup truck clung desperately to the sharp bends and turns of the winding road that dropped from the ragged escarpment above into the small town of Leaky.

Brand glimpsed the city from the towering cliffs and peaks from which they descended. When the courage to look over the edge of the cliffs strengthened him, the little village appeared to be a small town clustered against the banks of a glimmering river.

"Welcome to Leaky," Leon announced over the roar of wind and road noise rushing through his open driver side window. He pronounced it "Lakey."

Brand made no comment as he surveyed the flashing terrain passing by around him. His mind was blank. Everything he saw was a new experience with almost no reference from his clouded memory. His feelings were like a paraplegic with only phantom nerve sensations and tingling twitches. Nothing felt right. Nothing made sense to him.

Leon drove at top speed until he entered the town proper. As he passed the city limits sign Leon slowed to the posted speed, observing a surprising adherence to the traffic laws.

"Are the cops bad here?" Brand asked with relief, nodding to indicate the truck's speedometer.

"No license," Leon replied simply. "I got pulled over for a DWI and I refused to blow. They took my license, and now I am on probation."

Brand nodded. At that moment he felt genuine gratitude for law enforcement.

They were silent a moment more before Brand broke the pause in their conversation.

"So where does Dehra work?"

Leon grinned at him with raised eyebrows.

"You likey likey," he observed with a playful lilt to his tone.

Brand's expression remained impassive.

"I like her," he agreed, reluctant to encourage more fun at his expense from his loquacious companion.

"She works just outside of Uvalde at a high-tech manufacturing and testing facility. All very hush hush. She just started there last week."

Leon turned the little truck into a small strip center parking lot and pulled into a space before an office with a sign in front reading 'Temp Employment Agency.'

"She is on the day shift," Leon continued as he shifted the truck into park and opened the door. "Very hard to get on the day shift."

He stood, stretched, and closed the truck door. He moved towards the front door of the temp office. He paused in front of the truck.

"You coming?"

"Where?" Brand asked leaning his head out the open window.

"Inside," Leon replied vaguely.

After a pause in which Brand did not immediately emerge from the truck, Leon shook a warning finger at Brand, his smile removing any serious intent from the remark.

"No lethargy in our house, young man."

With a lighter tone Leon explained, "Everyone without a steady job checks in daily. Come on."

Brand sat back in his seat for a moment, reluctant to comply. With a sigh, he released the seat belt and opened the door.

Inside, Leon led the way to the tall check in-counter where he signed the sheet attached to a clipboard using a cheap pen taped to a string and tied to the loop of the clip board.

"New guy, Rose," Leon told the hard-faced woman behind the counter. "He lost his wallet. Can he just fill in the ID section until he finds it?"

Rose looked Brand up and down as if he were a dangerous suspect, and she was the desk sergeant in a police precinct.

"Alright," she agreed authoritatively. "But get me a copy of that ID as soon as you find it."

She handed Brand another clipboard with an application. Under Leon's direction, Brand filled out the form using his and Dehra's address. He wrote a variation of Leon's state ID number in the ID section then returned the clipboard to Rose. She scrutinized his information before directing him to return to his seat beside Leon.

Brand returned to the seat and leaned towards Leon.

"I'm not looking for a job," he said in a low voice.

Leon considered Brand soberly for a long moment.

"You may have a stack of hundreds now," he said in an equally muted tone. "But when that runs out, you will have a tough time finding a job locally without Beatrice's help."

"Is Beatrice the woman at the window?"

"No. That is Rose. Beatrice owns the place and handles all of the training, and the workplace conditioning workshops for incoming candidates, as she calls them."

"Workplace Conditioning Workshops? What does that mean?"

"You'll see soon enough," Leon assured him.

Brand considered Leon's answer for a moment.

"If you have been here before, haven't you already gone through one of these workshops?" he asked emphatically.

Leon considered the question for a long moment.

"The training is ongoing," he explained with the patience of experience. "There is never an end to inequity so there is never an end to the workshops."

Brand leaned back in the plastic chair.

"When do you have time to work?"

Leon rewarded Brand's continued naivete with a level look. "The workshops are the 'work'."

Brand was silent as he waited for an explanation.

"While we wait on a job, we take the workplace courses and get paid in exchange."

"How do they pay for this program? This doesn't look like an unemployment office."

"The biggest employer in Uvalde County is Tel Gōngsī de, where Dehra got her job."

"Tell what?" Brand asked.

"Don't worry. I'm better than most at saying it. We call it Tel Gong for short. They sponsor all onboarding activities."

A loud voice from the back of the room interrupted their conversation.

"Those who are here for the workplace course please come in and take a seat, the rest of you move out the back door to the busses. Your final on-boarding will begin at the plant."

"See," Leon said about the final statement."

A thin older woman with wiry gray hair and large, bright, blue framed glasses looked carefully around the crowded room.

Most of the lobby's occupants rose from their seats and moved to the frosted glass of the double doors at the back of the waiting room. Others shuffled to the back door, manilla folders in hand.

Through the frosted doors, the students entered a large classroom lined with several rows of chair/desk combinations which reminded Brand of a school classroom. He and Leon took their places in the middle of the room.

A young woman with ample hips moved down the rows depositing colorful workbooks and pens upon each desk. Brand opened the magazine style book and skimmed the contents.

He saw full color images of smiling people with perfect teeth and seemingly perfect lives. All the models in the photos appeared to be self-satisfied in a world of racial equity and balance. The chapter titles included: "An African American view of the White Workplace," "White Frailty, Bridging the

Ethnic Gap for Whites", and "Racism – The White Cancer – There is a Cure."

"What the shit," Brand muttered under his breath.

Leon turned a strained look upon Brand.

"Keep your comments to yourself," he warned with uncharacteristic irritation. "This is a paying gig."

Brand shook his head. He was at sea in his memory loss and in his struggle to keep up with the quickly changing circumstances of this strange and unexpected life.

The gray-haired woman took her place at an oak-colored lectern. She rested her hands lightly upon the edges of the tilted top and looked around the room, her gaze loitering briefly upon each member of her class.

Brand felt an unmistakable air of judgement as the lean woman's eyes settled in turn upon him.

"I am about to share a self-evident truth with you. We are all racists! By virtue of having white skin, we innately hate those who do not. To deny this fact is to attest to the truth of the fact."

She paused as this opening salvo sunk into the heads of her audience.

"Do not be offended. I am Beatrice Murphey. Beatrice Murphy is white. She is also a recovering racist."

Brand snorted as he attempted to cover his laughter.

Beatrice favored Brand with a glare at his outburst.

"Please hold your comments for the Q and A at the end of our lesson."

Brand stared at the floor. He wasn't embarrassed or ashamed. He was feeling an uncomfortable heat burning just under the skin. The sensation had come on suddenly. He felt as if he had been flash fried with a bad sunburn, but under his skin. He looked at the skin on his arm. It looked no different than before, but the heat beneath grew until shining beads of sweat bubbled from his pores. His vision darkened with a red haze. He heard a buzzing in his ears like an old man in the grasp of Tinnitus.

He ground his teeth, fighting back a groan, as his discomfort grew into real searing pain. With a panicked look around him, he leaped from his chair and fled to the double door entrance. He burst from the room and ran to the restroom down the hallway.

Beatrice and the class watched in silent surprise as the disruptor fled from the room.

Beatrice broke the silence.

"Someone please close the door so that we may continue."

Brand rushed into the restroom. He staggered to the long vanity, turning on the tap at the first of the three sinks. He bathed his burning arms and his reddening face with rapid splashes of cold water.

The water scarcely helped at all. The burn was under the skin and the cool water did not affect what he felt as a scorching pain. Growing heat seared his entire body as he desperately soaked his clothing and exposed skin.

With a wail, he fell to the cool tiles on the floor. He writhed under the intense searing sensation for several minutes until as suddenly as it had begun, the burning sensation passed.

He remained on the cool floor tiles for a moment, his breathing labored. The relief of the diminishing pain was like a cool wave breaking across his entire body. He rolled onto his back and sighed his relief. After a moment he stood, looking at himself in the mirror.

The red flush was gone, all that was left of the attack were wet clothes and his soaked disheveled hair. Perspiration no longer dripped down his face and neck into his shirt. He pulled a long length of paper towels from the dispenser and dried himself. He opened his shirt and pants and dried those areas as well as he could.

He buttoned his shirt and snapped his pants, leaning on the counter, spent and relieved. He looked at his face in the mirror. For the first time since this morning, he recognized the face he saw.

"Brand," he muttered in a low voice. "My name is Carson Brand."

Beatrice and the class turned their heads as the door opened. A more calmly composed Carson Brand returned to his seat. His clothes clung to him moistly, his hair was wet and matted, but his behavior appeared well in hand.

Beatrice eyed him suspiciously for an authoritarian moment, ready to deal with another outburst. Only after Brand had been seated quietly for almost a full minute did she reluctantly continue her presentation. After a moment of scanning her notes, she seemed to find where she had left off.

"Your white privilege," she continued, the familiar terrain of the text and its familiar ideology comforting her outrage at the class disruption. "Is something that you have depended upon your entire life. From being called upon first in school, to getting that big promotion at work, you achieved whatever success you have because of the color of your skin. The young black boy who was not called upon in school, the black man who was not promoted at your work. Their failure was suffered in order for you to succeed. What was the crime they committed? What sin did they transgress? Why were they forced to sacrifice so that you might succeed? What was their horrible crime? Having dark skin!"

Brand heard little of Beatrice's lecture as his mind cleared and his memories returned in a chaotic flood. The first to return were the memories of his imprisonment and torture. He suffered a punishing mental agony at the new memories. Without older memories he was left with little understanding what would cause someone to harm him. As additional memories took their place, they filled in the blanks. Understanding put the memories into context. Realization buoyed the cruel experiences with an understanding that helped assuage the anguish of those tortured mental images with a clarity of thought and an orderly distribution of the timeline behind it all. Within moments, as if a curtain had been slowly drawn, he remembered everything.

To Leon's view, Brand underwent a remarkable metamorphosis. He sat straighter in his chair and looked around the room with a new light in his eyes. His shoulders squared. The meekness melted away almost as if it had been a physical manifestation. Brand seemed out of place in the class, like a tiger in a sheep pen. Leon struggled to adapt to this new perception of this recent stranger in his life.

Brand turned his head, seeing Leon watching him curiously.

Leon held his hands up as if to ask, 'what is going on?'

Brand ignored the silent question.

"Until you open your eyes to the truth of your hate," Beatrice droned on. "You will never heal…"

"I don't have time for this," Brand said in a loud voice. "Lady, you are so full of shit your eyes are brown. Almost everything you have said so far is a lie. What you are being truthful about is that you are a racist – towards white people."

"Excuse me, sir," Beatrice interrupted authoritatively.

"Stop talking," Brand commanded. He looked around the room. "The rest of you can sit here and listen to this crap, but there is no amount of money that can buy my self-respect. If you can be paid to give this idiot a say in your life, then you are no better than the prostitute who sells herself to pay for her next fix."

Beatrice stepped forward bravely. Her spine straightened in righteous indignation.

"You sir, are the reason our race has taken so many steps backward and have so much to atone for."

She pointed a stiff accusing finger at Brand as she stalked towards him.

Leon found himself pitying the old crone as she advanced bravely. For some reason, the image of a mouse attacking a lion occurred to him.

"I will not allow your racism to ruin the steps we have gained here to…"

Brand stood from the little desk. He brushed the old lady aside as he left the room, knocking her into the line of desks and leaving the door ajar once again.

Sometime later, when Leon appeared at the entrance to the building, Brand leaned against the little truck, his arms crossed. Leon opened his mouth to reprimand Brand. Something about the man changed his mind. His eyes were harder. Leon looked Brand over thoroughly. No, that wasn't it.

He recognized before him a man who was extremely capable. That was the best description Leon could come up with. The pliable, meek Ben Franklin was replaced by a strong, self-possessed man with an unmistakable inner strength that presented itself like a beacon.

"Let's go," Leon said weakly as he moved around the truck to the driver seat.

Leon pointed the truck towards Uvalde. They drove in silence for many minutes. Leon drove at his customary high speed, the little truck fairly groaning as it careened dangerously to either side of the winding roads.

This time Brand exhibited no fear or annoyance at Leon's dangerous driving. Rather, he rode silently, examining his situation as his mind recovered the last of his lost memories.

10

RESPECT! THAT IS WHAT BILL WIATREK WANTED. That is what Bill Wiatrek would have! The goddam Chinese were demanding and rude. They made no bones about their dislike of Americans. They tossed around derogatory remarks and racist epithets with no regard for the offensive aspects of their careless comments.

Bill was not a follower of Woke doctrine per se, but he had been pushed as far as he would be pushed. His value to the Chinese communications conglomerate, and the Party, was not lost upon him despite the minimalizing context shown him whenever he communicated with them.

He looked around the large terminal hall as the Chinese executive spoke to him over his cell phone. The airport terminal was crowded but no one paid him the slightest attention. Bill's heated responses to the caller's flaccid entreaties failed to pierce the din of angry travelers, delayed more than two hours by a rainstorm that limited his view outside the large windows to only a few feet. Nestled against the walkway beyond the gate, the silver 737 appeared as the prow of a sinking ship, visible only from the front of the wings to the nose as the deluge seemed to draw the plane into its shadowy depths.

With a quick draw of breath, Bill realized that the caller was silent, ostensibly waiting for a response from him. Bill's face screwed into a mask of anger and frustration. His voice escaped him as a whine.

"Wang," he hissed. "I know enough to take the whole thing down. That includes you and the entire company. You had better start showing me the respect I am due. I developed the software for your network and the apps for your devices. I sure as shit am an important part of your plan. I suggest you remember that fact when you decide to talk down to this dirty American."

Ha Wang was silent for a moment. He was a Chinese COO and unused to this type of unrestrained criticism from an underling. He understood, however, that this was a delicate matter which had already been dealt with. He merely had to limit the damage for a few more minutes.

Bill's expression relaxed a fraction as he imagined that the Chinese executive struggled to compose himself in the face of his unwelcome tone and unprecedented demand for respect. When Wang did finally respond, Bill was impressed at his controlled tone.

"Think about what you are saying to me, Bill," Wang warned reasonably. "You have been generously rewarded for your work. Control your emotional outbursts and think of a future free from worry for money, or certain prison time."

Bill felt his face warm as uncertainty weakened his brittle confidence.

"Don't threaten me, Wang," Bill warned with as much conviction as his weakened determination could muster. "Your country's secret plans for world dominance makes my actions seem insignificant in comparison. If anyone learned that your Tel Gōngsī de was gathering meta, personal, and financial data from your phones, it would cause World War Three. If it was learned that your company and the Chinese Communist Party have established the infrastructure here in the U.S. for a *social credit scoring* system like the one that exists in China, you and your on-the-take politicians in Washington could find yourselfs in prison or in front of a firing squad."

Once more Ha Wang was silent.

This time Bill felt as if he had stepped onto a ledge hundreds of feet above a busy street. He sensed he had crossed a threshold from which he could not return.

"Look," he stammered. "I'm not saying I'm going to do anything. I only ask you for what you expect from me, a little respect - and some appreciation for the genius I brought to the table."

Bill felt his confidence grow as he laid out his value to the Chinese executive.

"Very well," Wang finally said after what seemed a long moment of reflection. "You are right. We could have been more respectful. I apologize for losing sight of the contribution you made to our efforts. Thank you for your hard work and talent. May we return to business for a moment?"

"Sure," Bill replied, pleased but uncertain of his footing with the Chinese executive.

"I need you to forward a copy of your work, as agreed, so we can tender your final payment. When can you do that for me?"

"I'll send the file right now, sir," Bill offered eagerly.

He took a seat in one of the scores of connected chairs filling the gate waiting area. He withdrew his laptop from its case and snatched open the device. He activated the computer with a flurry of keystrokes.

"Bill," Wang called over the phone.

"Yes," Bill replied vacantly as he pulled up files.

"Send it over your phone's voice line, please."

"Oh, yeah," Bill stammered as he deleted the email he was preparing. "Doing it now."

Bill closed his laptop, moving the phone from his ear. He quickly located the VTP app he had created.

Until his astounding breakthrough, data had required a separate bandwidth. He created the first protocol which combined analog and digital information simultaneously. He dubbed it Voice Level Transport Protocol. On the open market VTP would have guaranteed him a place amongst the pioneers of telecommunication. His technological creation was on a par with Time Division Multiplexing, by which multiple voice calls can be transmitted simultaneously on a single twisted pair of copper wires by slicing each call message into timed segments, inserting them in measured intervals on the same strand of copper.

He shrugged as he tapped send. The money would have to suffice.

"Received," Wang confirmed.

The phone went dead as the CEO ended the call without preamble.

Bill shut down his phone with an oath.

"Respect, my ass."

The overhead speakers in the airport crackled as the airline employee at the desk announced that they would begin boarding his flight.

Bill stood, gathering his carry on and laptop bags. He always flew first class. He would plane first. At least he got respect from the airlines, at Tel Gōngsī de's expense.

Bill snacked and drank a cocktail as the forty-five minutes passed during which the plane was fully boarded, and the doors were closed. As the plane pushed back from the gate Bill felt his stomach convulse like a python had been secretly stowed in his body cavity. His eyes grew red as blood filled them behind the blue corneas. His throat contracted, cutting off his oxygen. He died writhing on the carpeted floor of 1st class.

The plane returned to the gate.

11

DEHRA MASHED THE BRAKE PEDAL RECKLESSLY as she brought her car to a halt before the single-wide mobile home. Dust hung thickly in the hot afternoon breeze as she shut off the ignition and got out of the car. She struck the air angrily with balled fists as if invisible foes surrounded her. She slipped, her rage making her clumsy, as she strode from the car. She picked herself up, slamming the car door. Her eye makeup stained her cheeks where tears had nearly blinded her during her drive home. She mounted the stairs and entered the cool darkness of the mobile home.

Inside she found the two men sitting in the living room. On Leon's normally jovial face was a rare dark cloud of a frown. Dehra nearly forgot her emotional distress as she considered this uncharacteristic display of temper from her brother.

When her survey moved to the other man in the room, she saw a visibly altered Ben Franklin's face. There was an intensity in the unfamiliar hardness in his eyes. Maybe, she thought, it was the set of his square jaw, but he was remarkably changed from the hat-in-hand apologetic stranger with whom she had awakened that morning.

Leon was first to break the silence.

"What's wrong, Dee?"

Dehra favored him with a black look at the distasteful nickname. He apparently was not too distraught to set a familiar barb.

"I lost my job," she blurted.

Tears flowed once more.

Leon stood abruptly, alarm plain on his face.

"What...How...?" he stammered. "Dehra, what happened?"

"I don't want to talk about it right now," she cried as her attention turned to Brand, sitting aside on the leather lounger.

"What's on your mind, Ben?"

"Brand," the other replied. "Call me Brand."

Dehra considered this new development.

"So, it's starting to come back," she said in a tone weak with emotion.

"It's all back," Brand replied firmly. "My name is Carson Brand. I appreciate your taking care of me while I was out of it."

"Carson?" Dehra repeated the name like she was trying it on for size.

"Everyone calls me Brand," he said, pressing his original statement.

Brand stood, his movements hindered by lingering pains from his torture at the hands of the Cartel. The pain and the returned memories of the last few weeks were no longer soothed and dismissed by an overarching sense of well-being. Conversely, a raging fire of anger warmed his center like a freshly stoked blast furnace. He wanted to mete out retribution to those who had harmed him. He was keenly aware that he was not at full strength due to his injuries and malnutrition. Many of those injuries felt serious enough that he considered visiting a clinic for an official medical opinion.

His attention returned to the others. Both watched him with a sort of fascination. It was apparent to him that they regarded him with confusion at his transformation from helpless amnesiac to whatever they saw in him now.

Leon was the first to break the silence.

"So, what now, Brand?" He placed a significant emphasis on the name.

Brand considered Leon for a moment. He was not ready to commit much about himself to these new acquaintances. He looked towards Dehra.

"Are you alright?" he asked levelly, returning the focus of the conversation to her.

Dehra stood straighter at the unexpected turn of attention.

"I am not," she managed to croak as she fought the tears that defeated her efforts to hide them.

Leon shook his head doubtfully.

"I didn't do anything," Dehra declared indignantly. "They accused me of being a racist."

Leon punched the air in frustration.

"Didn't you learn anything from the classes, Dehra? You have to be careful what you say."

Dehra turned away from her brother. She went to the kitchen cupboard and collected a glass, filling it at the tap. She drank from the glass, her back to the two men.

Brand watched her back, his attention on his own problems. He remembered the class with a wry grin. He was impressed by neither the instructor nor Leon's commitment to the tenets of the course.

His attention returned to his own situation. With the insight of his recovered memories, he occupied himself with fantasies of violent retribution visited upon those who captured him and tortured him. He controlled the euphoria of his mounting rage with difficulty. DEA agent Kilgore had characterized this euphoric feeling accompanying his anger as *Blind Rage Syndrome*. Apparently, it was a thing, Brand mused.

The idea of Kilgore diverted his focus from his growing anger to his current dilemma. He was undecided how he should communicate with Agent Kilgore, his primary contact within the DEA. The last he had seen of the agent was at the bar in San Antonio, Rod Dog's Saloon. Kilgore had shown up unexpectedly with the news that Brand was officially a contractor for the Agency.

Moments after Kilgore's departure, Christina, the former cartel lieutenant, and his former romantic interest, appeared across the bar. Brand fumed silently. Their reunion had been a happy surprise until she escorted him out of the bar where cartel thugs captured him and spirited him away to a dark prison cell in Mexico.

With an internal wince and a flood of renewed rage, he relived the pain and humiliation of the rough treatment he had received during his imprisonment. Every ache that slowed his movements, every agony he felt when he breathed, each nightmarish memory of the torture sessions, was associated with a specific torment from Rabino.

That single name was all he knew of the sadistic giant who plied his manic skills upon him. He would build upon that scant information.

Brand emerged from his reverie. Leon and Dehra watched him silently and with great interest. Their expressions clearly conveyed that his grim intentions towards his foes had registered upon him a mien which the others found troubling if not frightening.

"Are you alright?" Leon asked hesitantly, placing a new cautious light on the danger he perceived from the changed Brand. It occurred to him that they might be in peril from this new friend.

Brand looked at Leon for a moment.

"I'm fine," he replied.

He shifted the attention again to Dehra once more attempting to divert the conversation from him and his dire imaginings of revenge and dark recompense.

"So why did they fire you, Dehra?"

She glared at Brand, her eyes darkening as she recalled the events of the morning.

"Unlike Leon," she began, leveling a hard look at her brother. "I don't buy into all of this woke shit that he sucks up like candy."

"Hey...," Leon protested.

"Let her finish," Brand interrupted authoritatively.

"Thank you," Dehra said with genuine gratitude. "But Tel Gong is dead serious about it."

"Leon told me about Tel Gong at the Temp Agency," Brand said.

"Leon took you to listen to that psycho. Well. that is the company I used to work for. They are a huge telecom company. This facility designs and implements the software package that serves their cell phone platform. I was working in the Vendor Affairs Resource Services Division. They call it VARS.

"I was a CSR in a large call center. CSR's sit in a giant cubicle city in front of computer terminals and answer inbound calls from vendors who require support for the software platform.

"Today was my first day out of training. I was doing great, handling my service calls without a glitch, when the screen lit up with an inbound. It had a strange call signature. I didn't know what to do so I answered it.

"The call connects automatically when I click the 'accept' icon on the screen. I clicked the icon, and my headset went live with an ongoing call. I guess it was a mistake in the call app because the conversation was live and ongoing when I picked up.

"The people on the call apparently didn't know I had joined because their conversation continued without a pause. It was the subject of their conversation that my manager asked me most about in the exit interview.

"I didn't announce myself on the call because I didn't want to interrupt. The two men seemed very serious. I wasn't sure what they were talking about, but I clearly understood what they meant in general. One of the men on the call was Ha Wang, one of the presidents of the company. The other was a guy named Bill; at least, that is what Wang called him. Anyway, Wang, who is the COO of Tel Gong, warned Bill that something Bill had done was placing the entire 'operation in jeopardy', or so he said.

"This Bill guy told Wang that he and some paid for politicians could be shot or thrown in prison He told him something about wanting to be respected and said his role in the deal was way less serious than the Chinese guy's plan to rule the world, or something like that.

"Wang took it pretty well and asked Bill to send him some files.

"Bill said he was sending the files. Wang said he got them then the call went dead."

Dehra paused, searching the others' faces for a reaction to the strange call.

Finally, Leon broke the silence.

"So why did overhearing a conversation make you a racist?"

"I don't know. I only know that I told my manager about the call and what I could remember of the conversation. He pulled me offline and made me wait in the break room for about an hour."

"Again," Leon pressed. "How does any of this make you a racist?"

"Look," Dehra explained slowly, so Leon could keep up. "I flagged the call in the que and paged my manager. All the calls are recorded for training and quality, so I played this one for him and told him that it sounded to me like our Chinese-owned company is spying on American citizens."

Brand eyed Dehra dubiously. He had been exposed to a lot more politically correct and politically driven speech than he expected would occur in Uvalde, Texas."

Leon seemed shocked.

"So, they fired you for overhearing an incriminating conversation," Leon summarized. "It's not like you have a copy of the conversation to release to the news. Why not just let it go?"

"Well," Dehra said in a lower tone. "I kinda did save a copy on a memory stick."

"What?"

"It seemed important enough for my manager to ask me if I had shared this information with anyone else, then took me offline until he had time to speak with upper management about it. I had a wild hair that I should have some proof that I wasn't making this stuff up in case it came to me losing my job – which it did.

"Here I am, unemployed again. I was fired without the required 4 step process: no verbal or written warning; no paid day off to consider whether Tel Gong was the right place for me; they went straight to, 'sign this form, pack your shit, and get out.' The reason for my firing, the form read, was uttering racist slurs in the workplace."

Dehra withdrew a paper from her back pocket and unfolded it, presenting it to Leon.

Leon read the form with a frown.

"It says here that you are intolerant of Asian-Americans and demonstrated anti-black sentiment in your workplace conversations with co-workers and on posts and comments on your social media accounts."

"I signed a privacy release for my background check, but I never thought they would try to use my posts or comments against me. I am not a racist. I have never posted anything that would be considered racist."

"Dee," Leon continued. "Whiteness is an inherent mental disease with all of us. We have been racist so long it is a part of our DNA, so to speak. The classes explained this and taught you to keep those urges under control. You probably didn't even know you were doing it at the time."

"Shut up Leon!" she shouted in frustration.

Leon looked at Brand helplessly, holding his hands before him in supplication.

"See what I mean," he whispered conspiratorially.

Brand considered Leon for a moment. He had no intention of being drawn into a useless ideological discussion with a woke indoctrinated kid.

"Not my problem," he said finally.

"Well, it is definitely our problem now," Leon exclaimed to Dehra pointedly. "We don't have thousands of dollars in cash hanging around like our carefree friend, Brand."

"We will figure something out," Dehra vowed weakly. She gave Brand a glance that conveyed betrayal at his dismissal of her troubles.

Leon collapsed onto the sofa beside Brand with a melodramatic exhalation and a pitiful look of despair.

"This probably ruins my chances of hiring on with the largest employer in the area. Thanks, Dehra."

Dehra turned away from them towards the sink counter, her eyes welling with tears.

Brand pursed his lips, controlling his instinct to comfort her. He had to remain focused on his priorities. He was convinced the cartel would come after him. They wanted him dead. He had learned too much about their operation to live.

Dehra's cell phone rang, interrupting the uncomfortable silence.

Dehra answered the call.

"Hello," she said with a contrived cheery tone. "This is she."

A brief pause ensued as she listened to the caller.

"No," she replied to a question asked by the caller. "Just my stuff. Some photos on my desk, a book, my lunch, and my insulated cup."

Dehra listened to her former manager on the other end of the call.

"Are you sure that is all you left with?" the manager asked carefully.

"Of course, I am sure," Dehra replied with conviction.

"So, you didn't accidentally pack any company property or data when you left?"

Dehra reddened as she thought of the memory stick.

"Is something missing?" she asked with heat.

"I'm not saying you took anything on purpose, Miss Duncan. I am only following procedures required with all off-boarding employees."

"My procedure when I am wrongfully terminated," Dehra returned pointedly, "is to tell my former boss to go fuck himself. Do you have any more questions or poorly veiled accusations to deliver with your procedures?"

"There is no call for that kind of language, Miss Duncan..."

"I don't work for you anymore so stop telling me what to do, Mr. Owens."

She ended the call, placing the phone carefully on the counter. She knew Leon would impart an insightful commentary about how she should have handled the call differently. She turned towards the two men in the room.

"Not a fucking word, Leon," she warned her brother. Her tone stayed his tongue for the moment. "Carson, what are your plans?"

Brand ignored her passive aggressive tone and her intentional use of his first name.

"Let's get a bite to eat. I'll buy," he offered. He wanted more time to formulate a plan for his next move. He sensed his position was precarious considering where he had spent the last few weeks. He needed to contact the agency, but he wasn't certain how to approach the issue.

Leon stood from the sofa.

"I could eat," he agreed brightly.

Dehra brushed at her tears, nodding her acceptance of his invitation.

12

AHIRAM LEVY SMASHED HIS HIGH BALL glass against the stone hearth of the cold fireplace. The impact exploded crystal fragments, amber liquid, and ice in all directions. With a remarkable restraint he narrowly avoided sending his phone to the same fate.

Instead, he yelled into the phone.

"The last time was the last time."

The voice on the phone responded with a calm steadiness as if Ahiram had only shared a calm opinion rather than expressing murderous rage.

"This is the last time," the voice assured him with a maddening calmness.

"You said that last time."

"Things change."

"Maybe things changed for you this time. Maybe I made the final decision."

"That would not be a prudent course of action."

Ahiram's tone steadied, conveying a new and significant meaning.

"Are you threatening me?"

The man on the other end of the call did not vary his tone, as if he were unaware of the veiled threat in Ahiram's words.

"Do I need to threaten you, Ahiram?"

"Do you dare threaten me?"

Ahiram's rage simmered now, seeking a small crack from which to boil.

"Let us speak reasonably, Ahiram. I only ask you to do this one last thing, then you are free to return to your beloved Israel. Return with additional riches. Return with our gratitude in providing us this one last service."

Ahiram, former Mossad operative and present-day mercenary, ground his teeth until his jaw ached. He didn't like the patronizing tone nor the oversimplification of what he was being asked.

With a mighty effort he controlled his rage, the heat of his emotion hissing through his teeth in acquiescence. His thoughts sought order in his tormented mind. He focused upon the melting ice and wasted scotch, dripping from hearth stones onto jagged glass shards.

"Send the information," he said finally, ending the call.

Two hours later the coded email arrived with the mission and confirmation of money deposited into his offshore account. An hour after that he looked to the weaponry strapped to his black assault uniform under a light jacket.

Out the window, a large sedan pulled to the curb. He emerged from his rented town home, entered the car, and settled into the front passenger seat. He greeted three similarly dressed men seated in the car as the driver merged the car smoothly into dense traffic onto a busy boulevard.

After more than an hour in sluggish rush hour traffic, they left Dallas behind, heading south. Ahiram estimated they would arrive at the operational area somewhere around 2 AM. He settled deeper into his seat, occupying his mind with pleasant musings of returning to his homeland and his long-missed wife and children.

13

BRAND AWOKE SUDDENLY. He lay in Dehra's bed, frozen in place, his senses strung tightly. He inhaled lightly and slowly. He detected the faint smell of gasoline. To his left Dehra breathed rhythmically in her deep sleep. He listened intently but heard nothing. He was troubled, unsure what had roused him from a dream of his old friend Bert.

In the dream he and his late friend sat together in an unfamiliar living room, in an unfamiliar house, watching a dark television.

Bert turned to him with a serious look and said, "You'd best watch your ass, tough guy."

Brand had awakened with a start.

He remained stock still, listening with tensed nerves. Still, he heard nothing…There! He heard a muffled sound outside the window on Dehra's side of the bed.

Brand slipped from the bedding. He gave only a moment's consideration to his nudity, dismissing it for the moment. He moved quietly, settling his weight carefully on the pads of his bare feet. He picked his way soundlessly across the floor, parting the curtain from the window frame enough to see outside. Below him, a man wearing dark clothing flicked a lighter, setting a small fire under the mobile home.

He saw the man more clearly in the new firelight. He wore a full-faced ski mask and black gloves. Brand made out the shiny leather of a slung holster in the growing light of the blaze.

The arsonist cast a cautious glance at the window but seemed oblivious to the slightly parted curtain. Perhaps the flame had spoiled his night vision.

Brand watched as the man moved quickly out of the fire's glow towards the front of the mobile home.

Another flickering light caught his attention from the other end of the narrow mobile home. Another fire was being set.

Brand moved towards the back door. He tried the handle and the door opened only a fraction of an inch before it jammed against an obstruction. The door had been barred from the outside.

He was trapped. It occurred to him that maybe he was not trapped, instead that he was being flushed towards the front door. His reasoning sped along crazily as he struggled to come to terms with assailants in clandestine uniforms setting fires to a mobile home, locking the occupants inside or maybe to drive them to the front door. How could the Cartel have found him so quickly?

He considered dressing to meet this foe. Instead, he made his way silently to the front door, the smell of smoke filling the air around him. He had to know the intentions of his attackers. The front doorknob turned easily. He pushed the door open no more than a fraction of an inch. The door moved without impediment. That confirmed that the assailants expected him and the others to flee the fire out the front door. His training and his common sense warned him of an ambush. He carefully pulled the door closed and turned towards the bedrooms in the rear of the trailer.

Brand arrived at Leon's bedroom first. He clapped a hand over Leon's mouth as he woke him from his loud snoring.

"Mmmmpff," a startled Leon managed through Brand's restricting grasp.

"It's me," Brand said in a low but authoritative tone. "Shut up and listen to me. The house is on fire. We have to get out of here, but there are men with guns waiting for us outside the front door. I need you to get dressed quickly and wait for me here. I will get Dehra and we will leave together. Do you understand?"

Leon tried to reply through Brand's hand.

"Nod if you understand?"

Leon nodded with wide frightened eyes.

"Don't make a sound while you get dressed, and do not leave this room until I return. I will kill you myself if you don't follow my instructions to the letter."

Leon nodded once more. His eyes reflected his growing fear. He surveyed Brand's nakedness with wide eyes. Brand realized that a portion of Leon's fear was of him as much as it was for the dire portent of the fire.

Brand was gone in an instant. Moments later, he returned with Dehra in tow. She wore a sweatshirt and jeans. He had pulled on jeans, tee shirt, and his shoes.

Leon was dressed and fully awake. Smoke floated just below the ceiling, growing denser by the second.

Brand led them to the hallway. He opened a narrow adjoining door, revealing an old water heater next to the air handling unit for the mobile home's ancient air conditioning system.

Brand knelt, testing the floor and the lower walls of the closet with pressure from fingers and palms. As he suspected, the floor gave under the pressure. He knew that old water heaters and air handlers leaked. Over time, particularly with the thin wall and floor components that make up mobile home structures, water rot is inevitable.

The exterior fires roaring with their mounting heat energy, and the increasing cloud of dense smoke, clearly indicated the fire had engulfed much of the mobile home. They were securely pinned within a metal-skinned death trap.

Brand knew the stories of many mobile home fires. There were rarely survivors. Mobile homes seemed to be built with the most flammable materials available based upon the speed with which they burned and the low occurrence of survivorship when they caught fire.

The popping of chemically treated building materials, cracking structural components, and melting electrical outlets, covered much of the noise of him pulling the water heater through the door and into the hallway. Water spewed from a crack in the copper water line as it bent under Brand's efforts.

He kicked a hole in the rot blackened flooring. He pulled Dehra towards the opening and helped her roughly through the ragged hole in the floor.

Leon required no coaxing. He was thin, and easily shimmied down the ragged opening, collapsing onto his stomach on the damp earth beneath the house.

Brand widened the hole but scraped flesh from his arms and shoulders as he scrambled below, flames chasing him from the hallway.

Brand saw Leon crawling towards the front of the mobile home, the dim light from the street beckoning through the lattice skirting. Brand grabbed his ankle and pulled him towards the rear of the blazing mobile home.

Leon kicked out with panic. Brand pulled again with an irresistible iron grip, causing Leon pain.

"This way," Brand uttered through his teeth. He was fully enraged at the attack on their lives. He was in no mood for Leon's rebellious hijinks.

They moved away from the exposed front of the mobile home towards the darkness of the metal skirting at the back of the trailer. They cowered as a loud crash and the whoosh of engulfing flames announced the collapse of the mobile home's thin wood and metal roof.

Brand kicked at two panels of the skirting, opening a passage to the outside and safety. He helped Dehra through the hole and to her feet. He saw her face dimly in the pall. Her cheeks were wet with tears, her eyes swollen. He was impressed with her silence and her courage considering the fear she obviously felt.

Leon stood, moving closer.

Brand grasped his bony shoulder.

"Take Dehra and head that way."

He pointed towards the woods behind the burning home.

"Get to the nearest house and call for help. I'll catch up with you as soon as I can."

"What is going on…?"

"Leon, I don't have time to break this down for you. Do what I told you. Take care of your sister."

Brand moved away towards the far end of the burning structure.

Leon glanced fearfully at the blaze then pulled Dehra away towards the woods.

The fire was at its apex and Brand had to keep a safe distance from the flames as he cautiously moved towards the front yard. Near the front corner of the mobile home, he crouched behind a utility housing for either electrical or telecommunications equipment.

He scanned the area before the burning building. A dark sedan sat idling across the street with the parking lights aglow. The fire's leaping blaze allowed him to make out dim faces of men in the car watching the fire. One of them wore a full faced stocking cap like the man he had seen starting the fire.

Brand looked to his right. The adjoining lot was filled with junk, old cars, decrepit trailers, and scattered household appliances.

He dropped to all fours and moved into the junk yard. With difficulty he made his way towards the street. The car faced his direction on the opposite curb, and he had no cover from which to approach the vehicle undetected. From his vantage at the edge of the lot, he saw no way to cross the street without being seen by the car's occupants.

Sirens sounded in the distance. He didn't have much time. The urge to assail the attackers consumed him. Desire for retribution burned in him with an irresistible force. He struck upon a less risky plan, although his instincts warned him, an equally reckless one.

He returned to the cover of the junk pile, moving away from the car towards the adjacent property. Climbing over a short chain link fence surrounding a yellow frame house, he straightened, walking openly towards the street.

The driveway was empty. He assumed the house was also unoccupied. The street was bordered by few homes, most abandoned. This explained the lack of neighbors' attention one would normally expect during a house fire.

Brand put his hands in his pockets and feigned guarded interest in the catastrophe. He did not look towards the car but kept his gaze on the fire. He heard the car shifted into gear. He casually blundered into the car's path in case the driver pulled away from the curb. The headlights flicked on, temporarily blinding him. He raised a hand to cover his eyes, looking directly at the car.

"Hey," Brand said with as much bystander interest as he could fake. "What happened, man?"

The driver rolled down his window.

Brand figured the others didn't want to expose themselves.

"Get out of the way."

Brand moved to the curb, towards the driver.

"Is there anyone inside?" he asked with as neutral a tone as he could muster.

"None of our business," the driver spat impatiently.

Brand was nearly at the driver's window.

He heard a voice in the car say, "Just drive."

Brand slammed a fist on the hood.

"Aren't you gonna call the cops or something?"

The driver cursed as he brought a pistol with a silencer out the window.

Brand felt his training take over as he stepped towards the gunman, grabbing the automatic with his left hand and the gunman's arm with his right. He held the element of surprise over an opponent restricted in movement and defenseless. He backhanded him in the face with his right fist.

The stunned driver released his grip on the pistol and the car brake. The car moved forward. Brand wrested control of the pistol from the stunned driver. He shot the driver in the face. The back door window broke as one of the passengers fired a silenced round at him. Likely due to the small 9mm caliber, the safety glass deflected the bullet away from its intended target.

Brand fired two more shots through the shattered rear door window, striking the near passenger. Brand ducked as a fresh volley of bullets erupted from within the car. He moved quickly around the back of the car which was picking up speed as it moved driverless and directionless down the dark street.

Both passenger side doors opened with a fusillade of covering fire as the occupants sought to escape the deadly confines of the drifting automobile. Brand fired several rounds through the rear window glass. The first broke the window, the last struck the rear passenger, his inert body folding onto the street, narrowly missed by the slowly rolling tires.

The front seat passenger, Ahiram Levy, flung himself violently from the auto and rolled clear of the moving car, scanning the area behind the car for the surprise assailant. He recognized in this foe skill and training. A lifetime of action under fire allowed his mind to work as he moved tactically into a defensive posture.

How, he wondered, did a trained combatant happen to be on the site of a clandestine operation?

His targets were known to be TC MOTS, short for *The Common Man on the Street* – rank civilians. He had expected no resistance. He and his team had remained only long enough to be certain there were no survivors. This man had appeared to be a curious neighbor.

Ahiram settled into a low defensive position, pistol trained and ready for instant suppression if the gunman appeared from behind the car, which continued to move slowly down the street. The former Mussad agent realized too late that the gunman was no longer taking cover behind the slowly moving car.

Ahiram shifted his aim to the top of the car, where the man plummeted mid-flight towards him from atop the car. Ahiram instinctively absorbed the attack with a collapse of his squatting posture and rolled with the impetus of the attacker. In an instant he was atop the attacker, grappling for advantage. The stranger was quick, bringing a knee hard into his thigh, the blow seeking the pressure point there. Ahiram accepted the blow in exchange for a fresh grip meant to gain immediate advantage over his opponent.

Brand turned his head away from the attack, countering with an evade and dominate technique, using the man's energy against him.

The move created a small separation between them. Brand brought a fist up and into his victim's throat.

Surprisingly, Brand felt the impact of a countermove from the smaller man. Brand had not counted upon a continued struggle after collapsing his foe's airway.

Brand grunted from the body blow, bringing a foot up hard into the man's groin.

His opponent fell to the pavement, writhing in the waning glow of the mobile home fire.

Brand looked around him. The sirens were close. He knelt, disarming his man with a deft gesture. He secured the weapons in his waistband and dragged Ahiram over the curb and into the brush beside the road. He struck him hard in the face, subduing him and discouraging further attacks.

Ahiram labored desperately to open his airway, clawing at his throat with both hands. His abbreviated inhalations came with a rattle and ragged moans.

Brand squatted a short distance away, watching the man struggle to breath.

As Ahiram regained minimal access to life saving air, he favored Brand with a hateful glare. Brand leaned forward and struck Ahiram heavily with the pistol butt, breaking his nose.

Ahiram's eyes teared and blood flowed.

"Don't give me the hard look," Brand warned. "You tried to kill me and my friends. You're not gonna like what comes next if you don't tell me what I want to hear."

Ahiram prepared himself for death. The man was not a true pro, or he would know that a lonely death in the dark is something all wet work operatives prepare themselves for. Threats would not work on him. The lie of life would not loosen his tongue. Instead, Ahiram recited the words he had rehearsed every day of his life since the day he took his first life. He would leave this world on his terms. Fear would not dictate those terms, neither would this foe.

"We are getting nowhere," he said as best he could with his injured throat. "Save your threats. Spare me your lies. Finish this if you have the nerve to do it."

Brand considered the man's words and his calm demeanor with curious interest. He recognized fear in the man, but also a strangely calm resignation. Brand knew instinctively the man would tell him nothing.

He glanced up as a firetruck arrived. The chasing police car stopped short of the fire, next to the black sedan, idling but jammed against a powerline pole at the end of the street.

Two officers in khaki uniforms and straw cowboy hats approached the car. Spotting the gunshot victims inside, their cautious demeanor changed to alarmed action. They drew their sidearms and spoke rapidly into shoulder mounted walkies. Brand's attention returned to the prostate man before him.

The other watched him with interest.

"Get up," Brand ordered, his decision made. "Walk to the street. Turn yourself into the Sheriff deputies and you live. Or I can end it for you now."

Ahiram stood slowly, clutching his throat.

Brand stepped back outside of foot range.

"Don't try it, tough guy," he warned. "It doesn't take much effort to pull the trigger on a silenced Glock. Go now."

Ahiram headed with an unsteady step towards the police car.

In their singular attention to the fire and the possibility of victims within the structure, the firefighters did not notice the man in black as he trudged past the firetruck towards the officers.

The deputies did however notice the approaching man and moved forward to meet him, guns at the ready.

Brand moved through the thick brush and into the dark woods beyond. The man he had captured was not Mexican. He did not seem to be a typical Sicario associated with the Cartel.

Why had he been attacked? If the man was a Cartel asset, how had he found him so quickly? Brand had been at large only a few days. He had escaped from the back of the dirt hauler truck in the darkness of night at the main signal light in town. No one had seen him arrive. He had kept a low profile.

He was no expert on Cartel operations, but he had been exposed to their violence and pursued by their assassins. Where were the Mexican Sicarios, the foot soldiers for the Cartel? These men seemed like a completely different kind of hard ass. The dark clothed man spoke with an accent, but it sounded more middle eastern than Mexican. He was no expert on dialect or accents, but he doubted there was some remote part of Mexico where they spoke with that accent.

His quandary lay within the knowledge that he was pursued by the Cartel. Had he pissed off someone else? Was there another force arrayed against him? He wanted to contact Agent Kilgore with the DEA. Surely the man could shed light on his predicament.

His concerns turned once more to Leon and Dehra. He had brought this upon them. They could have perished because of him. He had to get them to safety. Their home was gone. He doubted they had many options now. He committed himself to do what he could for them.

Brand put a quarter mile between himself and the fire before crossing the street, headed in the direction Dehra and Leon had fled.

14

LEON SAT ACROSS THE TABLE FROM DEHRA, sipping coffee. The small cafe seemed unreal to him in its calm routine. Those scant patrons who filled the few chairs seemed to be regulars, going about their day as normal. The buxom waitress bustled about with a smile and a wink as she refilled coffee cups and took orders.

Leon eyed Dehra who sat silently, the table empty before her. The ordeal they had just escaped seemed a fiction in contrast with the unaffected normality of the cafe. In that alternate reality the only palpable reminder of how close they had come to death was the heat and remaining nervous energy from his fear driven adrenalin surge. He wondered how those few early morning patrons could be oblivious to a life and death struggle played out only a few yards from them.

The waitress returned to their table.

"Are you sure I can't bring you something, sugar?" she asked of Dehra.

Dehra shook her head, her eyes fixed upon the white speckled top of the steel trimmed booth.

She wanted nothing to eat or drink. Her mind whirled with myriad imaginings of strange assailants trapping them within a burning mobile home. Chief in her troubled mind was Carson Brand. She felt with certainty that he and his mysterious past were the cause of this attack. She remembered his actions under the duress of choking smoke, inescapable flames, and a likely death. He had acted decisively and calmly. She guessed he was highly trained and vastly experienced in dangerous situations. His boasts at the bar about being a secret agent seemed to have some basis in truth.

Anger whitened her knuckles and furrowed her brow as she lamented the loss of everything they owned, and their narrow escape with their lives. All had been a result of their mysterious guest's unknown deeds in the past.

Less than a half an hour earlier, when they arrived at the café, she had insisted upon contacting the police, but Leon had confined her to the booth with another display of his unusually cautious judgement. He had demanded they wait for Brand.

She argued that Brand had told them to call for help at the nearest house. Leon remained unmoved, insisting that they wait for further information from Brand.

She acquiesced with the condition that they wait no more than a half an hour, then they would contact the authorities.

Leon agreed.

She looked up from her inspection of the cracked Formica covering the booth's table as Brand passed the window beside them and entered the café.

He spotted them and moved quickly to their booth, taking a seat beside Dehra.

Nothing was said at first as they sat silently, gathering their private feelings about the night's travails.

Brand broke the silence.

"Are you two okay?" he asked, looking each over in turn.

Leon nodded, wide eyed, as he surveyed this new man who had operated so coolly in a life-threatening situation.

Dehra watched her brother's silent worship of Brand with derision. By her estimation, Brand was no hero. He drew those evil men to them. Getting she and Leon out alive was small repayment for the damage done.

"Why were we attacked?" Dehra asked abruptly.

She shifted with a squeak of the vinyl bench seat as she looked more fully at Brand.

Brand shook his head, struggling to assemble his confusion into a reasonable explanation. He was grateful that neither of the others attempted to hurry his response. He exhaled as he decided on a direction.

"I have a lot of unanswered questions about that, but this is what I know."

He sat back in the booth.

"The team that attacked us was a pro hit team. They were waiting for us out front as the house burned. There were to be no survivors."

"What the f…"

"Leon," Dehra shushed her brother. "Let him finish."

Brand nodded his thanks.

"I am guessing that you two have figured out that I have a past, and you are thinking that you got caught in the crossfire. I tend to agree except…"

"You put us in danger." Dehra burst out with a fresh torrent of tears.

"Except," Brand repeated. "These guys don't seem to be associated with the people chasing me. These men were not Mexican, and they were well-trained."

"Mexican?" Leon sputtered. "What are you talking about? Mexican Mafia?"

"Yeah," Brand replied calmly. "They killed my best friend and now they are after me. I have dealt with their men a lot lately. These guys tonight were not like what I have encountered before. Cartel goons tend to be typical tough guys who happen to belong to the Cartel. They rarely have advanced training. Those who do are usually prior service military. That doesn't account for much in a special op's environment."

"What is all of this supposed to mean to us?" Dehra pressed him.

Brand considered the angry blonde for a moment, rubbing his chin in an unconscious gesture of considered self-scrutiny.

"It means that the only answer I have so far is I think you two are caught up in the crossfire between me and Cartel goons who want me dead. I don't know how they found me or, for that matter, how they found me so quickly."

Dehra laughed without mirth.

"So, you are in denial because the Mexican Mafia used different tactics and people when they attacked us, and they were better at locating you than you believe they should be. I've got news for you, tough guy. They are onto you, and we are all in mortal danger because you have a shitty past and your chickens have come home to roost."

Dehra shoved him rudely until he stood from the vinyl booth bench. She shouldered past him and shoved him again just for good measure.

Despite her efforts, Brand hardly moved under the assault. He was more undone by her underlying anger than he was by the physical assault.

She growled her frustration through clenched teeth.

"They are here, and you are fucked. By the way," she shouted. "So are we!"

Dehra turned on her heel and stomped away through the front doors and into the lightening gray skies of the early morning.

The few patrons sipping coffee and eating greasy breakfast food watched the drama, silently masticating like lazy cattle. Brand returned their looks for a moment before he walked out of the café.

Leon remained seated, a blank look on his face. He had never seen his sister so upset.

The waitress approached cautiously and slipped a green and white striped bill before him. She departed immediately, returning to the small table where she had been rolling silverware into paper napkins, and refilling empty salt and pepper shakers.

Leon glanced at the check before depositing a few rumpled bills atop it. He rose, rushing to the door to follow the others.

15

AHIRAM WALKED OUT THE FRONT DOOR of the Uvalde County Justice Center. The early morning was breezy and cool. He wore his black tactical clothing, but he no longer carried his holsters, knives, or tactical bric a brac.

The deputies had retained his weapon-related property for evidence. The surprising phone call from the fed had tendered his release but was not sufficiently compelling for him to keep his property. With the sight of dead bodies in their recent memories, the deputies refused to allow him to leave even minimally armed and / or dangerous.

He strode to an idling car waiting at the curb. He took his place in the front passenger seat. The driver, a beefy man in chinos and a long sleeve pull over, wisely made no attempt to engage him in conversation as he pulled the car away from the jail house.

The driver's cell phone rang. The big man glanced at the display before handing it to Ahiram.

"It's for you."

Ahiram answered the call.

"Yes."

"You have made a mess of this operation."

"I will handle it," he assured the familiar voice.

"Three of your team are dead. You were arrested. We had to call in a big favor to get you out. What makes you think you can handle this or anything else. If we hadn't intervened, you would still be in solitary confinement with no chance for bail or release."

"As I said…"

"Shut the fuck up, Ahiram," the voice commanded with unfamiliar anger. "You have lost any credibility. The targets were a man and woman with no idea you were coming. They are civilians. You had the element of surprise.

"We have activated a backup team. None of them crave retirement as you apparently do. None of them will end their careers as shamefully as you now have. If we could risk exposing you, we would have left you to rot in a Texas prison."

Ahiram underwent a remarkable transformation during the last part of the phone call. He was pale. His expression was strained. His breathing was shallow and labored. His words hissed into the phone with the timbre and rattle of his rage.

"We never saw the man and woman you wanted," he growled. "The man who attacked me and my team was well-trained and held the element of surprise. He killed the others with a gesture. He overcame me with little more effort. Who is this man? Who does he work for? How did he know we were coming? You might consider briefing your new team more thoroughly than you did us - with timely and relevant information as to the security measures the targets have around them."

The voice remained silent for a long time after Ahiram's impossible claims of a counter team or operative involved in the operation.

Ahiram glanced at the driver as he pulled the car into the driveway before a small house. Ahiram concluded it was a safe house.

"I'm killing your man for your disrespect."

The driver looked at him sharply, alarm plain on his face.

Ahiram swung a wide arc with his left arm, driving the phone into the driver's eye socket. He bent over the center console. With repeated blows, he struck the protruding phone into the dying man's skull until it would go no further.

Ahiram grimaced with surprise as he heard the voice's continued warnings against killing their man. The sound was muffled within the man's head, but still audible.

Inside the safe house he found a cache of weapons and tactical gear. He chose from the inventory, arming himself sufficiently to hunt for and defeat the unknown assailant.

He had no idea where to begin his search. If there had been another man and woman in the mobile home, and they had survived the fire, they could lead him to the man who killed his team. It was highly improbable that this man could hide with two untrained civilians. Civilians always leave a trail.

16

THE SUN WAS RISING WHEN BRAND ARRIVED at the curb across the street from the smoldering remains of Dehra's and Leon's mobile home. The only recognizable features of their home were Dehra's car and Leon's little truck.

Dehra sat on the hood of her singed car. She cradled her knees within her folded arms. She faced the blackened axles and floor framing which used to be hidden beneath the metal skin and corrugated roofing of her mobile home.

Brand stopped short of her place atop the hood of the car. She turned her head briefly, ascertaining who had joined her. Her expression grew unpleasant as she returned her gaze to the ruin before her.

"What do you want?" she asked without looking at him.

Brand did not reply.

They surveyed the spectacle before them for a long time.

Leon emerged from the woods. He moved past Brand and took a seat beside Dehra. He draped an arm over her shoulder.

"I love you, sis," he said weakly.

Tears welled in her blue eyes.

Brand shifted his feet uncomfortably. He felt miserable responsibility for their loss. He wasn't accustomed to being in the wrong. His life had been tumultuous since Bert's death, but the collateral damage had been limited exclusively to him and his enemies. These two people before him were guilty of nothing more than taking him in when most others wouldn't have. Their simple lives were ruined because of their kindness to a stranger.

Brand stuffed his hands in his pockets as his anger rose once more. He looked down. He withdrew his right hand, revealing the stack of hundreds he had stuffed there that morning. He had been so preoccupied he had forgotten about it.

He struggled with his decision to give the money to them, vacillating with uncertainty. He suspected, in their current state of mind, he might appear insensitive, thinking that a handout would make things right. He returned the cash to his pocket, vowing to wait for a better opportunity.

Leon looked back at Brand, interrupting the silence with characteristic candor.

"So how are you gonna make this right, Mr. Brand?"

Brand considered him but made no reply.

"You are responsible for this mess," Leon pressed brazenly. "What are you going to do to fix it?"

Dehra turned her face to Brand. It was clear that she wanted to curtail any further involvement with him, but the memory of the money he possessed silenced her for the moment.

Because he had been considering the very thing Leon pressed him for, Brand was nonplussed by the suddenness of Leon's outburst. The assured tone of entitlement with which it was delivered rankled him, nonetheless.

A defensive protest struggled to escape his clenched teeth. Finally, Brand sighed in surrender to the reason behind Leon's terse words.

"Let's get you two some clothes. Afterwards we can figure out where we can stay."

A police car turned onto the street, approaching them slowly.

Brand's tone registered an urgency his words scarcely needed.

"I am just a passerby who saw you two sitting here. I wasn't there last night. Tell the cop you managed to escape out the back door before the place went up completely."

Neither Leon nor Dehra acknowledged his request as the cruiser stopped on the street behind their cars.

Two sheriff's deputies emerged from the car.

"Are you Dehra or Leon Duncan," one of the officers asked. The other cop drew a cigarette from his pocket and lighted it.

"I'm Dehra Duncan," she admitted uncertainly. "This is my brother Leon."

She indicated her brother with a nod in his direction.

"I don't know this guy," she added, favoring Brand with a frown.

The deputies gave Brand a moment of scrutiny before returning their attention to the other two.

"Thank God you two were able to escape with your lives. Can you tell us what happened?"

Brand's attention was drawn to the nearby intersection where a dark colored car turned onto the street, approaching slowly.

Leon shifted his position to speak as Dehra interrupted him.

"We were asleep. I woke up and smelled smoke. I woke up my brother and we were able to get out the back door before the trailer went up."

Brand watched as the car passed the idling police car. He recognized the driver. He was the man he had released to turn himself into the cops. The driver met his gaze with an intense stare. The threat behind the look was unmistakable.

"Why didn't you two wait for the fire department to arrive?" The deputy asked.

"We didn't think about it," Dehra replied without a pause to think about her answer. "It was dark, and we had just escaped certain death. We wanted to get inside somewhere where there was light and people. We went to the café on the main road."

Brand watched the car move away and turn onto the next intersecting road and out of view. He listened to the exchange between Dehra and the deputy carefully. He knew a cursory look into her story would place him at the café.

"I saw them at the café and approached them," Brand explained. "She was crying, and they both seemed upset so I asked if there was anything I could do. We had a cup of coffee and I accompanied them here."

"Do you have some ID, sir?" The deputy asked.

"I don't," Brand replied honestly. "I've been down on my luck. I was just passing through and stopped for a bite to eat before moving on to San Antonio."

Both deputies gave Brand their full attention. The last stranger they had encountered was dressed in tactical attire and had contacts high up in the federal government. They were willing to consider any stranger to be more than he appeared.

Brand saw the heightened interest in him with concealed alarm.

"I'm a carpenter by trade," he continued by way of building upon his claim. "I would stick around here if I found construction work."

The deputies regarded his words with doubt.

"I don't have my tools," Brand pressed. "But I am a lead man and can do anything from framing and cornice to interior trim, if you know somebody looking for someone to do that kind of work."

"Are you from up north, son?" the smoking deputy asked with wry humor.

"San Antonio," Brand replied.

"I didn't think white men worked construction anymore with the rush of immigrants from Mexico."

Leon sat straighter at the blatant racism of the deputy's statement.

Dehra placed a restraining hand upon his knee.

"That's a big part of the reason I am on the road," Brand agreed, accepting the comment eagerly. His construction past served him in this hurriedly concocted alibi. "It didn't used to be that way."

The deputy shook his head at the deteriorating conditions at the border.

"You got that right, mister."

The other deputy interrupted their diatribe.

"What's your name, sir?"

"Matthew Kilgore."

"Mr. Kilgore, I doubt you will find gainful employment here. Move on immediately. I'm sure you can catch a ride on the main road."

To Leon and Dehra, he said, "Do you two have a place to stay?"

"We're working on it," Leon replied with a meaningful glance at Brand.

"We take care of our own," the deputy assured him with an equally significant look at the outsider, Brand. "Let us know if we can be of further assistance."

The deputies returned to their car.

"Who's Matthew Kilgore?" Leon asked Brand in a louder voice than was necessary.

Brand's silent gaze caused Leon to look askance uncomfortably.

They watched in silence as the patrol car pulled away from the curb, then moved out of sight.

"A friend," Brand replied to Leon's unwelcome question. "I don't know who knows what about me. My intent is to keep you two out of any more trouble. Let's find a place for you two to live while I get this sorted out."

17

AHIRAM WAS PLEASED AT THE EASY SUCCESS his hunch had yielded. His targets lived still, but their security man was with them. It was unfortunate that the deputies' presence prevented him from completing his task, but he was confident that he would be headed back to Dallas that evening, his mission successfully fulfilled.

He had a good look at the man who had taken out his team. He didn't seem remarkable at first view. He was maybe an inch over six feet, medium build with a hint of athleticism. The true strength of the man made itself apparent in the look in his eyes when their gazes locked as he passed. There was no fear or weakness conveyed in that look. Ahiram guessed the man was as eager for their next bout as he. The encounter would happen soon enough. Ahiram, however, had no intention of indulging some misplaced whim of honor in fair and open combat. He would catch his prey at his most vulnerable and finish him quickly and efficiently.

His clarity of purpose was defined as receiving the rest of his money and returning to his home country, to live out his remaining days with his family. He desperately wanted what so few in his line of work got. He wanted to grow old watching his children blossom into adulthood to raise children of their own who would gather at their grandpa's knee.

Ahiram possessed all the knowledge necessary to complete his mission here. He knew the types and colors of the two cars in the drive. He had a definitive recognition of his targets. He knew where they were at that moment. The security man was clearly identified in the clear light of early morning. The final component was to create the opportunity or wait for the first provided opportunity to dispatch all three.

The security man, the previous night, had caught Ahiram and his team by surprise. That advantage was a one-time thing. The Israeli was certain that man to man, in a straight up fight, he was the better. Nevertheless, Ahiram would determine the place and time of their next conflict. The advantage would be his.

He had willingly sacrificed the element of surprise for the surety of recognizing his targets. Consequently, his quarry knew what he drove and his face. His first task was to replace the dark sedan with something else.

He drove for a short while before he pulled into the parking lot of a grocery store. The lot was surprisingly full considering the time of day. Ahiram parked the sedan in the middle of the parking lot. He didn't want to risk the remote chance that the security man might spy the car by chance. He retrieved his duffle and abandoned the car. He walked the lot casually, taking quiet inventory of the autos around him. He knew that the cars parked farthest from the store typically were those driven by store employees. He walked directly to an older import. The fender was dented, and the paint faded from years in the Texas sun. The year model suited Ahiram in that it would be easy to start.

The driver side door was unlocked, a habit to which he had grown accustomed during his time in Texas. He squeezed the full duffle into the back seat, smashing empty drink cups and fast-food bags under the weight. He slid into the front seat, looking around cautiously before ducking low and overriding the ignition. The car started with a poorly maintained shudder, and he was back on the road, alert for either of the two cars he had seen before the burned husk of the mobile home.

His search was brief. Uvalde was a small town, easy to cover. The main highway linking San Antonio and Del Rio, ran through the central intersection of town. Ahiram was waiting at the light when he saw a dingy white import pickup speed through the intersection before him. He recognized the vehicle as the small truck he had noticed before the remains of the torched trailer house. The driver was the younger man of the two men he had seen before the ruined home.

Ahiram turned right on red from the left turn lane, taking up a cautious pursuit of the aggressively driven little truck. He gained on the vehicle until he was a strategically wise distance behind. He followed as the truck turned down a side street.

Leon parked at the curb before a white frame house with three cars in the driveway and one parked on the unmown grass of the front yard. He needed to replenish the meager stash of pot burned up in the fire. He hoped his dealer would extend him a short-term credit.

He circled his truck, stepping onto the curb when he heard a passing car stop behind him. He turned towards the street. A faded blue car idled roughly on the street. An older man with dark hair and a bushy moustache smiled at him.

"Can I help you, brother," Leon asked, taking a step towards the car.

"Very kind of you," the driver replied with an accent Leon failed to place. "That man I saw you with this morning, who is he?"

"What…"

A gun barrel peeked out the window, but the man's expression remained friendly.

"You and your sister were in the company of another man. Who is he?"

Leon recognized the danger before him too late.

"You'll find out soon enough when he kills you for this," Leon replied with shrill defiance. "Fuck you."

The pistol belched flame and Leon fell limply to the pavement. Ahiram opened the door and collected the boy's cell phone before he drove away.

18

BRAND SAT SILENTLY IN THE PASSENGER SEAT. Dehra sat stiffly behind the wheel of her car. Her lips were set in a forbidding line of consternation. She drove purposefully, both hands on the wheel. She pulled into a parking lot Brand indicated with a gesture. She parked her car in the shade of a porte-cochere at the entrance of an extended stay suites hotel.

Her cold eyes remained forward as she extended a hand towards Brand.

He dug in his pocket, withdrawing the wad of hundreds. He peeled off five and handed them to Dehra. Without a word she opened the car door and strode in businesslike fashion to the hotel office.

As he waited, Brand looked out the window at the empty hotel parking lot. He was uncomfortable with Dehra's anger towards him. The more she refused to cooperate with him, the more difficult it would be to protect her.

He accepted the blame for the attack upon them, but he was troubled by the details of the attack. The man he captured and turned into the sheriff's deputies was not Mexican. The others in the car appeared to be Caucasian, based upon the two faces he could see, and the skin tone of the face behind the ski mask of the third man. The man was arrested early that morning but was at large a few hours later. The Cartel could not affect so quick a release.

Besides that, he was perplexed at how quickly the cartel had located him. Even if they had concluded that he had escaped in one of the dirt trucks, how could they have known that he left the convoy along the way? And if they figured that out, how would they have known to find him in Uvalde? He knew the road well. There were many places he could have escaped along Hwy 90. If they knew enough about him to find him so quickly, why wouldn't they have suspected his location to be San Antonio, his hometown? Had the driver seen him and reported him? He remembered how dark the night was when he climbed out of the truck at the signal light in the center of town. At that late hour, there were no other cars on the road in either direction. He had ducked as low as his injuries allowed and had crept towards the side of the highway as the trucks air brakes whooshed and the truck moved away into the night, headed east on the highway. There had been no flash of the trailer's taillights as might have happened if the driver had noticed someone climbing out of his truck trailer. Brand shook his head doubtfully.

Dehra returned to the driver seat with a receipt and a large key with a red plastic oval attached. The number on the plastic disc read 215. Brand held out his hand. She handed him the receipt.

"The room is three hundred a week," she announced casually. "I will keep the change if it's alright with you."

Brand made no reply as he studied the paper. He assumed she was not seeking agreement or permission.

She put the car in gear and circled the building until she spotted the room number on one of the second-floor doors. She parked the car and killed the ignition. She sat motionless. Finally, she turned to Brand.

"What are your plans, Carson?"

Brand suspected she was trying to get rid of him. The allure of going it alone appealed to him. However, the image of the killer passing them in the dark car came to him with a klaxon bell warning. They were in danger in his company or on their own. His instincts warned him to maintain his vigilance over them.

"I don't want you around us anymore," Dehra said, strong passion hardening her words.

Brand shrugged helplessly.

He had no desire to debate the matter. His initial desire reasserted itself. He would be safer alone without Dehra and Leon to babysit. Maybe his instincts were way off base. Dehra's and Leon's safety might be better served if he separated himself from them. He opened the passenger side door and stepped onto the hot pavement of the parking lot.

Dehra scrambled out of the car. She was angry at Brand's easy dismissal.

"You bastard," she screamed. "You fucked us and now you walk away, easy as you please."

"You are not making any sense, Dehra," he countered. He was annoyed with her vacillating comments. "What do you want? More money?"

He peeled off several hundreds as he walked around the car towards her. He grabbed her wrist and stuffed the bills in her hand.

"I don't want your money," she cried, tears welling up in her blue eyes. "I want my life back."

"Sorry," was his weak reply.

She accepted the money and he turned from her. He walked away as she watched and cried.

19

DEHRA RETRIEVED HER SMALL TOTE from the back seat. She again fought an overwhelming sense of guilt for bringing the bizarre stranger into hers and her brother's lives.

Two days before, they had been happy. A renewed sense of well-being was the overarching tone of their lives. With a new job and hope for a brighter future, they had gone to the Purple Cow to celebrate. Meeting Carson Brand had seemed a continuation of the positive momentum they were experiencing. His strange appearance at the bar was troubling, but he was the first man she had met in a long time who had his own money and seemed like he would be sweet to her. Broke, abusive men had been her lot in life until Brand, or Carson, or Ben Franklin, or whatever his real name was, arrived. What a mistake. Now she was homeless, jobless, and devoid of hope for any sort of viable future.

She climbed the stairs to the door of her room and inserted the key card. The suite was nice compared to the messy mobile home, but the clinically neutral décor and perfect neatness of the space depressed her. She acknowledged that she wasn't much of a housekeeper, but her mess was familiar and held a singular significance of belonging to her.

This professionally cleaned and maintained habitat was as impersonal as the commercials she had seen for them. The guests were always neutral looking and mindless with their self-assured smiles and overly acted happiness in their new hotel room. The room was a plastic facsimile in a plastic world of make-believe.

She entered one of the two bedrooms. She retrieved her phone as she dropped her bag on the perfectly made bed. She texted the name of the hotel and their suite number to Leon.

She dropped the phone on the bed with a frown. Leon was probably scoring more drugs. It was a certainty he had not remembered to retrieve his stash during their hasty escape from the mobile home fire.

She returned to the bright central living area of the suite and dropped onto the rough upholstery of the firm sofa. She picked up the remote and turned on the TV. She felt a small sense of happiness that she would have access to cable, something they had been unable to afford.

She clicked the remote, shuffling through several channels. Most of the stations presented infomercials, reality show reruns and news. The few channels that offered programming with a plot were more ads than content.

She started at a knock at the door. She smiled as she remembered that she had not given Leon a key to the room. She wanted to see her brother, to let him know that she would fix this for them.

She opened the door a fraction. It burst open, knocking her to the beige carpeted floor. Rather than Leon, there was a large man dressed in black with a pistol in his hand. He closed the door and strode towards her. She dragged her butt across the carpet as she clambered away in a panic, trying to get her feet under her.

The man was fast and was immediately upon her, grabbing a handful of her hair in one hand and her shirt in the other. The pistol banged painfully against her rib cage. He tossed her on the sofa with ease.

"Where is the thumb drive?" he asked with an unfamiliar accent.

"What thumb...?"

The man slapped her with a gloved hand and shook her violently.

"Tell me quickly."

His voice held no anger nor emotion of any kind. His entreaty was matter of fact and promised reprisal if she did not comply.

"I didn't mean to…," she stammered as her emotions strained to comprehend the sudden attack.

The man slapped her again. This time he pressed the cold black automatic against her cheek. The pressure caused her pain.

"It's in my car," she said with a sob. "It's in the center console. Please don't hit me again."

Ahiram was satisfied that she told him the truth. He pulled the silencer from his left cargo pocket and quickly spun the device onto the barrel of the pistol. He moved to the side as he reached for one of the sofa pillows. He disliked the idea of killing a woman, particularly an attractive one. He would cover her face when he did it.

Desperately, Dehra kicked with her right foot. She caught the man in the groin. It was not a direct shot to his nuts, but it was enough to cause him to collapse to the floor, clutching his groin.

She clawed her way off the sofa and made a bee line for the door.

Ahiram managed to hook her ankle with a strong finger, tripping her. She fell to the floor. With remarkable agility, aided by adrenalin, she regained her feet and made it to the door. She stumbled again as she struggled to turn the knob. She heard the silenced report of the pistol as she staggered. The bullet punctured the door just above the knob.

She pulled mightily at the door, and it slammed open.

Another bullet splintered the door jamb next to her left hip before she gained the outside walkway. She turned the corner, placing the wall between herself and the gunman.

She nearly fell again as she saw Carson Brand with a gun in a two-handed grip, extended before him in a ready to fire posture. He approached swiftly, crouching next to her. He leaned his body against her, shielding her from the intruder's imminent attack.

He pulled her to the concrete decking of the walkway, extending his gun hand before him. The gunman emerged through the door, bringing his silenced pistol to bear as he stepped around the corner.

Brand's pistol belched flame. The report hurt Dehra's ears. She saw the gunman fall heavily. Brand fired again. The bullet struck the gunman with a meaty thud. Dehra saw the gunman shudder as he died.

Brand lifted Dehra to her feet. He dragged her away from the room.

Dehra struggled in his grip.

"I'm not leaving my stuff behind," she warned him in a voice that conveyed a strength she did not feel.

Brand released her arm, following her back to the room. He waited outside, scanning the parking lot as she collected her things from the bedroom. When she returned, he grabbed her arm once more and pulled her along. She risked a sidelong glance at the dead man on the landing. A puddle of blood spread beneath his black clothes. Brand grabbed her purse and rummaged around quickly until he located her car keys. He got in the driver seat, and without protest she moved to the passenger seat.

Tires squealed as Brand sped the car towards the street.

"We have to find Leon," Dehra said with a sudden realization.

Brand frowned as he gave his attention to the road.

"Did you hear me?" she asked.

"Leon's dead," Brand told her with a certainty she wanted to doubt but knew she could not.

Dehra's hands fell helplessly into her lap.

"How do you think he found you?" Brand muttered by way of an explanation.

Dehra sobbed quietly.

Brand drove east on highway 90. Neither spoke for a long time. Finally, Dehra mastered her sorrow for a moment.

"It wasn't you," she said in a wavering tone.

Brand made no rejoinder, watching the traffic around him.

"He asked me where the thumb drive was."

She watched Brand for a reaction. He remained stoic at the wheel.

"The one I took from Tel Gong."

"I got it," he said grimly. "We don't need to talk about it right now."

"We need to," she insisted.

Dehra felt an irresistible urge to make things right between them. The anger and false accusations in her parting words to him were still fresh in her memory. This stranger driving her car was all she had remaining from her former life.

"I was wrong about you."

"I know you were," he agreed. "I was wrong about it too. Now we know that this is bigger than we thought."

"Bigger?"

"Your former employer sent a hit team after you for what you heard then copied on that call. This isn't some drug lord vengeance thing. This is big. You are probably caught up in some Chinese spy shit. We need to disappear until I can get us some answers."

"How can you get answers?"

"I've got friends who will know what we are into."

"You just killed a man, Carson. Are you a cop? Are you a killer? I just want to go home. I don't want to do this anymore.?

Brand gripped the steering wheel until his knuckles hurt. His position was uncertain even to him. He was no cop. He didn't consider himself a killer, but he had killed. He was certain of two things. There was no going home. There was no choice in being involved or not. He had learned early that once you crossed the line between being a regular guy and an outlaw, your fate was sealed. The only remaining difference depended upon who you kill and who your actions benefit.

The man he shot at the hotel was an operative like he had seen in the movies. He was convinced that in doing so he had crossed another line which could not be uncrossed.

Dehra was an unintended victim. Her story was one he had seen too often. The lines of normalcy are not invisible but blurred. She made a choice, and that choice would weigh heavily against her. Maybe she should have ended the call when she realized that she was not supposed to be party to it. That could have been considered avoiding trouble. Copying the file onto a memory stick was action taken. Her actions were willful and indicated intent.

Brand was no legal expert, but he had avoided an accounting for his actions only because he had found himself in remarkable predicaments in which he had no choice but to act to survive.

The Feds had provided him cover only because it benefited their mission to do so. Brand was not naïve enough to believe that their mission couldn't change without notice. Something as far removed as an election, a foreign act, or even a change in social norms could place him firmly opposite of those same people who now channeled his actions for their benefit.

He was not confident that killing the assassin at the hotel would not place him in a harrowing position, even with an agency that supported him to the point of training him and contracting him to work on their behalf.

Agent Kilgore had admitted as much to him when one of his subordinates lobbied to have Brand jailed for the rest of his life. Kilgore hand-carried Brand through the process. Throughout their time together Kilgore had made no mystery of the fact that Brand would abide in a nether region where he would operate outside of the law in order to aid law enforcement in their work. It was clear that Brand would be lost if he did not cooperate with the DEA to the letter.

Brand's confident claim of assistance from well-placed friends was not shored in a certainty he could name. Sometimes you had to take a risk. This was beginning to look like one of those times.

Dehra's phone rang. She looked at the screen.

Brand glanced at her curiously.

She shrugged then answered the call on speaker.

"Hello."

"Ms. Duncan." an authoritative male voice said. "This is Bruce Anderson, Deputy Sherriff. I need you to come into my office today."

"What are you talking about?"

"I think you know, Ms. Duncan. You are in a huge mess. Where are you now? I'll come to you."

Dehra looked at Brand, anguish creasing her brow.

Brand reached out a hand to her.

She looked at his hand in confusion.

"Ms. Duncan?" the deputy's voice sounded from the phone.

Brand gently took the phone and ended the call.

Dehra sat back in her seat, giving the view from her window her full attention. After a few long moments of silence, she sat straighter in her seat. She gave Brand a level look.

Brand was not in the mood for what he knew she would want to discuss.

"Maybe he didn't kill Leon," Dehra said without looking away from the terrain passing by her window.

Brand sighed and shook his head. Denial.

"Maybe," he agreed without conviction.

"So why did we leave before we made sure my brother is alright?"

"Dehra," Brand said levelly, keeping his eyes on the road. "He is not alright. I know something about the guy I shot. He was not hesitating to put a bullet in your head. He tried to do the same to me last night during the fire."

Brand looked at Dehra, assessing how close she was to breaking down. He was not confident in her emotional strength.

"I'm sorry," he said in a softer tone. "Your brother is gone."

Brand leaned against the driver side door as her sorrow erupted at the truth she was desperately trying to deny.

He knew how she felt. He had lost so many of those he loved in his life. He was a teenager when his parents were swept off the road during a flash flood.

It had been only a few months ago that he lost his best friend and his girlfriend in the same week – both murdered.

Dehra sobbed.

Brand glanced at Dehra with an impatient look. He had cried for the last time in his teens when his parents died. He learned early that crying did nothing but ensure you hung on to a memory that would serve only to weaken you and cause you pain.

His best friend Bert, and Natalie his girlfriend, left a gulf in his life, but the hole was nothing to him. He hadn't given it much thought until now. He knew he should feel their loss with profound grief, but he didn't.

When they died, he felt only anger.

In the case of a physical injury, he heard that the body produces a natural anesthetic, numbing the wound temporarily. He had assumed similarly, that after the insulating emotional and mental shock of losing those two had passed, he would grieve. As time passed and he accepted their loss, the reality washed over him like a salty wave, but the tears did not come.

Unwelcome, his memory took him to that night so many years before when his parents perished, leaving him alone in a bleak and stormy world.

With a heavy knock, the police officer had confronted him at the front door of their modest home overlooking the swollen waters of Canyon Lake. After a short but well-practiced professional soliloquy, the grim faced, dripping police officer told the frantic seventeen-year-old boy that his parents had been lost to a flooded low water crossing.

Lost? His mother and father had not been lost. They died.

His recollections receded further into the past. That dark Sunday morning was the last time he would ever see or speak with his mom and dad.

Despite the rainstorm being touted as the 'storm of the century', his mother had insisted they go to church. Brand's habit of stubborn resistance guaranteed that he could rarely be convinced to join them. Their continual fight in the face of his dogged determination had eroded his parents' will until over time their coaxing was reduced to nothing more than rare impotent appeals.

That Sunday, breakfast had been surprisingly pleasant as there was no effort to convince him to join them, probably due to the threatening weather conditions.

His dad possessed uncanny skill in the kitchen. Brand used to tell his friends he had never eaten a bad meal in his life. That morning he had yielded only a slight regard for his parents as yolky fried eggs, thick salty bacon, scratch biscuits and sausage gravy occupied his full attention.

He had responded to their attempts to chat with a begrudging brevity as he labored to feed the metabolic blast furnace that was his teenaged body.

After failing to get much response from their single-minded son, his mother and father leaned into the pelting torrent, umbrellas straining against the wind, bibles clutched protectively close to their breasts as they made their way to the car.

They never made it to the little white frame church. According to a witness in a following car, they were swept away by a 6-foot wave as they descended into a low water crossing.

The police led search for their bodies had taken the rest of the day.

Brand had been unaware of any trouble other than consternation that his parents were uncharacteristically late from church.

With their bodies' recovery came identification leading them to knock on the door of the dark house where a lone teenaged boy waited.

Even now he reeled at the jagged ending to what should have been a lifelong relationship. His father had been his hero, a great example and guide for him: the smartest and strongest man he had ever known.

Only a fortnight prior, Brand had returned from basic training. The senseless combination of his father's busy schedule, and the impertinent hard-headedness of a teenage boy's never allowed him to tell his father the stories of his time at Fort Sill.

Brand regretted the continual strife between he and his parents. He never forgave himself for the natural plight of a young man test driving his manhood at the expense of his parents' eagerness to help. They only ever endeavored to understand their boy's fears and doubts. They did all they could to connect with him. He couldn't see anything other than authoritative parents wanting to push him to do things he didn't want to do.

Their goal to raise him as best they could, as with all their other goals, would remain unfinished. Brand's singular preoccupation with a meal rather than making the most of his last moments with his parents would haunt him from that day forward. The loss felt like an amputation, complete with phantom pains and glimpses of the elusive shadows of those he lost in every crowd.

Brand glared at the dark road ahead. He pushed the weakness of self-indulgence from him. He was beyond self-pity. He recognized at some level that the grief that had strangled his young heart had hardened him. He had grown brittle and hard.

Even prior to this new and bewildering journey of the last few months, he had felt little regard for those he harmed. Most recently, he gave little consideration to those few who had lost their lives at his hand.

He glanced at Dehra, her head nodding to the rhythm of the road as she slumped in an exhausted sleep.

He knew how she felt, but he couldn't experience the sorrow.

She was reading a chapter from the same book we all read, he mused. It was as simple as that. No point in complicating it further with wasted emotional energy.

This moment was to him like so many others, played out repeatedly with varied results. No matter his resolve, regardless of his intentions, he felt helpless to avoid what fate demanded of him.

He reasoned that he was on a path not of his making nor his liking. Some powerful force manipulated controls beyond his reach, dragging him irresistibly towards some unknown end. He was certain of this unseen control, like a ponderous weight tied to him, dragging him towards the cliff edge of a bottomless chasm. Perhaps through a dogged resistance against the inevitable end planned for him, he could find some small gap by which to escape. He doubted he could ever return to a normal life. Maybe he would find some blind corner where he could conceal himself from whatever endeavored to consume him.

Brand favored Dehra with a longing look. She told him she wanted to go home – to a home that no longer existed. He wanted out. What would it be like once more to awaken on a Saturday morning with nothing to occupy him besides a bowl of cereal on a worn sofa in front of the TV?

Brand laughed aloud at the dark irony.

What Saturday TV could distract him from what he had seen? His was an all-access pass to an unfiltered reality. Taking a life changes you. The veil is removed. Where would the spirits of those he had ended sit? They were always with him. That living room would be crowded.

Brand shook his head, clearing any remaining grim humor.

Fuck them.

20

DEHRA AWAKENED TO A WORLD HEAVY with sorrow. Her dreams had been exclusively about Leon. She could not avoid believing that she was the cause of his death.

Brand had offered no words of comfort. She doubted he could have convinced her otherwise. Her actions at Tel Gong had set the wheels of fate in motion. Those wheels now spun her far away into a terrifying reality.

He left her there more than an hour before. He seemed to have changed during their drive. He was grim. He no longer monitored her moods as if he feared she would go off like a time bomb. She had to admit to herself that she was reluctant to indulge in those occasional fits she employed to get her way. She suspected that with Brand it would not go well for her. She didn't know why she felt the way she did. She could only describe the change as that he seemed more formidable in some way. He had not been aggressive or in any other way unpleasant, but she instinctively knew he was not to be screwed with right now. He never said it. She just knew it.

The sign outside the building identified it as a federal office building. She remembered him mentioning that he had contacts in the government that could help them. He was likely acting upon that option. He didn't give many details as he left her in the car.

She reclined the passenger seat as rain began falling intermittently from a bruised sky. Brand was somewhere in the glass and steel building before her. She eyed the keys dangling from the ignition. The impulse to drive away and disappear into a fantasy world of obscurity beckoned.

She knew with a certainty she could not explain that there was no world where she could hide from this. Brand was her only remaining vestige of the familiar – of hope, yet he was not a comfort. She craved the familiar in this unfamiliar place. The unknown terrified her with an unreasonable sense of foreboding.

Wouldn't the Sun once more dawn over the same world? She asked herself.

Despite her loss, she was still the same girl.

That was not true. She turned the windshield mirror towards her. She might look the same – albeit a little worse for wear – but she had changed at the most fundamental level. She studied her eyes in the mirror. She saw something darker there.

She returned the mirror, approximating its original direction and angle.

Everyone says, time heals all wounds, she thought. I just have to do the time. She enjoyed a temporary solace in that fantasy before Leon's memory once more soured her mood.

She checked the time on her phone. Brand had been gone for a long time. She wondered what he was doing.

21

BRAND MADE HIMSELF AS COMFORTABLE as he could in the hard chair, the handcuffs biting into his flesh in a way that could not be relieved no matter what position he tried. The other man in the narrow interrogation room watched him casually. He was obviously a junior agent judging from the lack of concern he exhibited. Brand had some experience with federal agents. Those with field experience were continually alert and constantly concerned with not underestimating potential danger from a prisoner.

Agent Spencer had cuffed Brand, confining him to the small room. His orders to the junior agent had been brief.

"Watch him."

Brand stewed in his hatred of Agent Spencer. The agent hated Brand even more. Spencer had made his feelings clear the first day they were introduced. Brand's handler within the agency, Matthew Kilgore seemed to be Brand's only friend in the organization, although his alliance came with clearly defined boundaries and dangerously narrow limitations.

After leaving Dehra in the parking lot, he entered the wide lobby. At the guest sign in he asked for Agent Kilgore. After identifying himself, Brand was set upon by a half-dozen agents, and delivered roughly to the interrogation room. Spencer arrived shortly after.

"Where have you been, Mr. Brand?"

"Where's Kilgore?"

"He's not available. Answer my question."

"Fuck you, Spencer."

That had done the trick. Spencer cuffed him and shoved him into the steel chair.

Brand judged his time in the room at nearly two hours with no follow-up visit from Spencer and no sign of Kilgore.

He looked at the agent before him.

The man returned his look for only a few seconds before averting his eyes. Either he knew something about Brand, or he was nervous.

"What's your name, Agent?" Brand asked levelly.

"Keep quiet."

"Has anyone told Agent Kilgore that I'm here?"

"I said keep quiet, prisoner."

"Prisoner my ass. Spencer is an asshole with a hard-on for me. I am a contractor for the DEA. Can you please get word to Agent Kilgore that Carson Brand is here?"

"I told you to shut up," the agent repeated with heat.

"Or what?" Brand challenged.

"Or I'll shut you up."

"Why don't you try that one on for size," Brand invited. "Better make sure I am still cuffed when you do."

The agent uncrossed his arms and approached Brand, a menacing grimace on his face.

"I won't be cuffed forever tough guy," Brand warned. "Take your best shot and make it count. I promise you that I will take mine when I get loose."

The agent rapidly crossed the short distance between them and grabbed Brand's shirt. He pulled Brand towards him, his chair teetering precariously. The agent drew back a fist. He halted the impending blow as the door opened and Agent Kilgore entered, Spencer on his heel, an angry sneer painting his face.

"Still making friends, Brand?" Kilgore asked mildly. "That's enough Phillips."

Agent Phillips settled Brand's chair back to level. He eyed Brand with his remaining unreleased hostility.

"Later, smart mouth," he muttered.

Brand memorized his face for later reference. He said nothing in return.

"Uncuff him, Spencer."

Spencer moved behind Brand, tugging his arms painfully as he released the cuffs. He shoved Brand into the heavy table occupying the center of the room.

Brand leaped backwards, toppling the chair. He spun his body as he launched himself at Spencer.

He managed to land two hard punches in the middle of the agent's face before the other two men tackled him to the floor. Spencer fell backwards, his arms outstretched in a defensive gesture.

Brand moaned a low dangerous growl as he struggled with the agents, trying to get at Spencer. The latter scurried backwards against the green painted concrete wall at the back of the room.

The two agents strained mightily to restrain Brand. Kilgore was rail thin but surprisingly strong. Phillips struggled to place an effective hold.

"Calm down," Kilgore ordered Brand through clenched teeth. "I don't want to have to toss you in a cell for a few days to cool you down."

Brand mastered his anger by degrees. He felt a fire deep within him, and he wanted more than anything to throw Spencer on that flame and destroy him. His understanding of the power Agent Kilgore wielded over him aided much in ratcheting down his rage.

After a moment Kilgore nodded to Agent Phillips and they released Brand, apprehension easily seen on their faces.

Brand rose slowly to show his control returned.

Spencer was again on his feet.

"I want to press charges, Kilgore," he complained bitterly.

"You can do that after I write you up for insubordination and conduct unbecoming."

"What...?"

"I don't want to hear another word from you, Spencer. Get out of here before I open a file on you."

Spencer growled unintelligibly and left the room, muttering and fuming.

"Sit down Brand," Kilgore ordered, indicating the chair he had previously occupied.

"Here in an interrogation room?"

Kilgore eyed him with a dangerous look.

Brand held up his hands to show his acquiescence. He took the proffered seat.

Kilgore sat across the desk. Phillips remained standing, eyeing Brand suspiciously.

"The last time I saw you was at that bar in San Antonio," Kilgore began. "I was shaking your hand and welcoming you to the family. Then you disappear without a trace for two months. You appear here with no call and no warning. Explain."

"No more than five minutes after you left, I was kidnapped by the cartel and dragged to Mexico where I have been beaten and tortured for two months. I managed to escape and here I am."

Kilgore was unable to hide his surprise.

"Are you serious?"

"As funny as it seems to you, yeah I am serious."

"I didn't mean not serious as funny."

"Well, I'm not laughing at all."

"I guess not. You'll need to file a report, and we will need to debrief you. I realize it sounds a touch insensitive, but you may have been exposed to information that might help us."

"That's fine," Brand agreed dismissively. "I've got bigger problems to tell you about."

"Is that right?"

"I think I may have stumbled onto an international plot to spy on American citizens."

"Bullshit."

This last was from Phillips.

"Agent Phillips, get out," Kilgore commanded.

The agent obeyed immediately. Brand guessed he was unwilling to join Spencer in Kilgore's doghouse.

Once they were alone, Kilgore leaned back in his chair.

"It's good to have you back in one piece, Brand."

"Thanks. Sorry about the Spencer thing."

Kilgore waved off the apology.

"You two have been spoiling for a row since day one. I know how Spencer can be."

Kilgore shook a finger in Brand's face, smiling to take off the edge to the gesture.

"Don't do that again. He is a DEA agent, and you are a lowly contractor."

"Understood. Brand agreed.

He liked Kilgore despite the threats and the rough treatment.

"So, tell me about this plot."

Kilgore produced his phone and activated the voice recording app.

"Aren't cameras on us now?"

"It helps me to get all the details," he explained.

Brand took a long breath.

"I received information that a Chinese owned telecom company has developed an app for their phones that monitor their customers' location, conversations, and habits. The company is called Tel Gong."

Kilgore relaxed his posture, disappointed in Brands information.

"Every social media platform does the same thing. I wouldn't call it a plot. It is more a marketing scheme."

"I thought the same thing until a hit squad burned down a mobile home with me in it, then tried to kill me on the street."

"When did this occur?"

"Yesterday."

"Where?"

"Uvalde, just down the road."

"You're leaving something out, Brand. I need all of the facts."

Brand remembered Dehra, waiting in the parking lot. He again was reminded how innocent people are drawn into dangerous situations with tragic results. He felt a strange reluctance to bring her name into it.

"You know I have a knack for being in the wrong place at the right time. I believe it was a case of mistaken identity."

Although misleading, the statement was technically true.

"So why aren't you dead?"

"I surprised the team before they could complete their mission."

"How surprised were they?" Kilgore asked knowingly.

Brand looked at his hands.

"They don't feel surprised anymore."

"I would rather not get the story from the local news tonight. Give me the complete story, heavy on the details please."

Brand related the account of the previous 48 hours, excluding the amnesia and Dehra and Leon's names from the tale. He also left out the existence of the memory stick.

"Wait here," Agent Kilgore commanded and left the room.

Kilgore returned a half hour later and sat once more in his seat.

"Your exploits are clogging the wire with local law enforcement. I've got our intel assets on it. We should know more details about the hit team shortly.

"Early reports indicate an international organization. The dead guy at the hotel is former Mussad. The others are Russian soldiers of fortune types with Interpol rap sheets. What were they after, Brand?"

Brand shrugged.

"I thought they were cartel assassins at first. I am as surprised as you are that they are something else."

"I believe you are jerking me around. What are you not telling me?"

Brand wanted to protect Dehra, but he wasn't willing to jeopardize his relationship with Kilgore to do it. He decided to proceed with enough vague information as to seem oblivious to Dehra's actions.

"The only thing I left out was meeting a girl at a bar and going home with her. It was her mobile home they torched to get to me."

Kilgore settled more comfortably in his chair.

"Finally, some honesty. The news mentions a female accomplice. Who is this girl?"

"What does she have to do with this?"

"I think you know," Kilgore said with too much certainty for Brand's comfort.

"Shit, Kilgore," Brand exclaimed in surrender. "I think she learned more about Tel Gong than they wanted her to know. Up until the moment that I shot that Mussad guy, I truly believed I was the target. She worked at their plant in Uvalde, and she overheard a phone call and was fired. That didn't seem to be a killing offense. I wasn't certain until they went after her directly. I shot the guy at the hotel while defending her."

"I want to talk to her."

"I'll see what I can do."

"What does that mean?"

"You said it yourself. Local cops are all over this thing. It won't take them long to bring her in if she hasn't gone into hiding."

"You are a shitty liar. Is she outside?"

Brand shrugged.

"I don't know where she is."

"What's her name?"

"Dehra Duncan."

"Can you call her?"

"I don't have a phone, so she never gave me her number. The cartel took all of my stuff when they captured me."

"How did you get here?"

"I hitched a ride."

Kilgore was not satisfied with Brand's explanation. After a moment sizing him up, Kilgore rose from his seat.

"Follow me."

Brand obeyed silently.

Kilgore led him to his office where he circled the desk and rifled through the lower drawers in his desk.

He straightened and slid a flip phone across the desk to Brand.

"Hang on to this burner, that way I can contact you when I get this thing sorted out."

He opened the top drawer, withdrawing two treasury envelopes.

"Got any money?" Kilgore asked as he tossed the envelopes onto his desk.

"Pocket change."

"You earned a couple of checks during your training at the Pod and field time."

Brand nodded at the memory of his training and the field mission at the Golden Stallion night club. He gathered the checks and the phone.

"Thanks."

"What's your plan?" Kilgore asked, leaning on his hands.

"I don't have any. Can I get another vehicle?"

Brand had been issued a pickup prior to his kidnapping. He was certain it was no longer parked at Rod Dog's where he had been kidnapped.

"Call me tomorrow and I'll see what I can do."

"Thanks."

"I need to talk to the girl, Brand. Don't put yourself sideways with the agency. You have a history of waging crusades for damsels in distress. This one's not worth it."

Brand nodded and left the office.

He opened the flip phone and powered it up. After the network logo faded, he keyed Dehra's number into the text app and messaged her to drive east where he would meet her at the nearest convenience store. He closed the phone with a slap and pocketed it and the envelopes.

He didn't want to lie to Kilgore about knowing her cell number. He had read her number on the hotel register paperwork earlier. At least he hadn't lied about his phone or her giving him her number.

22

HAORAN WANG LEANED BACK STIFFLY in his chair as the tech fitted his lavaliere microphone, concealing the wiring within his expensive suit coat. His attention was split between annoyance for the sound tech's familiar proximity and the producer's prep questions for his upcoming nationally broadcast interview.

"The Great Reset is bullshit," he replied with heat at the producer's prep question.

"You can't say that on the air."

"I'm not on the air," Ha returned pointedly. "If this interview is meant to use me as a tool to advance another of your network's conspiracy theories, I'm leaving."

"Mr. Wang," the producer assured him with a contrived tone of patience. "We ask the questions our viewers want answered. We don't participate, nor do we endorse conspiracy theories. Your company and the Chinese government have been linked to a secret organization called *the Lexicon* whose aim is to control the world's commerce by establishing a central world bank and a worldwide *Social Credit Scoring* system. Your country's well recorded human rights violations against the *Uyghurs* are no secret. We could do a ten-part series on that alone. You may want to give your side of the story rather than leave it to our journalists to control the narrative."

Ha considered the smug, young, blond, woman with the radio earpiece and the trite manner as she tapped data into her tablet. He liked her perky curves and blue eyes, but the pleasant features of her appearance were not sufficient to overcome the brittle facade she projected. To his eye, she was another overindulged American girl whose only accessible emotion was impatience. His formal education at the Nanjing University, and more recently his training with the MSS, taught him that Americans, particularly young American women, had no conception of position. This uniquely American ignorance among young females produced the typical angry teenaged girl persona so popularized in American film and TV.

Ha Wang disliked American women because of their propensity to act out snidely and bitterly despite the uncontrolled wealth and privilege heaped upon them in an overly generous American society. Chinese women understood innately that orderly Chinese society placed certain requirements of decorum and self-control upon them which must be satisfied. *"Sincerity with Aspiration, Perseverance with Integrity"* was more than just the motto of Nanjing University. It was a condition of attendance to the prestigious institute of higher learning.

In this matter above all, Ha Wang was the authority, and he had no patience for violation of this principle, nor time to educate an arrogant American female on the nuances of being a proper lady in public.

"Get out." Ha ordered the producer without heat. "Call me when I am needed on set."

The producer looked up from her tablet in alarm.

"Your rider from your company requires we preview all questions prior to the interview, sir."

"I am aware of our agreement with your network. You have prepared me sufficiently."

The producer hesitated, her lips parted in readiness for whatever her thinking could come up with to convince the Chinese businessman to conform to her wishes. As nothing occurred to her, she locked her teeth in an insincere smile and left the green room.

Ha was left to wait only a few minutes before he was led to the set where busy crew hastily moved equipment and set it into place while well-coiffed on camera talent breathed deeply and spoke with producers prior to the beginning of their news programs.

Ha took the chair indicated by the thin young man with the headset. The attractive host of the show was seated across the glass table from him. Her impossibly blue eyes surveyed the Chinese businessman with a scrutiny he was not certain was flattering. Seemingly satisfied, she flashed him a professional smile and shook her blond hair. A man stepped forward of the cameras and raised a warning hand towards them.

"And three, two…"

"Good evening," the host said with a surprisingly strong and authoritative voice. "I'm Sharon Bright and you are watching the Bright Spot. Step out of the darkness. Join us in the Bright Spot."

Music filled the studio monitors as the viewing audience watched the introductory graphics on their screens. The man with the headset counted down once more then pointed at Sharon Bright.

"Chinese telecom giant *Tel Gōngsī de* has been prominent in the news cycle lately," Sharon read into the camera. "With talk of market dominance which threatens to relegate the big device manufactures to minor players in the global telecommunications game, talk of antitrust and shady international commerce practices is running rampant. With us tonight to answer some of these troubling questions is Tel Gong Chief Operating Officer for American continental markets, Haoran Wang. Mr. Wang, welcome to the show. How do you answer the numerous allegations crowding the news cycle these days?"

"First," Ha began. "Thank you for having me on Sharon. I appreciate your standing alone amongst the many news networks in setting the record straight with me and my company. It is disconcerting how quickly unsubstantiated claims and unfounded allegations can gain traction without any interest in interviewing the victim of these lies. We have adhered to all US and international trade laws. Despite our operation being more heavily scrutinized than any of our competitors, we have complied with every demand made of us.

The claims by our domestic American competition are prompted only by their losing billions in market share to a company that has created and manufactured groundbreaking products and software platforms they could only dream of, and their former customers love."

"Thank you for that Mr. Wang," Sharon Bright said with a quick smile. "Speaking of groundbreaking tech, what of the claims that your company stole R&D from the big three telecom giants?"

"Sharon, this sort of thing is common in any industry where innovation and groundbreaking technological advances are introduced. Look at the big three American auto makers during the 70's. In an industry where American automobiles were engineered with a built-in obsolescence to fail at one-hundred thousand miles, the Japanese auto manufacturers introduced a better manufactured, more reliable, and longer lasting automobile to the American market. The American auto manufacturers claimed their designs had been stolen and slightly modified to cover the theft. It is certain that when the man who invented the wheel introduced it to the stone age world, there was a guy with a square stone block screaming and raising a club claiming theft of his next idea for the wheel."

"Are you claiming to have reinvented the wheel, Mr. Wang?" Bright asked pointedly.

"You are such a dumb whore, Sharon," Ha mused calmly. "I told your hot little producer that I would tolerate no tomfoolery from you."

Sharon Bright stared at him for a long moment.

"Mr. Wang," she repeated. Are you claiming to have reinvented the wheel?"

Wang emerged from his reverie, his imagined response fresh in his mind.

"Sharon," Ha said mildly. "I was making a point with a little light humor. Of course, we have not reinvented the wheel. That is what makes our breakthrough so special. The technology was right before our noses, ready to be discovered. We at Tel Gong have built our success upon locating and implementing those opportunities overlooked by the huge money-focused corporate behemoths. The world is changing quickly. Tel Gong is leading the way towards that change."

"Fascinating," Sharon Bright commented. "Do you expect that your company will continue to trend, as you say, towards change, or do you see the dynamics of the market bogging you down possibly with litigation or international trade limitations?"

Wang shook his head, clearing the impulse to say what he was compelled to say to the arrogant host.

"Of course, we will continue to meet all challenges head on and in a measured and meaningful way."

"Is there any truth to the rumor that you and your company are funded partially by the Oligarch conglomerate, The Lexicon?"

"I don't know what you are talking about, Sharon. I assumed conspiracy theories were below you and this network. You might want to back off the online videos and embrace real reporting."

"So, you claim that you or your company have no ties to The Lexicon, or anyone associated with it?"

"Sharon, is it your intention to gin up baseless rumors or are you trying to boost your ratings with this nonsense?"

Sharon Bright made no reply for a moment. Finally, she smiled at the Chinese executive.

"Thank you Haoran Wang, COO of Tel Gōngsī de."

She shifted in her seat as she faced a different camera.

"Next up, does the president have all of his marbles or is he the empty-headed fool we all suspect he is? We have our Bright Ideas panel up next to discuss it - right after this short break. Stay with us. You don't want to miss this."

"Cut to commercial," the director announced. "Two minutes people."

Wang pulled at the lavalier microphone clip, tearing the wires from his suit. The sound tech rushed to rescue his equipment from the angry COO.

"Get out of my way," Wang shouted as he shoved the tech out of his way and departed the studio.

23

BRAND SPOTTED DEHRA'S CAR PARKED near the car wash in the convenience store parking lot. She sat outside of it, on the hood. She watched with open interest as Brand approached.

He looked around cautiously, finally leaning against the car beside Dehra.

She handed him her fountain drink without a word.

He nodded and pulled from the straw.

"I guess that didn't work out like you hoped," Dehra observed as he returned her cup.

"We are both still at large," he responded with little optimism. "It seems that the hit team that came after us is an international team of merc's.

"Merc's?"

"Mercenaries," he explained. "I think you are in very deep shit right now. My contact there wants to talk to you."

"Why don't we do that?"

"Maybe we should," Brand agreed with consideration. "I have a feeling we should know more about what you are up against before we act too definitively."

"I'm in deep shit? What I am up against? So, there is no more we in this thing?"

"I'm standing right here Dehra."

"I'm just listening to you, Brand."

Brand watched Dehra carefully as he considered what their next strategy might be.

"I know this town," he said finally. "Let's get settled somewhere. We can rest and figure out our next move."

They drove to the northeast side of town where they checked into a small motel. Brand remembered it as the same one where he and Christina had stayed before she betrayed him the first time. Unlike the final betrayal, he had managed to rescue her and escape with their lives that time.

It was after nightfall when Dehra and Brand parked before Rod Dog's Saloon. The bar had been a familiar haunt when Brand was a regular guy. He hoped Karen was working. The bartender was one of the last vestiges of his old life. He craved normal right now.

They entered the glass front door bearing the image of a cartoon dog with a cocktail. Inside, they took seats at the oval shaped bar.

Karen beamed as she approached them. She sat a bourbon rocks in front of Brand.

"What will you have?" the dark-haired bartender asked Dehra.

"The same," Dehra replied, nodding towards Brand's glass.

With a surprised arch of an eyebrow, Karen poured the cocktail.

"Dehra," Brand announced. "This is Karen. We go way back. You can trust her."

Karen and Dehra uttered their responses to the introduction.

I'm surprised you are working tonight," Brand commented grateful that he had been wrong.

"You are lucky, mister. I had to cover."

Brand nodded his agreement.

Karen leaned on the bar close to Brand.

"What happened the other night? Our cameras recorded some pretty upsetting footage."

"We can talk about it later," Brand replied. "Dehra and I are handling a situation right now. I'll catch you up in a few days."

"That's not going to get it done, Brand," Karen disagreed pointedly. "Since Bert died you have been acting pretty mysteriously. Everyone has noticed. Those guys who jumped you a couple of months ago were no joke. Are you in trouble?"

Dehra listened in rapt attention. She was getting a much-desired insight into the mysterious stranger to which she had attached herself. It was obvious that Karen wielded a unique power of persuasion over the strong-willed Brand.

"Karen," Brand said with a measured tone. The strain of controlling his emotions was obvious in his face and body language. "I can't talk about it here - in the bar."

Karen gave him a puzzled look. In all their years of friendship she had never seen this grave side of Brand. Her bartender's intuition served her well here.

"It's OK Brand," she said with what Dehra recognized as almost a maternal reaction. "You're good here. How about another drink?"

Brand nodded, his eyes upon the bar.

She was disappointed that she would get no more insight into Brand, but Dehra saw more deeply into the complexities which made up her companion. Strong emotions boiled just below the surface. She had thought him stoic and brooding. Karen's brief conversation with him quickly and easily summoned a tortured and highly impassioned man.

Dehra guessed he had seen much during the time Karen had described. Whoever this Bert was, his mysterious death was obviously what had sent Brand on this path which, Dehra guessed, was grim and deadly.

She had seen only three deaths in her life. Her mother had passed when she was young. She witnessed the other two during her brief few days with Brand. Much of the security she felt from Brand's protection over her evaporated with her glimpse into the pain he carried and how closely he held it.

Leon's memory rushed forward to take its place, dominating her thoughts and causing her acute pain. Dehra's face contorted as she fought her grief. She mastered herself enough to down the bitter drink before her. The burn of the bourbon helped to neutralize some of the raw ache of her brother's memory.

Unbidden, Karen refilled her glass.

Dehra looked up from her internal battle in thanks to the bartender, her eyes glistened with moist regret as she forced a smile.

Karen's expression assured Dehra that she and Brand were a pathetic pair amongst the music and frivolity of the patrons around them. She imagined herself a pariah in her troubled state. She suddenly wanted to get away from everyone and everything. If she could only have a few moments of solitude, maybe she could figure a way back to the place before, where Leon was alive, and killers weren't after her - where she wasn't in the company of a torn-up stranger who killed with alarming ease and without any sign of remorse.

Dehra glanced at Brand and started violently. He was watching her as she grappled with her tortured feelings. His blue eyes were bright with his observation of her. His expression gave her the distinct impression that he read her doubts.

She averted her eyes as she collected her myriad thoughts, tucking them away from his view.

"Relax, Dehra," he said softly. "We can't do anything about this now. We'll figure it out together."

She wanted so badly to tell him to fuck off.

She knew he was not solely responsible for their predicament, but to her it was no coincidence that soon after he had arrived, like a harbinger of death, Leon's life had been lost and her life had been tossed into this unfathomable abyss.

She knew the memory stick and its contents were the true source of their troubles, but it was difficult to separate Brand from the negative based upon the time frame alone.

She sneaked a glance at Brand. He no longer watched her. His gaze roved casually around the room, stalling briefly as the actions or the revelry of a patron caught his attention.

Dehra focused upon her half empty glass as shame worked at her senseless anger towards her companion.

An unwelcome voice in her head reminded her that she would have been as dead as Leon if Brand had not saved her life - twice. The truth of the conclusion did little more than galvanize her anger towards him.

She downed the contents of the highball glass, nodding to Karen for a refill.

Without any sign of judgment, Karen freshened her ice and refilled her drink.

Dehra mused that either she was mistaken that Karen held a dim view of her, or the bartender was a pro and kept her feelings cleverly concealed. She exhibited no judgement, only professional regard.

She was a pro, Dehra admitted to herself. What she and Brand were going through was not normal nor in any way acceptable by any measure.

Dehra lifted the glass to her lips.

Her self-loathing was sufficient to fill the void for the moment.

Her third cocktail joined the heat of the previous two, lightening her mood as the booze took hold. She glanced at Brand once more. She guessed he was avoiding looking at her. He seemed uniquely dialed into her moods and more accurately, how she responded to him through them.

She smiled despite her efforts to remain dour towards him. Hard ass or not, he was no different than any other man in his deference to her and his reluctance to anger her.

"You have any cash for the jukebox?" she asked, leaning against him playfully. "I'm broke."

Brand fished a handful of smaller bills from his pocket.

"Sure," he replied.

She plucked at a five bill in the stack.

"Keep it all," he insisted. "You can't walk around without spending money."

Dehra's blue eyes darkened once more as she decided how to react to his charity.

"Dehra," he asked with a sigh, watching her emotional selection process with weary helplessness. "Can't you just take this and put some music on without chewing my ass out?"

Dehra grinned in spite of herself. She accepted the stack of bills and moved to the merrily lighted juke box.

Brand watched her go with a cautious eye. His gaze lingered only a moment as she coursed through the selections on the machine.

Finally, he returned his attention to the bar. Karen stood before him, arms akimbo.

"I don't have but a moment or two," she warned. "Catch me up. Just give me the broad strokes."

Brand shook his head doggedly.

"There is no short version of this," he said firmly. "I will tell you everything someday. Today can't be that day."

Karen opened her mouth to assert her will.

"I promise," he said. "It's too hard right now. You will have a lot of questions; anyone would. This isn't going to happen now. I am sorry, Karen."

"This is not going to help get you out of the friend zone, pal," she said with a characteristic grin by way of dropping the subject.

Brand was grateful that she was ratcheting down the pressure on him.

"I've got as much of a chance of getting back on your good side as Bert would have had."

Karen shared a grim chuckle with Brand. His late best friend was a shameless ladies' man, notorious in his zeal for female conquests.

"Your probably right. How about a refill? Your girlfriend is one ahead of you."

24

MICHAEL CERVANTES SAT IN THE passenger seat in the leading vehicle of the two black SUV's. Two armed men sat in the back seat. The four occupants of the dark vehicle rode in silence. Cervantes bolstered his confidence with the likelihood that his quarry would be careless enough to return to the very place he had been captured months before.

He hadn't shared his plan with the others on the team, nor with Castillo, knowing his assumption would be ridiculed. In Castillo's case, he would most likely have been killed and beheaded.

Once more he felt anger and resentment towards the cartel boss fire him deep inside his chest. He hated the man with a physical pang. Someday he would end the man - someday soon. He shook his head, clearing his mind of all other than his goal for the evening.

He had followed his plan since the day he carried the heads of the guards out of Castillo's office. The task had been unpleasant but not uncommon. Cervantes was used to his boss's theatrics and hardened by a history of many foul deeds requiring an iron will and strong stomach.

With no additional contact with anyone at the compound, he had departed the following morning. Despite the lax security on the U.S. side of the border, it had taken several days to get into the country undetected then to connect with his team on the north side of the river. Their operation was firmly entrenched in Texas. The cartel owned much property and employed many Americans.

The cartel operation centers were better protected than the American border to be sure. The security protocol necessary to make contact with the American-based operations was more hazardous than the clandestine crossing through one of their many tunnels, and undetected by the border patrol.

He had waited two full days outside of the little cantina in Falfurrias before one of the local cartel thugs had visited the designated meeting spot, allowing him to gain access to the infrastructure of the American run cartel network.

Forty-eight hours later here he was, speeding towards his target. He was confident that the American, Carson Brand, would be in his hands before morning.

Cervantes considered himself a student of human nature. His instincts had served him well during his short career with the cartel. He knew that the only instinct stronger in human beings than survival was the need for the familiar.

This powerful desire is the reason solitary confinement is such an effective punishment in prison. The need for a man to be among those things with which he is familiar is why those *pendejos* could not survive more than a couple of weeks on Vancouver Island in that reality show on TV. The American would return to the bar. He had no home and no friends. He would return because he had nothing else.

Cervantes settled back into his seat, satisfied his plan would succeed. Castillo would not place Cervantes' severed head on the floor before his desk – at least not this time.

The two SUVs hurtled down the dark highway just south of San Antonio, the glow of the city's lights beckoning them.

25

BRAND ENJOYED THE FEEL OF DEHRA'S body against his as they danced. He glanced towards the bar where Karen stole quick looks his way more often than he deemed necessary. He was unsure why he felt mild embarrassment at the attention.

He and Karen had dated years before until she had found out he was married at the time. He was no longer married but she kept him firmly in the friend zone, nonetheless.

Dehra nuzzled his neck, bringing his attention back to the pleasantness of her company. He was certain that her passion was bourbon powered, but he was pleased anyway. They had showered at the cheap motel before arriving at the bar. He was glad based upon their proximity to one another. Before his shower, he was getting pretty rank by his estimation, and the dancing might have gone differently.

The song ended and he led Dehra back to their seats. A country song began and several of the patrons took inspiration from them and moved to the dance floor.

Karen brought fresh drinks to them.

"Thanks, Karen," Brand said, trying to gage her mood.

"You're welcome," Karen returned with a professional tone which was impossible to read, and from which he could not interpret an underlying meaning or intent.

"I don't think she is that into you," Dehra observed with uncanny intuition.

Brand tried mightily to cover his discomfort at her pinpoint assessment of his predicament.

"It's not like that," he stammered, trying to make a reasonable excuse for his concern.

"No judgment here, Brand," she said deliberately with obvious enjoyment at his discomfiture.

Brand gave his attention to his drink.

"Besides," Dehra purred mischievously. "I like a little competition."

Brand looked at Dehra once more with a deeper appreciation.

"You want to get out of here?"

"I don't know," she replied uncertainly. "What do you have in mind?"

"Maybe a late meal and a good night's sleep?"

"Nothing more?"

"What else is there?" Brand asked with manufactured innocence.

Dehra opened her mouth to fill in the blank when she saw he was playing with her. Her expression sobered dangerously.

"Nothing else if you keep messing around."

"Alright," he surrendered with raised hands. "I'll be good."

Brand fished several twenties from his pocket and counted them out on the bar. He made certain to estimate their bill high and leave Karen a generous tip.

He waved at Karen as he stood from his seat, drawing Dehra along with him.

Outside, he led Dehra to her dusty car. It was parked in front of the bar, a few spaces distant from the front door.

26

CERVANTES POINTED TO THE MAN and woman leaving the bar as they entered the parking lot of the strip center.

"*Ahi ellos estan,*" he said to the driver.

The driver accelerated dramatically to place the truck behind the dusty sedan, blocking the couple's escape. The following SUV driver expertly arced the black truck around the lead vehicle, boxing in the man opening the driver side door.

The black SUVs screeched to a halt and men boiled out of the vehicles, sprinting towards Brand, pulling pistols from their clothes. Brand reached under the front seat of the car, withdrawing the nine-millimeter automatic he had taken from the driver the night of the mobile home fire. A glance at Dehra revealed she was frozen in surprise and fear at the attack.

He sprinted towards the large group of approaching men. He struck the first to arrive in the face with the pistol. He felt a solid blow strike him on the back of his head.

He knew instinctively there were too many for him to defeat them all.

Another man struck him with the full weight of his body. Brand planted his leading foot and flipped the man violently over his hip onto the pavement. He blocked a fist aimed for his exposed face, collapsing the attacker's larynx with a chop blow with his left hand.

Suddenly he was beset by several men at once, knocking him to the ground in a thrashing and tangled pile of straining arms and legs. The men attempting to subdue him grunted with their effort. They snatched the gun from his hand, and he was struck hard on the side of the head by an unseen foe.

Brand was well in hand when the parking lot exploded in a myriad of blinding headlights and red and blue flashing strobes. Over the grunting of startled cartel thugs, he heard shouted orders and the gravelly shuffling of tactical boots.

"Everyone on the ground," a stern voice commanded.

"Drop your weapons," another shouted.

Brand heard the muted concussion of an automatic weapon. One of the cartel thugs fell to the pavement with an inert thunk. That served to take the will out of the group, and he felt himself released as the cartel goons assumed prone positions on the warm pavement.

He joined the others on his belly, his hands in plain sight.

A familiar voice said, "On your feet Mr. Brand."

Brand recognized Agent Kilgore's voice.

"Check on your lady friend while we clean this up."

Brand stood, relieved at the unexpected outcome of his capture.

He saw Kilgore standing at a distance while a large contingent of DEA agents secured their prisoners.

He nodded gratefully to Kilgore then looked for Dehra.

She was also on the ground on the passenger side of the car.

"It's okay," he comforted her. "Let me help you up."

With his assistance, she stood, looking around her at the tactical team moving like a stop motion cartoon within the strobing, colored lights.

"What's going on?" she asked, near tears.

"That's my Fed contact, Agent Kilgore," he explained, nodding towards the agent who watched them with a mildly amused look on his face.

Brand led Dehra around the perimeter of the police activity towards Kilgore.

SAPD squad cars arrived on the scene, securing the surrounding area as the feds cuffed and stuffed the cartel members.

Brand stopped before Kilgore.

"You used us as bait," he accused the agent.

"You lied to me," Kilgore parried. "The burner I gave you is monitored."

He produced a phone similar to the one he had given Brand earlier.

"*Drive east*," he read. "*I'll meet you at the nearest gas station.*"

He slapped the flip phone closed.

"Luckily for you both we tracked the phone."

"Yeah," Brand agreed sarcastically. "Lucky. You used us for bait."

"You need to decide if you're on team good guys or if you are on your own team, Brand. Bloodying the noses of cartel henchmen and saving damsels in distress are not components of a sustainable business model. If we hadn't suspected that the cartel would track you down, and traced the burner, you would be dead – or on the way to a place where they would have killed you both."

Brand had no rejoinder. Kilgore was right.

He looked at Dehra.

She watched him silently, her eyes filling with tears at the prospect of how this could have ended if not for the federal agents. He saw clearly that she no longer trusted him. Her look of disappointment was hard to weather, but it also annoyed him.

He never proposed to be a hero. He had accepted long ago that he was more lucky than skilled. This characterization of his efforts as somehow being heroic or selfless was misguided and irresponsible. If Dehra believed it, she was tragically mistaken. Hearing Kilgore say it aloud was embarrassing.

"What now," Brand asked simply, placing emotional distance between himself and the ill-conceived criticism.

"Miss Duncan will come with us so we can get her version of the events of the past week or so."

Kilgore looked directly into Brand's eyes.

"Keep the phone on you," he warned with a serious look on his face. "We'll be in touch."

Brand dug the motel key out of his pocket. He handed it and the car keys to Dehra.

"In case you need to get your stuff," he explained mildly.

Dehra accepted the keys and looked at the ground. It was clear that she felt he was abandoning her, despite the Feds offering him no choice in the matter.

Brand lay a hand on her arm. She looked at his hand like a horsefly had landed on her. She looked at him with an unpleasant twist to her mouth.

"I'll find you," he promised impotently.

"Don't strain yourself," she said, shrugging his hand from her arm.

Kilgore shook his head as he turned to lead her to his car.

Brand watched him close the rear passenger door behind her then move to his seat in the sedan. He glanced at Brand before driving away.

Brand turned towards the bar where a large group of spectators watched the action before them. Karen was among them.

"Everyone, close out your bar tabs," she announced, turning towards the glass front door. "We are closing for the night. There's been enough entertainment for one day."

Brand walked towards the bar doors, circling the police perimeter as the final cleanup of the arrests concluded in the parking lot.

He was struck by the stark contrast between death-certain activities outside the bar and good times being had within the bar. So much of what he had seen since his life transformed from regular working guy to fugitive from the cartel, and part time fed contractor, had given him a unique perspective on how most people perceived their protection from the horrible dark forces in life.

Even considering his contribution to that horrible dark world, he seemed to dance in and out of that normally invisible region with the regularity of a neutral observer rather than a regular participant who impacted those events significantly.

Much of his reluctance to share his experiences with Karen was founded in the doubt he would be capable of explaining the past few months adequately enough to convey the bizarre details as he perceived them. He knew his recounting of the events would appear deluded in his interpretation.

When he had time between deadly altercations to do so, he gave his role in this new and deadly existence much consideration. He had lost so much in his life that the idea of alienating or removing what remained was terrifying to him.

In the shrinking realm of what used to be normal for him, Karen's role in his life was taking on a huge significance. He did not know why specifically. He only knew that she was the last vestige of a life lost to him. He was surprised to realize that the idea that he could end up alone was terrifying. He shook his head in disbelief at his misgivings. Terrifying? Was that the word he would assign to what he felt?

Perhaps not, he thought. If he were bound hand and foot on the flat deck of a barge, connected to a heavy chain and a sinking anchor feeding into the murky water beyond, terror might not be the emotion he would feel. Dread?

He entered the bar, turning sideways to allow departing patrons access to the door. He took his former seat, watching as Karen cashed out the last of her customers at the big old-fashioned cash register in the center of the bar.

She left the area inside the circular bar through the access panel on the other side of the bar top, following straggler customers to the front door.

"Thanks for coming by," she called to them as she followed them to the door. "We will be open regular hours tomorrow."

Brand heard the rattling of keys as she locked the front door. In a moment she returned to the cash register where she removed the cash drawer. She placed it on the bar across from Brand, counting out the receipts for the evening. He sat quietly as she separated coins and cash into piles and logged credit card receipts.

After a time, she concluded her count then deposited the cash into a blue bank bag.

She returned the drawer to the cash register and dropped the bag on the clipboard where she had logged the credit card receipts. She leaned against the bar as she assessed her feelings. Finally, she looked up, holding Brand's eyes with a stern expression.

"I don't really know you anymore, do I?" she asked with an edge to her words.

Brand sat back in his bar chair. He hadn't expected her to react this way. It occurred to him that he didn't really know himself if he were to be honest.

"Either you talk to me, or you need to go," she warned. "And when you go, it is for good."

Brand was stunned by her brutal ultimatum. He had not considered this tactic. He guessed she might guilt him or even entreat him with heart felt caring, but he never believed she would threaten to end their friendship.

His expression changed as he realized the finality of her demand. He felt anger rising within him. It occurred to him that she was adopting the normal manner of those who wanted something from him. They predictably resorted to threats and cajoling ultimatums. He was not pleased that Karen, his true and loyal Karen, would join those who believed he could be manipulated with threats.

"For good," he repeated in a throaty growl, as if tasting the bitterness of the threat behind the words.

This was a major crossroads between Karen and him.

Karen, this bar, San Antonio for that matter, were familiar, and in many ways a home to him. He considered quickly how he would lose all ties to what he once was if she left him.

What?

He couldn't believe this was the truth. He knew he cared about Karen, but was she truly that important to him? Sure, they dated for a short time many years before. For years since then he frequented that bar because she worked there. That very night his one hope was that against the odds she would be working the bar. He focused upon her a look that caused her gaze to waver.

"Alright," he agreed with a commitment to honesty no matter the outcome. "I'll tell you whatever you want to know."

"Right here and right now?" she demanded with a renewed strength of conviction.

"Right here and right now," he agreed doggedly.

27

KILGORE LED DEHRA THROUGH THE BACK door of the building where she had waited for Brand earlier that day. They took an elevator to the third floor, where he led her to a large interrogation room. One wall was covered by a large rectangular mirror.

"Can I offer you something to eat or drink?" Kilgore asked, pointing at the chair he wanted her to occupy.

She sat obediently.

"I could use a burger, and fries, and a Coke, if that can be arranged," she replied without hesitation. She felt the effects of the bourbon still. When she drank, she always got the munchies.

Kilgore pressed a button on the triangular device in the center of the table.

"Handle that for me," he said into the device as he looked towards the mirror.

Kilgore took the seat opposite Dehra. There was a knock at the door and a sturdy woman in a dress suit and conservative shoes dropped a folder on the table before the agent.

"Thanks," he said as she took the chair beside him.

"Now then," he said, resting his elbows on the table, touching his fingertips together. "I am Agent Matthew Kilgore, and this is U.S. Attorney Carla Saunders. We will ask you a few questions. You will answer honestly to the best of your ability. Is that clear. Ms. Duncan?"

"Do I need a lawyer here?"

"You are not under arrest at this point. Of course, you have the right to legal counsel at any time you see fit. However, it may serve to lengthen your stay with us. If you choose to continue without council, I recommend you cooperate as much as you can until you feel you want to be represented."

Dehra thought about this for moment.

"Who is Carson Brand?" Dehra asked abruptly.

Kilgore opened the folder and thumbed through the pages within as he formulated his response.

U.S. Attorney Saunders watched Dehra silently.

"That is a good question," Kilgore replied slowly, halting his search on a sheet of paper in the folder.

"Thanks," she said sarcastically. "I'm glad I asked a good one."

Kilgore glanced up from his studying.

"You will need to control yourself, Ms. Duncan. I understand that you are under a considerable amount of stress and grief, but you will understand soon enough that you are in more danger than you think. Carson Brand is no longer your concern."

"What do you mean more danger?"

"Be patient, please. I will be as clear as I can as we continue our conversation."

Kilgore thumbed through a few more pages in the file until he found the one he wanted.

"Tell me about your job at Tel Gong," Kilgore continued, ignoring the question.

"I worked in the help desk phone room," she explained, obviously uncomfortable with the subject.

"Are you in possession of any proprietary information involving the firm?" asked the U.S. Attorney Carla Saunders.

"What? No."

Saunders shook her head impatiently as she interrupted Kilgore.

"You told your boss that you overheard a conversation you were not invited to. The servers logged a data upload of that same conversation onto a storage device at your terminal.

Upon further inspection, that device has not been located. Ms. Duncan, do you have said device in your possession?"

"No, ma'am."

Saunders glanced at Kilgore who jotted a note on the page before him.

"Dehra," Kilgore said cordially. "Let me tell you what we know. You worked at Tel Gong, as you call it, for about two weeks. Your first day on the floor you eavesdrop on a private conversation containing high value company secrets. You made a recording of the call and denied doing so when your boss asked you directly and now when we are asking you directly. You met Carson Brand at a bar and brought him home. You told him that you not only made the recording but told him you made a copy of the call. Since then, you have been on the run from some very bad men. Corporate espionage is a very serious crime, Ms. Duncan."

"I was not eavesdropping. The call came to my que by accident. Being new I didn't know what to do about the call."

"Your first reaction was to make a recording of company secrets?" Saunders asked disbelievingly.

"I made the recording to have some recourse in case I was fired."

"You admit you made the recording after claiming that you didn't," Kilgore accused. "Lying to the FBI is a serious crime, Ms. Duncan."

Saunders leaned forward, holding a restraining hand up towards Kilgore.

"Let's take a step back - all of us," she recommended soothingly. "We understand your reasoning for what you did. We even understand why you would lie about it. What we don't understand is why you enlisted the aid of a known killer to escape and then evade the Sherriff's department when they ordered you to give yourself up. Call me crazy, Ms. Duncan, but that doesn't seem like the actions of an innocent employee who overheard a simple conversation on the phone."

Dehra closed her mouth with a clicking of her teeth. The interview was going in a dangerous direction. She had no idea how telling the truth about a simple mistake could make her sound like a criminal.

"Am I under arrest?" Dehra demanded.

"You are now," Kilgore admitted with a deliberate tone.

"What?" Dehra screamed. "On what charge?"

"Ms. Duncan," Saunders announced. "You are under arrest for suspicion of crimes against the state including espionage and treason. Please stand up."

"No! I'm not a criminal. I only had a job. I didn't do anything."

Kilgore moved around the table and cuffed Dehra.

"Ms. Duncan, you have the right to remain silent…"

Dehra's eyes welled with tears and her body shuddered with the despair of being caught in a situation she could not control and did not deserve.

28

BRAND SAT NEXT TO KAREN AT THE BAR. Both sipped from the glasses before them. He had his usual bourbon rocks. She drank beer on the rocks.

"I had no idea, Brand." Karen said helplessly.

"No one does," Brand said without emotion, draining his glass. "Can I get a refill?"

Karen slid the bottle over to him.

"Help yourself. Why did the DEA guy take your girlfriend?"

Brand refilled the glass and replaced the bottle on the bar. He dug in his pocket, withdrawing the memory stick.

"Probably to get hold of this," he replied.

"What's on it?"

Brand shrugged.

"Whatever it is, it is important enough that a kill team came after Dehra and her brother. Then Kilgore took her in for questioning. The last part is why I think this drive is something big."

"Is it the launch codes for nukes or what?" Karen asked half-jokingly.

"Dehra said it is a recording of a phone call between two employees with the company she was fired from. Something about gathering info on American citizens."

"That is some unbelievable conspiracy shit."

"Agreed. But here it is."

He held up the drive, turning it in the dim light.

"So that is why the feds used you as bait for the Mexicans?"

"I've been thinking about that. There is no way they could have known the cartel was going to be here. I think the Mexicans were just in the wrong place at the wrong time," Brand confided. "I think the feds were here to take Dehra into custody. If it was about the cartel, they would have taken me with them."

"I'm no law enforcement expert, but it seems strange that you are being allowed to do what you say you have done with no legal repercussions."

"Kilgore has given me cover since the beginning. He told me once that I am able to get in where he can't legally go. I guess that access has value."

"That also means you are breaking laws he can't legally break."

"I'm not sure a law can be legally broken, but I hear what you're saying. I thought of that. I am aware that it wouldn't take much for me to find myself an outlaw."

Karen leaned away from Brand as if to get a better view, as if she were witnessing an unbelievable oddity.

"Are you hearing what you are saying? What you just told me is that you will eventually be an outlaw: not if but when. You need to get out of this before it is too late."

Brand nodded but made no rejoinder.

"And what about the Mexican gangs who are after you? Do you think they will stop with this one try to kill you, or capture you and kill you?"

"Karen," he replied wearily. "You are wearing me out. Can we take a break? I told you before, that two minutes was not enough. We have been at this for a while. You have a lot of questions, and it has been a long day. Besides, I have to get my stuff out of that motel room and find somewhere else to stay."

"Why can't you stay there?"

"If the feds haven't already gone by to pick up Dehra's things they will soon enough. It won't be long before they come looking for this memory stick."

"You have to give it to them. You're not thinking of doing something else with it, are you?"

"I 'm not sure what I should do," he said, looking at the drive in his hand. "Something about it is not making sense."

"The drive?"

"No. Why is the DEA so interested in a non-drug issue? Why did they want Dehra so badly? Is there something to this spying on Americans story? Why didn't Kilgore turn this case over to the FBI?"

"He probably knows what he is doing. Remember, tough guy, you are not a federal agent."

"That's true, but I had a friend who is FBI and there was a definite line of demarcation with the handling of some terrorists I came across. I got my ass chewed for crossing jurisdictional lines then. Those lines seem to have been discarded here."

Brand pocketed the drive.

"If what is on this drive is true then the plot could go all the way to the federal government, which would explain why jurisdictional lines might be crossed. Maybe none of us are safe."

"The girl!" Karen accused him with the intuition upon which women rely. "You are still protecting her, aren't you?"

Brand shrugged.

"I like to know what I'm doing and why I am doing it. When I figure it out, I'll decide what to do with this thing then."

"If this is an international conspiracy and federal agents are acting like mafia hit men and thugs…Brand, if what you say you suspect is true, then she is already gone. Think about it. If the information on this drive is so incriminating, based on your fed friend crossing jurisdictional lines, someone is trying to get her out of the way – maybe even kill her. She was taken by the feds. They probably won't let her go without getting the information on the drive. Even then, she might be in too deep to be allowed to get away. "

Karen stood without finishing her beer.

"By the way," she said as she moved to tidy their mess. "Everything I just said applies to you too."

"Yeah," he agreed, impressed with her intellect. "I'm starting to see that."

Karen shook her head at him.

"I have never seen you afraid of anything. It must be nice."

Brand frowned. He could only be so honest.

"It's nice," he agreed without conviction.

He was concerned about his future. He was reluctant to describe his feelings as fear, but he knew a small amount of dread held a place deep within him.

"Why don't you stay with me tonight," Karen offered as she collected the keys to the bar.

Brand nodded.

Once outside, Brand nodded to the empty spot where Dehra's car had been parked.

"The feds took her car, probably looking for the thumb drive."

Karen looked askance at Brand once more. She feared he was taking huge chances with little benefit, even if he got away with them.

29

HA WANG STEPPED OFF THE SLEEK PRIVATE jet plane and onto the tarmac of a small air strip in a region of squat concrete and steel warehouses and manufacturing buildings near *Nanchang,* the capital of *Jangxi* Province in west central China. The dull gray waters of *Poyang-hu* glittered dimly in the distance.

Two MSS men in expensive suits waited near the jet, standing beside the idling *Hongqi* luxury sedan.

Ha strode to the car and placed his thick leather carry-on in the trunk, then took his place in the back seat.

As they drove away from the small airport, the MSS agents sat in the front seats, remaining silent during the forty-five-minute drive to the city's downtown district. As they travelled past utilitarian industrial areas, then ramshackle shanties, arriving finally in a region filled with tall residential towers, Ha experienced a familiar calming comfort at once more being among his own people in his home city.

Soon the sprawl gave way to the glass and steel geometry of office buildings crowding against the precisely organized waterfront. The wide river *Gan Chiang,* which quaked in the strong winds crossing its expanse. Those same gusts rushed to the waterfront where they collided with the downtown structures, billowing against the sides of those modern tall buildings like flood waters against a shiny dam.

The car pulled into the busy circular porte-cochere before the *Crown Plaza Nanchang Riverside* hotel. Accompanied by the

MSS men, Wang left the expensive car parked out front as they made their way to the hotel lobby.

Ha quickly checked in at the front desk, leaving his MSS escort behind in the lobby. As the sleek elevator rose to the top floor, he regarded the others in the car mildly, as if sharing the elevator was distasteful.

His room was a corner suite overlooking the *Nanchang* Bridge crossing the *Gan Chiang River*. He placed his carry-on bag on the bed and carefully unpacked it. He opened his laptop and keyed in his security credentials gaining access to the Tel Gong intranet site. He keyed in his arrival code and immediately his cell phone rang.

A voice on the phone spoke in precise Mandarin. Ha could not place the dialect.

"10 minutes."

"Understood," he replied in Mandarin into the dead phone line.

At precisely 10 minutes after the call, his laptop pinged, and a strobing tab appeared in the web window. He maximized the tab and joined the web meeting. Three meeting participants were online. Wang recognized one as the CEO of Tel Gong. The other two were unfamiliar to him.

"Hauan Wang," the CEO said, opening the meeting. "What is the status of your U.S. operation?"

"Sir," he replied uncertainly. "I have not been introduced to the others in this meeting."

"These men are from our holding company and the governing authority. Now, be forthcoming."

Wang surveyed the stern faces on his laptop screen. He had never briefed anyone above the CEO, especially members of the "Party."

"As a whole," he began brightly. "We are progressing along planned telemetry guidelines. We are getting some pushback from American pundits and journalists. This is to be expected due to the freedom of their news outlets and the natural suspicious ignorance of the American people. That being said, I just finished a quality on-camera interview with a major news outlet."

"Yes," one of the other men agreed. "We saw the interview."

"Then you should be pleased that we have things well in hand with our planned operations bearing fruit."

Silence greeted his optimism. He continued with forced confidence.

"The situation involving the breach is in process. The perpetrator is in custody and thus far there is no data drive."

Simultaneously, the three men leaned nearer their screens, like dancers following a choreographed movement.

"I have not ruled out its existence for caution's sake, but the spy would have given up the device to save her skin. She was arrested and the authorities are searching for the disk."

"It is critical that the data disk never surface," the CCP official said with the authority of the Chines Communist party behind it.

"Understood," Wang agreed uncomfortably. His position was precarious in this matter, and he was not losing sight of the danger it presented to him personally. His tenure with MSS and his high-level security clearance did little to alleviate his misgivings for these strangers attending the meeting.

"What of the team you sent?" asked the same man. "We are hearing that local authorities in Texas are investigating the incident, claiming as many as six people died. Is there any truth to this rumor?"

"The rumors are accurate," Wang admitted. "The spy and her brother were in the company of a stranger who defeated the team."

"Are you not concerned that a single man defeated a sanctioned clandestine team? Wouldn't that kind of skill indicate a federal agency might be involved?"

"He is not affiliated formally with any of the agencies with which we communicate. He appears to be a rogue civilian. I believe he is romantically involved with the spy, this Texas woman."

"Texas woman?" the Party official repeated with a mocking sputter. "This Texas Cowboy must be contained. Moreover, we need to know who he is and who he works for. Could he be in possession of the data drive? There are too many questions for us to so easily dismiss this issue as being in hand."

"We are in the solution as we speak, sir. The woman is isolated and under control. Her brother was eliminated by the first team. I have dispatched a second team to handle the Cowboy, as you say. The first team was unaware of the new man and his abilities. This stranger is no longer aided by the element of surprise. They are searching for him particularly. In the unlikely event he possesses the data, it will be recovered when he is eliminated."

The CEO and the two officials blanked their images and muted their audio.

Wang endured several minutes of dark silence before the CEO's image appeared once more, this time without the other men.

"Ha," the CEO said soberly. "Personally, I don't believe this incident amounts to much. Those who manage the big picture believe otherwise. We are but a small cog in the machine. We cannot become the faulty cog. You have been specially trained and prepared for your work in the United States. I endorse your use of a follow-up team. However, the others believe this may be an instance in which we activate our hidden network and enlist the services of more formal channels. I have been assured that the American assets we control can be used to handle this."

"We agreed that was a last resort, sir," Wang responded doubtfully.

"Mobilize those resources and call off the team. We believe this situation could prove highly volatile and it is, decidedly, too risky to trust in sanctioned undercover solutions."

Wang was silent as the gravity of this directive sunk past his defensiveness and his fear. Once kindled, this fire could not be extinguished. He felt a coldness in the pit of his stomach. From this moment his actions could very well change the world as everyone knew it. If revealed, what he was about to put in motion would never be viewed as benevolent or selfless.

Further, if discovered, he would be a loathsome character in the prism of world history.

His time in the west had taught him many things, the first of which was that Americans are trusting to the point of tragedy. The second was that once roused from the deep sleep which renders them oblivious to the forces arrayed against them, they rally as one. He knew that Americans, to a man, would fight to the last breath to defend the very nation their freedom of speech allows them to demean and marginalize.

These same lessons caused him to doubt the will of those in the U.S. government he would have to count upon to rally behind his efforts, especially if they got wind of the devastation of the plan he advanced with the aid of their participation.

Hauan Wang nodded towards the laptop camera, unable to speak for the moment.

"You are here for more than a video conference," the CEO advised. "Approach the remainder of your work here with the same reverent sobriety you are exhibiting to me now. You have been trained. You are in your position precisely because of your ability to perform in this task. You will not fail."

The CEO's video panel went dark, and the call ended.

Wang remained as he was for several moments, watching the blank screen as if for answers. His thoughts went to the mysterious stranger who had thus far thwarted his efforts. Who was he? What danger did he pose to the success of his operation? What did he want?

As he leaned back, watching a towed barge make its way along the steely waters of the *Nanchang*, Ha committed himself to the dangers of his appointed path. To do otherwise was to ensure his own death as surely as he must ensure the death of this new foe.

With a deft gesture, he summoned his cell from a pocket and keyed in the number code which would call off the hit team dispatched to eliminate the stranger.

He reluctantly admitted the benefit of the CEO's and the others' decision. He wanted no more media attention focused upon his efforts. More dead bodies ensured renewed police efforts and guaranteed more difficulties.

Mobilizing highly placed American governmental assets would pose a great hazard, but not so great as the likelihood that additional corpses in Texas communities might sway the fragile loyalties of those he needed to move on his behalf.

He pushed a doubtful future from his thoughts as he prepared for his work – the work that would change the fabric of nations.

30

DEHRA HAD NEVER FELT SO BETRAYED – so lost. Her first night in permanent housing in general population, or Gen Pop, as they called it, had been a sleepless one. She closed her eyes to the cold gray concrete walls and the steel springed bed in her cell. She learned that her locked cell was a vast improvement over mixing with the other inmates. She was locked up in a county jail, but she felt like she was confined to a state prison, complete with all the hard ass bitches she could handle.

According to her jailers, she was safer locked in her cell – at least until the new wore off her. Her looks and her figure seemed to play a major role in the risk to her personal safety. The women's block was much less crowded than the men's block, so she was assigned her own cell.

She knew little about being a criminal. What she knew of being in jail was only what she had seen on TV. The heroes and heroines in those shows were badasses, easily intimidating the inmates. Compared with these hardened inmates, she was no hero nor was she a baddass. She was merely a frightened girl in a horribly cruel place.

She fought hot tears for what seemed the hundredth time since the federal agents had delivered her to the large holding cell where she had been in-processed. She couldn't decide which was more terrifying, the jeers from the men across the way in their holding cells, or the taunts of the women in the hold with her.

Once the heavy steel door closed her into the women's hold, she had given her back to the others in the cell and focused her attention on the activities of the jailers and the beat cops who, at frequent intervals, brought handcuffed men and women into the in-processing area for drop off.

In the wide hall between holding cells, a score of county personnel typed on computers, filled out paperwork, or moved forms from one end of the long two-sided workstation to the other. Everything ran systematically.

Their demeanor appeared blandly business like. Dehra was certain that many of those suspects brought into in-processing would not regain their freedom for months or years. Despite the grim reality of the future for those in the cells, the officers treated everyone the same - as if it were no big deal.

Waiting miserably in her cold cell, she felt that it was indeed a big deal. She had no idea with what she was being charged, save for overhearing crosstalk where the term *Federal Hold* had been mentioned. The threatened charges of treason and obstruction appeared on none of her paperwork.

Neither agents Kilgore nor Saunders had given her any indication how long she would be in jail. Her limited communication with the jail personnel yielded no information. Their dispassionate by-rote replies to her emotionally charged questions frustrated her.

With growing heat, she remembered Carson Brand. He had set all of this in motion with his appearance in her life. It could be no coincidence that with his arrival came attacks, Leon's death, and her arrest. Born and raised in Uvalde, her life had been one of bucolic peace at a languid pace. The arrival of Tel Gong as the county's largest employer had been a great opportunity for her to elevate herself and Leon from the squalor in which they had lived since her mom's passing.

If recording a conversation warranted a team of assassins, then why was it that Brand was set upon by goons in black SUV's instead of her? By his own admission, he had vouchsafed a dangerous, if not a criminal life, prior to his arrival. It was inconceivable to her that her life would go from quiet, normal, and carefree, to deadly in only a day or two.

No matter the outlying considerations, Brand brought danger and death to her and her brother. He was the reason she languished in a cold jail cell while he wandered freely wherever he was now.

As the chow bell rang jarringly, her door ground as it opened. Inmates' voices raised as they made their way to the chow hall.

Dehra groaned as she raised herself from her bunk. She felt hunger pangs deeply buried below the discomfort of her fear and dread of once more joining others in Gen Pop.

31

THE INTAKE FORMS LISTED HER NAME as Audrie Pyle. Those who knew her on the street called her "Rock Pile." Her partner LaQuisha had given her the *nom de gure*.
That LaQuisha could come up with some funny shit, she thought with amusement.

The deputy who handcuffed her after the fight had to daisy chain two sets of cuffs together to bind her wrists behind her back. The task was doubly difficult because she had been hopped up on adrenaline when she was arrested. Audrie was still sweaty and breathing heavily from her fight with the two biker dudes in front of the bar when the deputy cuffed her.

The bikers were tough and put up a fight – at first.

Good ole LaQuisha learned from the beginning of their time together that among Audrie's attributes was her ability to take a punch.

The two bearded men could throw a punch, but they didn't have the stomach for how many they would have to deliver to defeat Audrie.

It never went that far. It didn't last long this time either. She was able to crush one man's testicles with a hard kick, a classic LaQuisha move. The other fell under her weight onto the rough pavement as she pushed through a fusillade of lefts and rights.

Audrie beat the man senseless on the ground with her giant fists. She consumed her remaining rage energy grinding his face into the gravel aggregate of the pavement until his skin looked like he had fallen from his bike at speed, landing on his face.

As she remembered the fight, Audrie grinned a crooked sneer at the jail guard. LaQuisha would have gotten a laugh out of those pussy bikers if she were still alive.

Guilt and regret gave her eyes a dangerous glimmer.

The jail guard eyed Audrie's bruised face and glimmering eyes warily as he removed her cuffs.

"If you are any way other than calm and cooperative, we will do this with you on your face. Do you understand?"

Audrie grinned a round meaty smile. Brandishing ragged gray teeth.

"You scared?" she asked the guard with her characteristic direct glare.

"Shut up and behave," the guard warned her. He was authoritative but she saw the fear.

Audrie memorized the guard's face. She hoped to see him again so she could collect payment for his attitude.

LaQuisha always said, 'You don't get nothing for nothing. You fuck up, you pay up.'

The guard guided her to the fingerprint station with a hand on her broad shoulder. Audrie was over six feet tall, at least five inches taller than the jailer. His hand rested well above his shoulders as he guided her.

His view of her neck revealed a graphic-novel-worthy mural from her chin into the top of her brown crew neck tee shirt. Her huge round arms were as illustrated as her neck. Her hair was docked short and dyed pink – an ironic touch by the jailer's estimation.

He clutched her big left hand in both of his as he helped her coat her fingertips with the solution that allowed the digital print recorder to recognize the swirls and lines in her fingerprints.

She allowed him to manipulate her hands and palms on the glass screen with the numerous red laser lights crossing beneath.

Next, she was directed to follow the red line marked on the floor to the medical section where she submitted samples for her DNA evidence. All inmates provide samples for the National DNA database. After that, she was tested for HIV and COVID, then instructed to take a seat on the steel bench in the hall outside the medical section.

Soon, another guard escorted her to the intake women's holding cell for processing for permanent housing.

Audrie Pyle was known to law enforcement. She was a convicted felon with a rap sheet filled with nearly every violent crime short of murder. She was flagged the moment she was arrested. She would not be offered bail, and she would wait in a cell on the block for her court date.

Audrie stopped just inside as the guard slammed the door of the women's hold. She surveyed the dozen women in the cell for a moment before she moved to one of the long stainless-steel benches attached to the walls. The three women occupying the bench watched her warily as she approached.

Audrie paused before them for a short moment before, unbidden, the three women rose, deciding to find seating elsewhere. Audrie lay down on the bench, appreciating the three warm spots beneath her. Her experience taught her that she would wait in holding for as many as twelve hours before she was housed.

While the other women in the hold, most awaiting release on lesser charges, sat alert, craving freedom, Audrie fell immediately asleep to memories of LaQuisha's broad face and ready smile.

Her growling snores filled the room.

It was late, way past lights out, when Audrie finally settled on the cot in her cell on the women's block. The block was never silent. She lay back on her cot listening to the unintelligible sounds of inmates' murmuring conversations, the sliding and banging of steel doors, and guards communicating at full daytime volume over radios and to one another. All these sounds were familiar – almost a comfort.

She really missed LaQuisha.

She was awake when the lights came on at 6 AM. She pulled on her crocs and waited at her cell door. At 6:15 the bell clanged, and her cell door slid open with a grinding whir of an electric motor, and the scraping of steel wheels supporting the heavy slab of steel.

A stern voice sounded over the crackly PA system, explaining the rules of Gen Pop, and instructions for chow time.

Audrie had heard it all before. She strode with heavy strides towards the chow hall.

As she fell in line with other inmates headed to breakfast, Audrie reminded herself that there was always talk on the block. Despite LaQuisha's insistence that the flow of information could keep you alive in here, Audrie hated the talk. Everyone knew everything about everyone else on the block. Her doubts hardened her expression because she knew that her presence was known and that her crime was known. She also knew that she had very little time to do her thing before everyone knew what her thing was, and she would not be able to do it.

She entered the low-ceilinged, concrete block chow hall with the shiny beige paint and the red warnings on the walls. She grabbed a fiberglass tray and walked the line, trustees filling her plate with unappetizing food.

As she moved along the line, she was alert, keeping her head on a swivel - as LaQuisha used to say, eyes like a potato. She took a seat at a table at the back of the room so she could see everyone who entered the chow hall.

Dehra pulled a tray from the stack and moved along the serving line, avoiding the trustee's lustful eyes. She would keep her head down until she was out of there. She just wanted to go home. She would give the federal agents any information they wanted. Instinctively she knew that was their plan all along: weaken her resolve until she cooperated. She wanted to cooperate.

At the end of the serving line, with her tray filled, she pulled a cup from the stack. Her gaze rose as she looked towards the beverage dispenser area.

A large woman with pink hair rushed towards her at a surprising speed. Dehra dropped her tray and took a step back.

Violently, the huge woman was on her, crushing her against the wall with her huge body.

Audrie grabbed Dehra's head in a huge hand and bashed it against the concrete wall. The sound of her skull cracking was clearly heard in the noisy chow hall.

Dehra lost consciousness on the third impact with the wall. She was dead before the guards managed to pull Audrie to the floor and cuffed her.

"Add that to my sheet, motherfuckers," Audrie screamed as she struggled against the guards' efforts.

32

BRAND ROSE QUIETLY, trying not to disturb Karen who slept in the bed beside him. He pulled on his jeans and moved silently towards the kitchen.

Karen's house was small, nestled in an older treelined neighborhood. Brand noted that the house was unusually quiet. He remembered from the time they dated, that her niece and her younger brother were frequent visitors, liable to show up at any hour. He had learned the previous night, while catching up, that Karen's son was in college and made only rare appearances. He liked him and was disappointed at missing him.

Brand pressed the brew button on the coffee maker, leaning against the countertop, watching the machine work.

Karen appeared, wearing a thin wrap.

"Early riser still," she observed, taking a seat at the raised bar opposite Brand.

Brand nodded as he watched the coffee's slow progress towards the fill line on the carafe.

"Last night doesn't let you out of the friend zone," she warned him. "I was only there for a friend who needed a shoulder."

Brand looked up from his monitoring of the coffee pot's progress. He was unable to suppress a grin at Karen's humor.

"There he is," she announced brightly. "It's always sunshine and puppies around here. I knew you would eventually remember that."

"Sunshine and puppies." Brand repeated gently.

Another relic of his old life presented itself.

He looked at Karen with genuine warmth. Despite the misgivings he entertained the previous night, she was the truest friend he had ever had. Their history was sometimes checkered, but she was a cornerstone of his life.

Bert had been his best friend from childhood, but he was never one to resort to aimless sentiment or pointless emotion. He was not one to count on when anyone needed a shoulder, as Karen said. Karen had always shown genuine concern for him. Even when he had lied to her about being married, she had forgiven him. He never learned why she had. He eventually wrote it off to what he perceived as her strongest attribute – her unflinching faith in him. He allowed himself to believe that she also felt a deep, but unproclaimed love for him.

He knew this imagined investment of deeper feelings from her was hubris, but he found no other explanation. He would never reveal his feelings to her or anyone else. He took comfort that his silence on the matter limited his emotional liability to a self-serving fantasy within which he alone drew comfort and some degree of happiness.

Brand decided Karen was dear to him no matter where his life took him; no matter how much he suffered. He promised himself that he would not forget that.

The coffeemaker beeped, victorious once more in its task. Brand filled two cups, passing one to Karen.

"You sure know how to treat a girl," she chided him, sipping from the cup.

Brand blew on the hot coffee before sipping gingerly.

His mind raced ahead to his plans for the day as he tried to figure a way to ask Karen for a favor.

"You working today?" Brand asked.

"Of course. I have to be there to open at eleven," she replied with her usual smile. "Remember, I had to cover last night."

"It sucks to be in charge," Brand sympathized.

Karen favored him with an amused look over the rim of her cup, then sipped her coffee.

Brand suspected she was waiting for him to say or do something, as if he were a subject in some secret experiment of her own design.

Her lips tightened into a thin smile as he inhaled his intention to speak.

"Do you think I can borrow your car today?"

Her expression did not change as she heard the question.

"Are you going to blow it up or drive it through a crowd of pedestrians?"

Brand was relieved. Her humor prefaced agreement.

"I'll fill it up before I return it this afternoon," he promised, ignoring her question.

"Thanks. I'll take the bike in today," she said.

"You still have that motorcycle?"

"I do," she replied with characteristic brevity.

Brand laughed.

Karen was unflappable and unchanged.

"Thanks," he said with genuine warmth. "I really appreciate it."

"Brand," she began with a sigh and a dimming of her smile. "I don't know any other way to talk to you. You are going to end up dead or – best case – in jail for the rest of your life. I don't understand why you can't see that."

Brand grimaced at Karen's persistence to continue her protests from the previous night.

"I know you believe that, and I know you cannot be convinced otherwise, but there is a lot about my life you don't know."

"I know who and what you were before your best friend and your girlfriend got killed. You told me a lot about what you have been doing with your time since then. The math is not hard, sweetie. You have a choice to make, and you need to make the right one."

"I don't have a choice!" he blurted more forcefully than he should.

Brand clicked his teeth together audibly and shook his head. He had never raised his voice to Karen until that moment.

"I'm sorry."

Karen watched her friend helplessly. She knew that among Brand's faults, he did not know how to quit or be disloyal. She knew he was thinking of the blonde – Dehra. He was a blind crusader when it came to a woman in peril. She doubted it was anything more than a misplaced sense of duty – more likely a sense of responsibility for placing her in danger. Karen knew his self-blame was ill placed and groundless. His story placed Dehra firmly behind everything that was happening to her.

She pulled her car keys from a rack on the wall and tossed them to Brand.

"Don't wreck my car," she warned him as she went to her bedroom to find her helmet and motorcycle jacket. A moment later she walked by him and out the front door with no further comment.

Brand pocketed the keys and returned to the bedroom where he donned his socks and shoes. His concern for Karen's ire faded as he occupied himself with the plan, he was formulating to rescue Dehra from the feds.

33

KILGORE WAS SURPRISED. Agent Spencer grinned, obviously pleased with his boss' discomfiture. There was no love lost between Brand and himself. Instinctively, Spencer knew that Brand was close to an unfortunate ending with the DEA. Spencer was pleased to be a part of it in any way he could avail himself.

"He is in the lobby now?" Kilgore asked incredulously.

"As we speak," Spencer said once more.

"Have him escorted to my office," Kilgore ordered.

"I'll handle it personally," Spencer announced, a little too enthusiastically for Kilgore's liking.

Spencer took the elevator to the lobby floor where Brand waited, leaning against a wall adorned with nondescript corporate art.

Brand pushed away from the wall as he saw Spencer approach.

Spencer stopped before Brand, looking him over head to toe in an overly dramatic manner meant to make Brand uncomfortable.

Brand's instincts told him Spencer knew facts Brand did not. The agent's authoritarian manner was probably more a result of that knowledge than an extension of their long-standing dislike for one another.

"I need to see Kilgore," Brand announced unnecessarily.

"That's good," Spencer agreed. "He wants to see you too. You might want to watch your step tough guy. You may learn that you are not as smart as you think you are."

"That would still make me smarter than you," Brand returned with annoyance.

Spencer grimaced, fighting the urge to throttle the contractor.

"Fuck you, outlaw," Spencer managed to hiss through his teeth.

Brand smiled and nodded.

This only served to further anger the DEA agent.

"Let's go," Spencer growled, turning on his heel.

Brand followed him across the lobby to the elevator bank. They took the first car to the upper floor where the DEA offices were housed. Spencer turned to Brand as the elevator hissed to a stop.

"I need to frisk you, outlaw," Spencer said with grim satisfaction.

Brand considered the agent for a moment.

"Not going to happen, Spencer.

"We can do this the easy way or the hard way – up to you."

"Spencer," Brand said with a stern, level look at the agent. "If you press this thing I will go to jail, and you will not outlive the injuries you will sustain today - up to you."

Spencer paused as he weighed his options. Finally, he strode from the elevator.

Brand followed him to Kilgore's office.

Inside, Kilgore motioned Brand to a seat and Spencer out of the office. When the door closed behind Spencer, Kilgore circled his desk and took a seat in the second chair before his desk, beside Brand.

"I need to talk to you about Dehra," Brand said abruptly.

Kilgore nodded as though he anticipated this.

"Do you? Alright, let's talk. What's on your mind?"

"I'm willing to trade intel I possess for her freedom."

Kilgore said nothing, waiting for the rest.

"She doesn't know anything. She was just a civilian, in the wrong place at the wrong time."

"It's too late," Kilgore said soberly.

"What do you mean too late?"

"You can't help her now."

Brand's mouth fell open as his imagination conjured the worst.

"Is she in jail?" Brand asked.

"She is gone," Kilgore replied. "We placed her in witness protection."

Brand leaned back, relieved that Dehra wasn't in prison.

"Can I see her one last time before you hide her?"

"Like I said, Brand. She is already gone."

Kilgore stood stiffly and returned to his desk chair.

"Speaking of this intel. I presume you have the thumb drive with the overheard conversation on it."

Brand saw no further reason to lie about it.

"I do."

Brand pulled the memory stick from his jeans pocket and tossed it on Kilgore's desk.

"I found it in her car."

"We towed the car," Kilgore corrected him.

"Before that. She didn't know I took it."

"I see."

Kilgore raised the drive to eye level.

"This thing has caused a lot of trouble. It's good to have it in secure hands."

Kilgore paused for a minute before dropping the drive on his desk. He looked at Brand.

"I'm glad you came here without my having to bring you here. I have an assignment for you. I need you to go back to Uvalde and take a job with the Tel Gong plant there."

"You want me to do what?"

"You will have an assumed name and new credentials. We believe your girlfriend uncovered a deep state plot to steal Americans' information."

Brand held up his hands in confusion.

"I thought you guys were the Drug Enforcement Agency. Since when do you perform international espionage stuff?"

"I see you learned from your FBI friend," Kilgore observed. "The DEA doesn't do that sort of thing, and you won't be working for us in this matter. This is a covert op under the direction of the NSA. You are on loan to them."

Brand sat back in his chair, crossing his arms stubbornly.

"I cashed those checks today. That is pretty low pay for the danger you are expecting me to deal with in these little field exercises. We need to talk about a rate increase, especially since you want me to step up to covert ops guy."

"Seriously? That is your comment after what I have told you?"

"No. I have a lot of comments, but I also remember the constant threat against me and my freedom if I don't comply. You guys have plenty of money in the fed, so I figured it was not a big deal to expect what you expect twice a month."

"I'll work on it. Do you need money now?"

"Nah, I'm good."

Brand inhaled deeply as he sat straighter in his chair.

"You realize these people probably know who I am if they are sending hit teams after me."

"We don't think you were the intended target. We believe they were after the Duncan's. Those who saw you are no longer able to identify you."

Brand nodded in grim agreement.

We took the liberty of applying online for you. Your first interview is Monday morning at 9am. The position is in their physical plant. That is the group that oversees maintenance and repairs."

"I know what a physical plant is," Brand replied wearily.

"Your construction experience will help you get the job. Maintenance personnel get access to all areas within the plant including the administrative offices. Here is a copy of your resume."

Kilgore retrieved a stapled document from his desktop and handed it to Brand.

"Familiarize yourself with this so you can pass the interview. We have updated your tax records, employment data, and web presence, to reflect the accuracy of this information. Additionally, we improved your credit rating."

"Why are you monkeying with my finances?"

"You may not know this because you have been unemployed for so long…"

"Self-employed," Brand corrected proudly.

"Whatever," Kilgore responded impatiently. "Most potential employers check prospective employees' credit ratings to help verify their reliability. Pay a fucking bill once in a while, Brand. Your credit rating was sub-600."

"What is it now?"

"780."

Brand nodded, impressed.

"So," Brand continued slowly. "What am I looking for?"

"Get settled into the job for a few days. NSA will contact you with further details. I'll work on raising your pay scale here."

"Thanks. Can I get another car from the lot? I'm driving a borrowed car right now. I was told not to wreck it. I would like to keep the promise I made."

"Goddam, Brand. When you put your hand out it stays out. I'll call over to the lot. Pick what you want. I also would like your promise not to wreck it."

Brand left the room.

34

BRAND PARKED HIS DEA DRUG SEIZURE car in the parking lot before the large Tel Gong industrial building outside of Uvalde. He selected the car from a DEA capture lot. It was a non-descript gray sedan. Brand didn't bother to lock it as he made his way to the entrance.

He wore jeans, steel toed boots, and a black tee. It had been a long time since he had held a JOB, as he called it. He owned his own company most of his life. Before his life spun out of control, he framed apartment complexes and large homes. In those days he had a crew, tools, and the respect of his clients. Now he was a vagabond, dodging cartel hitters, and a life behind bars.

He passed the interview with flying colors due to his background and experience, aided by a solid work history courtesy of the federal government. Despite abandoning Beatrice's sensitivity training class that day so long ago, he was given credit for the racial sensitivity course.

He entered the front door where a stern sentry at the security desk demanded identification. After a suspicious inspection of his credentials, the guard directed him down a nearby corridor where he found the offices for Human Resources.

Brand entered a busy office filled with bustling activity and well-dressed office personnel. He identified himself as a new hire for the physical plant. He filled out a few final documents, was issued his security access badge, and instructed to sit in the small waiting area until his supervisor arrived to escort him to his workstation.

Moments later, a sweaty older man arrived, out of breath and wide eyed from the strain of his journey.

"You Brand?" he asked.

"Yes," Brand admitted with a faint smile.

"Let's go."

With that, the heavy-footed supervisor led him through a maze of administrative office corridors, through heavy double doors, and into the plant's production area. A wide hallway with glassed clean rooms on each side led at length to another set of heavy double doors which accessed the shipping receiving warehouse. A right turn, and a few more moments of walking brought them to a steel door with a small plaque identifying it as the entrance to the Physical Plant.

The supervisor pointed at a wall lined with gray lockers.

"That one's yours with your name on it. I'm Bruce Anderson, your direct supervisor. Change into the work clothes inside the locker and report to my office over there."

He pointed to a steel door with a wired glass window in the upper half as he walked in the same direction.

Brand moved to his locker. Inside he found four changes of blue work uniforms. He donned the heavy button-down shirt over his tee and pulled on the stiff dungarees. He tightened the belt as he stood then went to the supe's office as instructed.

He entered, standing behind one of the two chairs before the supe's desk.

"Sit," the seated man instructed. "Let's cover the rules and your duties."

Brand sat in the nearest chair.

"Alright," Anderson said as he read his computer screen. "You are Carson Brand from San Antonio – long commute for you."

Brand didn't respond.

Anderson looked at him doubtfully over the flat screen monitor.

"We don't tolerate tardiness or absenteeism. Is being here on time going to be a problem for you?"

"Nope."

"No, sir."

Brand shook his head.

"No, sir."

"Do we have a problem here?" Anderson asked heatedly.

"Not yet, sir," Brand replied nonplussed.

Anderson considered Brand for a serious moment. He seemed unsure whether to press the new man or just to let his lackadaisical attitude go. Instead, he cleared his throat and read from the company S.O.P. on the computer screen.

"As a new hire with Tel Gong Communications Corp. you are on a 90-day probationary term of employment, after which time you will be evaluated for permanent placement..."

Brand quelled a yawn as the sweaty supervisor droned on, reading from the web site text. His entrepreneurial instincts rebelled against the limited opportunity of the position - despite it being only a cover. The corpulent supervisor with the deprecatory manner was a frustrated egotist using his limited authority to fuel his frail sense of self-worth. Brand ignored the supervisor as he droned on, reading from the text on his screen.

Brand emerged from his reverie to see that the supervisor had finished reading the required information and was awaiting a reply from him. Brand waited silently, knowing that any reply would draw even more ire from the moody supervisor.

"I say again," supes repeated. "Do you understand the terms of your employment, and do you agree to those terms?"

"Sure."

"I need a yes or no."

"Yes," Brand replied impatiently.

"Was that attitude, Mister?"

Brand stood from his chair and circled the desk with a deliberate gait.

Supes stood uncertainly at the move.

Brand drew closer until his face was close to the corpulent supervisor's face.

"You haven't begun to see attitude, chubby," he warned. "If I have any more trouble from you, other than normal guidance on how to do my job, I will come see you after work and demonstrate bad attitude. Am I clear?"

Supes hesitated, unsure how to proceed. He opened his mouth to reestablish his authority.

"Think about your next words, Supes," Brand warned. "If you fire me now or at any other time, I will pay you a visit at your home, or at the bar, or at the restaurant with your family. I have a job to do. Let me do it and avoid any more trouble. Understood?"

"Yes sir."

"Good. I want us to get along."

Brand stepped back, giving the man some space.

"So where do you want me to start?"

Three days later Brand was on the shipping dock repairing a high-capacity shelf strut which had been bent from an impact with one of the many stand up forklifts speeding around the warehouse areas. He shored up the weight above, before he removed the nut and bolt assemblies that held the component in place. He locked the height in on the temporary brace and leaned back, wiping sweat from his brow. He was surprised to see a lean black man standing nearby watching him work. Likely due to his focus on the repair, he had not heard nor noticed the arrival of the newcomer.

The lean man nodded at Brand and motioned with a nod indicating that Brand was to follow him. Brand trailed behind the man, following him to one of the side doors which led to one of the many climate-controlled storage facilities where sensitive product was staged prior to shipment. Brand appreciated the comfortable 72-degree air-conditioned room after working on the hot warehouse floor.

"I see you are settling in nicely to your new job," the man said with a grin.

Brand did not make a rejoinder. He was unsure who the man was. He might be the contact he was promised by the feds. He could be a coworker playing with him.

"You are Carson Brand?" he asked uncertainly.

"Yeah," Brand replied simply. "What do you need?"

"I don't need anything," the lean black man replied testily. "You need to listen carefully and do exactly what I tell you."

"Okay."

"I am your contact with the NSA. You will keep your eyes and ears open. We want you to keep alert for a man named Ha Wang. He is the COO of the company and a Chinese operative. We want you to place this tracking device on his car and place three high frequency audio recording devices in his office.

The contact crossed the distance between them and handed him the small electronic devices. He returned to his original spot.

"The tracker works best under the car just ahead of the rear bumper. The bugs are best under desks, tables, or chairs. Be discreet."

"James Bond shit," Brand muttered, turning the electronics in his hand.

"Don't get caught double-oh-seven. I gotta go. Wait two minutes after I leave before you leave this room."

The lean man left without another word.

Brand pocketed the devices and left the room immediately. He returned to repairing the shelf strut. As he worked, he reviewed the short meeting with the NSA contact. He didn't like the flippant manner of the man. He also didn't trust him. Like Spencer, for whom he harbored a seething dislike, the lean man seemed amused at Brand's role in their covert mission. The new man did not openly display his derision as Spencer did, but his amusement was easily detectable below his hastily relayed instructions.

Brand grabbed a hammer and beat the thick flange plate into shape to accept the new fastening system he was installing.

The spy stories he had watched on TV and at the movies seemed much sexier than casual meetings in storage rooms and arduous repair work in a hot warehouse. The idea of planting a bug seemed absurd in the harsh light of reality. Were international bad guys hiding in every corner? Uvalde

Texas seemed, in his estimation, the least likely place to be selected as a hub of espionage for any evil doer.

Brand ratcheted the new connectors in place then boxed his tools. He lowered the temporary support bracket carefully. The strut held securely. Brand shouldered the bracket and gathered the toolbox. He returned to his work area.

Inside the physical plant locker room, he saw Supes watching him through the window glass of his office. He was on the phone trying to cover a dark look for Brand. The man had made no further nuisance of himself, but Brand knew the strength of his threat was temporary. His days there would be few. Supes was a bitter man with little self-esteem. Anger for the man who had bettered him would soon overpower any remaining fear. The salve of time would dilute the man's memory and diminish his fear.

Brand had no interest in making good on his threat if the man turned on him. The effort wasn't worth it. Besides, he was not emotionally invested. His actions had been spontaneous, spurred by his tumultuous emotions and the immediate need to get the man off his back.

Brand actuated his phone screen and googled Ha Wang of Tel Gong Corporation. His man's information was in the first search result. He studied his photo and on-line bio with interest. The man was a Chinese national who seemed to be well connected in the Chinese government based upon the multiple photos taken with Chinese heads of state and national celebrities.

"Uvalde," Brand muttered under his breath. "The Chinese spy capital of Texas."

Brand darkened his phone and went to lunch.

35

MICHAEL CERVANTES WAS RELEASED from jail and delivered to I.C.E. Those men on his team who had no warrants for previous offenses had already made bail and were in the wind. Unlike him, they were US citizens and were subject to standard judicial treatment. He was a Mexican citizen and was subject to federal international laws pertaining to illegal aliens.

As with the others in his group, he had endured days of incarceration and many hours of interrogation from federal agents. They were keenly interested in two things. They wanted to know about his boss, Fabian Aleman Castillo, as he knew they would. Interestingly, they had many questions about his relationship with the American, Carson Brand.

One of the DEA agents – an Agent Spencer – seemed quite driven in his pursuit of Cervantes' knowledge about the man.

Cervantes reviewed the questions as he sat among other illegals on the crowded seats of an I.C.E. transport bus. Amongst the rough clothes and disheveled appearances of the others on the transport, he was conspicuous in his dark slacks, tight black tee shirt and *Durashock* boots.

He also was the only passenger intent on returning to Mexico. The others, mostly laborers, would be processed and released with court dates they would never make. All would find homes in America.

Cervantes knew there was no hiding from the cartel. American officials, as a matter of course, misplaced their detainees. The organization never lost a man – at least not a live one.

Spencer's questions led Cervantes to believe that their American prisoner had been working alone, or at least without the approval of the DEA. Although confusing, Cervantes gathered that Carson Brand's affiliation with the federal government was tenuous – possibly unofficial. Cervantes heard of criminal informants, but the American was not a part of the cartel, traitor or not. Conversely, as an unknown adversary, he was an enemy of the cartel, marked for death.

Cervantes gave no information, per se, but his answers in that regard seemed to please the DEA agent. Did Agent Spencer want the American dead? Cervantes was able to learn through their conversation that Brand was holed up in Uvalde, Texas, not far from the Mexico border. The information had been carelessly dropped in a way that led Cervantes to believe the DEA agent wanted him to know the man's whereabouts. Again, Cervantes was puzzled.

Why?

Cervantes ruminated on this question as he watched the semi-arid expanses of the Rio Grande valley pass below the humming wheels of the transport bus.

A shaggy haired child stared at him, fascinated with this lean, thin man in the black clothes and military style boots. He inspected Cervantes up and down unabashed.

Cervantes grinned at the boy. He laughed grimly. That small boy could easily end up a sicario in the service of the cartel. The youth smiled in return.

Cervantes' grin faded as his fears progressed.

Because of his cartel affiliation, he knew he would be returned to Mexico and transferred to the authorities there. Cervantes was committed to reporting the failure of his mission and this new information to the boss, despite the danger. He hoped Castillo would allow him to return and finish the job he started rather than have the Mexican police kill him. He wanted the chance to share the intelligence he had learned, then return to the U.S. to finish off the American.

The bus arrived at the processing station in McAllen, Texas where the bus was emptied, and the passengers began the slow expatriate processing procedure. Cervantes was experienced with the immigration system in the US. He would suffer some delay because he had been deported no less than a half dozen times, but he would be delivered to Mexican authorities with little delay. Deportations were so rare with the new open border policies, that the C.B.P. personnel were happy to return one every now and then.

Six hours later Michael Cervantes was handed off to the Mexican border officials who treated him much worse than the American officials. He was confined to a dingy cell with no food or water overnight. He was transported to a high-walled prison for another two days until he was released to men in uniforms. They were not police or Federales. They were disguised cartel muscle.

He was cuffed and stuffed in the back seat of a hot dirty white sedan. A few hours later he stood before Castillo himself.

"You failed me again," Castillo announced with displeasure plain upon him.

He was not concerned with minutiae or giving his true intentions away. Cervantes would be a severed head on his office floor before the day was through. The guards were trusted servants and gave no attention to anything other than the bloody tasks required to be one of Castillo's personal guards.

"I have failed you, Don Castillo. I deserve to die by your hand. I made a pact, and I did not meet my portion of the bargain. Do with me as you will."

Cervantes' admission to his failure and submission to be punished by death surprised Castillo. He expected whining, excuses, and begging.

Castillo narrowed his eyes as he worked out this puzzle. His prescience was taxed with the conundrum before him. He detected no subterfuge in the man. He seemed genuinely contrite in his failure and deserving of the punishment for that failure.

"Kill him," Castillo commanded the nearest guard.

The guard immediately lifted a machete above his head for the killing blow.

Cervantes showed the expected amount of fear but did not break down and beg.

With a gesture Castillo stopped the guard as he began his downward stroke. Castillo moved forward, pushing the guard out of his way.

"What is this, Cervantes? Are you playing with me?"

"Hefe, I don't know what you mean. You are a man of your word and so am I. I know what is in store for me. I made peace with it when I was handed over to the federales."

"Get on your feet," Castillo ordered.

Cervantes looked into Castillo's face then stood as bidden.

"You have passed a test – a test that would have cost your life if you had failed. Tell me the details of your failure with Carson Brand."

Cervantes gave the cartel boss a full accounting of his actions after he left Mexico. Castillo asked few questions, and those few were only to confirm details. When Cervantes finished the boss moved behind his desk, sitting heavily in his heavy leather chair.

"This man works for the DEA. He is under their protection as we speak. We will have to wait for the right opportunity to exact our revenge."

"Senor, I know where he is today. I know how to get close to him and complete what you have started without dealing with the American federal government."

Castillo leaned forward, his fingertips pressed together before him like a Hollywood villain.

"Why didn't you say this before?"

Cervantes took a deep breath.

He would live today.

36

WANG LEANED BACK IN HIS LEATHER CHAIR, a shocked look on his face. Since he had returned from China, the results of his global plan were becoming apparent with alarming speed. Even global financial markets were reacting to the ripples of change implemented in the US. The speed of the international reaction to his behind-the-scenes manipulations caused him a giddy lightness behind the eyes, like one feels while descending a steep run on an out-of-control roller coaster. He characterized these early signs as the prow of a tidal wave gaining momentum – beyond anyone's control to stem or direct.

He was struggling with his reaction to these unseen forces when he learned that the American – the very American he had sought since the leak at Tel Gong - was presently working at the very facility where the data had been leaked.

He slammed his desk phone onto the plastic cradle, ending the call with the HR manager at the Uvalde plant, despite the manager being mid-sentence. How could this man, so quickly after his attack on the hit team, have passed through HR requirements then hired into the company? Wang had not placed him on any watch list, nor had he been able to learn the man's identity It was obvious he was working for someone in authority. Which authority?

Was this an attack upon him? Was this man an agent of a law enforcement agency outside of his control?

Wang scoffed at the idea. He had set the wheels in motion to ensure he would have no outside police involvement.

Suddenly it occurred to him. This man must have been delivered to him as a result of lighting his American resources. It was obvious to Wang that the man had been working for a law enforcement agency and was being delivered to him for disposal.

Wang breathed a sigh of relief, confident in his analysis. After a quick confirmation with his sources, he would handle this man swiftly and deftly.

He picked up the phone and dialed the Uvalde plant. He instructed HR to forward to him all employment documents for the new man.

Three minutes later Wang opened the attachments in the messaging app on his laptop. The man's name was Carson Brand. He was a former construction contractor for state government projects. He was hired by Tel Gong days before. Wang reviewed the new man's resume and credit statement. Both had been obviously tooled.

Ha closed the laptop and picked up his phone. He called his contact at the Department of Justice.

"Give me what you have on Carson Brand," he said without preamble.

"Carson Brand is handled, sir," the contact said. "You aren't in Uvalde now, are you?"

"I'm in Seattle."

"Stay away from the Uvalde facility for a few days. We've got this handled."

"You already said that."

Wang hung up.

He grinned without mirth as he witnessed once more how his controls at the highest levels of power would eliminate the new man without his direct involvement. His fears that American officials may not fall in line because of some senseless loyalty to an unsustainable governmental model was baseless.

He felt a confidence he had not dared allow himself previously. Those hidden forces in place in the US government were already doing his work unbidden.

37

BRAND RETURNED TO HIS RENTED mobile home just east of Uvalde. He had learned where Wang officed and when he was scheduled to return. He had gotten himself on the white box crew, taking part in the renovation of the new office spaces being prepared for the onboarding executives, arriving to the plant by month's end.

Supes had appeared heartily pleased to move Brand to the remodeling crew and off the maintenance department roles. Brand figured the move cut at least a week off his tenure with the plant. Without daily reminders of what awaited supes if he screwed up, he would grow emboldened, then act on his false confidence.

The renovation crews worked at night, after office hours. Construction was always noisy and obtrusive, disruptive to day-to-day office operations.

Brand was pleased that he would be able to complete his mission outside of working hours. The sooner he planted the devices, the sooner he could get back to San Antonio. Karen waited for him there. She was a new part of his move back to his old life, but she was an important part. He hoped he could build on it.

His thoughts went to Dehra. He wondered where she had been placed in witness protection. He hoped she would find some happiness. It rankled him that her last impression of him was someone who had betrayed her – set her up for death at the hands of the cartel, then arrested by the feds.

Maybe he would see her again. He knew little about how the witness protection program worked other than what he had seen on TV, but maybe it wasn't so clandestine as to prevent him from seeing her again.

He poured a bowl of cereal and flopped in front of the television. He had to be at work in three hours. He wasn't sleepy but hoped he would not become so later when the hours of wakefulness passed into his normal sleep cycle. With the dangerous task of planting the bugs at hand, he doubted he would grow bored.

Brand arrived at the plant just before 7 PM. He reported to the night shift manager for the remodel crew. After a few cursory questions, the man was pleasantly surprised at Brand's construction knowledge and assigned him to the trim crew on the third floor – the same floor as Wang's office. Brand wasn't one to look a gift horse, and all that, but he was surprised at being delivered exactly where he needed to be his first night on the crew.

He reported to the crew chief who directed him to work the perimeter stairwell where he would install the rich paneling at the upper walls and stair landings.

Brand arrived at the stairwell where a stack of building materials and power tools were stored nearby. He was alone.

After a careful search of the area to confirm he would not be joined by other workers, he quickly made his way past the dust curtain and onto the occupied wing of the offices. He searched the door placards for the CEO's name.

He figured he would be able to plant the listening devices quickly. He didn't know how much time he had before someone checked on him, so he located the restrooms in case he had to use them as a hurried excuse for his absence.

Wang's office was easy to locate. It was conspicuous at the end of the hall corridor. Tall double wood and etched glass doors reached just short of the 12-foot-tall ceilings. He noticed that all the doors along the corridor were secured with only door handle locks. There were no deadbolt keylocks above the handles, not even on Wang's doors.

Brand returned to the tool area where he secured two flat blade screwdrivers. He knew that most door handle and knob locks were spring secured allowing him to jimmy the door from the outside.

He returned to the corridor and made his way warily to the tall double doors at the end of the hallway. As he went, he checked the doors on either side in case he had to hide from a curious coworker or security guard. All were securely locked.

He paused before the double doors to Wang's office. He produced the screwdrivers from his back pocket and squatted before the double handles. On a whim he tried the door handle. To his surprise, the handle turned easily. It was unlocked.

He released the handle slowly, ensuring he made no noise. His instincts were firing like static electricity in a dark room. Why were Wang's office doors unsecured? Every other door along the long corridor was locked except for the office of the COO of the company.

He rose to his full height. He reviewed the events leading to this moment in a suspicious study. Even a cursory accounting cast the past few days in a curious light: Kilgore handing him off to the NSA; the amused half-ass bugging instructions by the lean man; easily landing the transfer to the renovation team; assigned to the very floor where Wang's office was; the COO's office – the only door unlocked on the floor.

Brand unconsciously shifted the screwdrivers in each hand to an aggressive hold.

This was too easy. His life experiences had taught him one thing above all. Nothing was easy. There was always a snag or a hurdle to overcome. By his estimation, this spy shit should be even more difficulty ridden.

He slowly backed away from the doors, senses alert. His nerves were strung on steel wires as he strained to detect anything which might indicate a trap being sprung. He heard nothing other than the usual noises of the air-conditioning system and the distant sound of the night air moving normally amongst the trees.

As he turned to flee, all of that changed.

The double doors whooshed on well-oiled hinges as carpet-muffled footfalls gathered and rushed towards the doorway.

Brand risked a glance behind him as he picked up speed. At least a half dozen dark pursuers in black ski masks sped down the corridor towards him. He saw no firearms in their hands. Brand hit the stairwell at full speed, leaping down the dozen or so stairs to the landing half a floor below the third-floor landing.

The dark pursuers flooded the landing as he made his turn to jump down the remaining flight to the second level. The men behind him leaped as he had, landing in softer staccato blows on the half floor landing.

Brand made the ground floor in two more leaps. He slammed against the doorway into the first-floor corridor. The door didn't budge.

He looked through the narrow windows in the doors. The hallway was dark and empty. He looked down. The door handles were chained and locked.

The pursuit hit the landing and they were on him.

Brand buried the left-hand screwdriver into the nearest man's chest. It sunk to the red plastic handle forcing a groaned exhalation from the victim. Brand took the brunt of two of the assailants with a spin, collapsing his weight to his right side.

The men slid over him, grasping for a renewed purchase.

Brand caught one of the men in the cheek with the right-hand screwdriver. He felt teeth break against the steel rod.

A solid kick knocked him flat against the locked doors. He grabbed the nearest man in an arm lock and spun his weight, using the man as a pivot. He spun his torso in a counterclockwise direction, allowing his mass to snap the man's neck at the jaw.

Now it was three to one. He had no time to consider the odds, he knew instinctively that he could not defeat three well-trained assailants.

He saw the flash of a thin evil looking blade.

"Shit," He muttered as the blade plunged into the meat of his right thigh.

He broke the man's nose beneath the hood with a hard right at close range. A second man grabbed him from behind in a choke hold, interlocking his hands securely.

Brand grabbed the knife buried in his leg and pulled mightily. It resisted an instant, causing him great agony, before it pulled free. Brand kicked at the man before him as he shifted the knife in his grip. He brought his right hand sharply up and behind him, narrowly missing his own ear with the blade. He felt the crunch of the point enter the man's head.

The attacker's grip weakened and fell from Brand's neck. Brand retained his grip on the knife handle as they separated, drawing the blade from his victim's skull.

The latter shook his head, trying to clear his senses. Brand plunged the knife into his heart.

Brand dropped to the floor, anticipating an attack from the man behind him.

Too late, a sharp knife blade sliced along the top of his right shoulder blade. The pain was like a searing hot flame drawn across his skin.

Rage boiled up in him in a scorching flood. He was on the man, crushing his face with blow after blow. Brand tore the mask from the beaten man. He drew back in shock.

The stricken face he saw belonged to Agent Spencer of the DEA. Brand struck him hard in the face two more times. He tore the masks from the closest two men. He didn't recognize them. He had expected the team to be Chinese due to the company's connection to Asia. Spencer and these two were Anglo.

He moved to the door where one of the men stirred with a groan. Blood leaked onto the floor tiles below his mask. Brand remembered him as the man who had suffered a broken nose. He unmasked him. He recognized the lean black man who had met with him and given him instructions to bug Wang's office. Brand punished him with two hard blows to the face.

He dragged him across the landing and dropped him roughly beside Spencer. The latter was regaining his senses and made a move to renew his aggression towards Brand. Brand kicked him in the balls.

"Stay down, asshole," he growled in a low menacing tone.

The lean man watched him, fear obvious in his expression.

Brand guessed that the agent was not familiar with him. Spencer had probably discounted him in the briefing prior to the attack.

"Who sent you to kill me?" Brand demanded of the lean man.

The agent looked around at the others lying motionless around him.

"They can't help you," Brand assured him. "Talk or join them."

The NSA man considered his situation gravely. He watched Brand for some inkling as to his plans for him. Finally, he shook his head in surrender.

"I was only following orders."

"These are your last words then," Brand said with a clear finality the man understood.

Brand retrieved a nearby knife.

"Wait," the agent begged. "The people who want you gone are…"

"Shut your fucking mouth, Childs," Spencer spat through his pain. "You'll kill us all."

"If I see you again," Brand warned Childs. "I will kill you."

"I believe you," Childs agreed earnestly. "You won't ever see me again."

Brand moved a short distance away where he pulled up the bulging black sweater of one of the dead men. He found a concealed pistol. Brand collected the pistol and checked the breach and magazine for rounds. It was loaded – the clip full of bullets. He pocketed the pistol, returning to the living agents.

"Who are the people who want me dead?"

Childs shook his head like a man who had abandoned any hope of living beyond this moment, even if he lived through this interview.

"The rumor is that…"

"Shut up!" Spencer yelled at the man.

Brand kicked Spencer in the balls once more. The agent doubled over with a groan.

"Continue," Brand commanded.

"The rumor is that the Chinese government has people among the higher ups in the DOJ, NSA, FBI, and the DEA. They have been ordered to eliminate you. You must have pissed off someone in the Chinese Communist Party and they have activated their domestic resources to stop you. I would guess that you have started some kind of international incident, and both countries are trying to put a lid on it."

"How high does this thing go?"

"That is the wrong question," Childs replied. "It is apparent to me that it goes all the way up to Washington. Your problem is how low does it go. You have no place to turn, Mr. Brand. When lower tiered agents and office level supervisory staff are sent after you, that means you are one man against all the law enforcement agencies. You are fucked."

"It sounds like you are too," Brand observed wisely.

Childs swallowed a bit of blood running from his nasal cavity into his throat.

Brand watched Childs for a moment, deciding whether he should kill the man or not. Finally, Brand grabbed Spencer by the collar of his dark shirt, dragging him to the emergency exit doors at the other side of the stairwell.

Outside, he hauled him uncaringly across the rough pavement of the parking lot to his car. He opened the trunk and shoved the weakly struggling agent into the compartment. In the haze of his pain Spencer moved his hand towards his waistband. Brand punched him in the face and lifted his shirt. He quickly located the agent's service weapon, a Glock nine-millimeter. He stuffed the gun in his pants then slammed the trunk closed. He moved to the driver door. His injured leg and shoulder hampered him with a growing stiffness and acute pain. He felt the sticky warmth and smelled the rusty bitterness of his own blood as it dripped below his work shirt.

He fell into the driver seat. He applied pressure to the puncture on his thigh, fearing it the more serious of his wounds.

He managed to get the car in gear and moving towards the highway. His mind whirled at the portent of what he had learned that evening. Spencer! Why was he trying to kill him? Child's confession revealed that Brand was targeted by the feds.

He recalled Spencer's cowardly attack from behind. If he hadn't dropped to the floor, Spencer's blade would have plunged into the center of his back – a killing blow.

Spencer hated him, but he was a federal agent, sworn to uphold the law. Their many confrontations had always ended with the threat of arrest and prison, not death. Spencer was by the book. As far as Brand could tell, he wasn't an assassin or a mercenary. So why had he been on a hit team? Why did he try to kill him? How does a federal agent revert from officer of the law to killer with a single order from higher up? Why wasn't he trying to arrest Brand rather than trying to kill him?

"Shit!" Brand yelled, filling the confines of the car with his wail.

By the time he arrived at his mobile home, the effects of his wounds were plain. He was weak, red spots floating before his eyes.

He pushed the car door open and staggered to the trailer house. He pushed the door open, slamming it behind him. He went to the pantry where he retrieved a cheap drug store first aid kit he had purchased after he had nicked himself with a utility knife at work a couple of days before.

He moved to the kitchen sink and drank deeply from the tap. He pulled the two pistols from his waistband and dropped his pants. He laid the guns on the kitchen countertop. He removed his bloody shirt. His shoulder was covered in dried blood. The slice had been no more than a scratch. Looking down, he saw that the leg wound oozed blood at an alarming rate. Brand tore open two alcohol wipes and attempted to clean around the wound. Fresh blood immediately covered the cleaned area.

Brand opened a round package of brown first aid wrap. He placed a white gauze pad over the puncture then bound the wound tightly, although not so snugly as to cut off circulation. He pursed his lips in pain, satisfied that he had slowed the bleeding. He hoped he would lose no more blood.

He drank once more from the tap.

Without bothering to pull on his clothes, Brand donned his work boots and returned to the car.

Inside the trunk Spencer was conscious. He made a weak attempt at attacking Brand. Even in his weakened condition, Brand managed to beat the agent with a flurry of hard blows to his face and neck. Once more subdued, Brand dragged the agent roughly from the trunk, allowing him to drop unaided to the hard compacted earth of the dirt driveway.

He pulled him uncaringly up the few stairs and into the mobile home. Brand yanked the power cord free from a nearby lamp and bound the agent's arms tightly behind him. He shoved Spencer against the wall, falling heavily into the old armchair across from him.

Spencer spit blood through red teeth, and his cut and splattered lips.

"You've done it now, criminal," the agent growled. "You just attacked and kidnapped a federal agent."

Brand eyed Spencer dangerously, unable to muster the energy to beat him further.

"Is Kilgore in on this?' Brand managed to ask.

"In on what?" Spencer spat angrily.

Brand stood with effort. He crossed the space between them and kicked Spencer hard in the ribs. His steel toed boots struck the agent hard, placing his ability to breathe on the endangered list of his bodily functions.

Brand returned to his seat.

"You fuck with me again and I will end your suffering."

Spencer finally regained his breath. He panted for a long moment.

"What do you think?" he whined through his fear and pain. "You went too far this time. What did you think was going to happen? You can't just run around hurting and killing people. You're a rabid dog that needs to be put down."

"Since when does the federal government send hit squads after criminals?"

Spencer laughed grimly at the failure of his "hit" squad.

"You're in way over your head, criminal. It won't end until you are dead and buried somewhere where you will never be found. You heard what the NSA agent said."

"Is that why you put Dehra into witness protection?"

Spencer looked at Brand with genuine confusion.

"What are you talking about?" he spat with derision. "We didn't put her into witness protection. Your trailer trash bitch was killed in lockup by some pink haired dyke."

Brand was struck mute.

Spencer's expression changed from confused to amused. He was enjoying Brand's pain.

"You are about a dumb shit, Brand. Did Kilgore tell you that shit about witness protection? That's rich."

Brand rose stiffly from his chair.

Spencer grinned through his bloody teeth as Brand approached.

Brand dropped to his knees. Spencer's grin faded like the setting sun.

Brand pushed the agent to the floor, wrapping his hands around the man's throat. Spencer's face registered genuine terror. He tried to speak but air no longer passed through his neck. His eyes bulged and his ears roared as air and blood ceased to flow.

Brand felt a fiery rage fill him. He wanted to feel the life flee from the agent. His vision dimmed as his rage took him. The terror in the agent's eyes fed his need for vengeance. He bathed in his rage like a fiend in blood.

Reason found a small place in his fury. Tears welled in Brand's eyes as his grief found purchase. With a groan, he released the man's throat.

Spencer's breath rattled wetly as he sucked loud labored pulls of precious air. His vision cleared as the red veil dropped from his eyes, leaving only sweat and tears behind.

Brand limped to the kitchen sink. He drew a glass from the drying rack and filled it with tap water. Silently, he drank the contents dry. He glanced across the room where Spencer sobbed as he fought to regain his wind.

Brand replaced the glass on the rack, picked up Spencer's Glock, and returned to the prostrate agent. Brand helped him to a seated posture. Spencer eyed the pistol warily. The whites of his eyes shone, his brush with death widening them.

Brand returned to his chair across from the agent. He sat gingerly, holding the pistol in his lap.

"I suggest you watch your mouth, Agent Spencer."

Brand's words were weak and gravelly with the strain of his fading fury.

The agent swallowed with difficulty. He made no rejoinder.

For the first time since meeting him, he felt terror at what he had seen in Brand's eyes. Brand was without remorse. Spencer saw that now. He had believed him only a sullen ne'er-do-well, benefiting from a long string of lucky circumstances. He saw now that there was an inner rage that powered him. He knew innately that he should be dead there on the floor. He didn't know why he had been spared. To the point, he was not certain he would live through the encounter still.

"I'm sorry," Spencer croaked.

Brand considered the agent with a mildly curious expression. He recognized a marked change in the man. He was beaten. Brand saw defeat – and something else.

Fear.

"Tell me what you know, Spencer. I don't want to hurt you anymore, but I will if you don't talk to me."

Moving his neck to relieve the tightness and pain he felt in his throat, Spencer grunted to clear his throat.

"I'm not your enemy," he began in a raspy voice.

Brand leaned forward in his chair, his demeanor embodied his intolerance for any further deflection or misleading talk. Still fresh in his memory was Spencer leading a team of killers against him, ending with Spencer trying to bury a knife in his back. He was not an enemy He was THE enemy.

"I'm going to be completely honest with you," Spencer assured him hurriedly. "Kilgore sent me to join the wet crew. It's true I didn't object to the opportunity to get you out of my hair, but I didn't volunteer for the job. Kilgore acted on orders from higher up in the fed. You have obviously pissed off someone in the upper echelons of federal government bureaucracy."

Brand leaned back in his seat, a grimace of pain painting his face as he considered the agent's words.

"What about this claim that the Chinese are involved?"

"I haven't heard that slant to it until Childs told you that. I only know that you have been classified an enemy of the state – terminate on sight."

Brand knew innately what he heard was truth. It was the why that confused him. There had always been a cloud of mystery around why Kilgore had pursued him to work covertly with the DEA in a capacity the head agent ostensibly called a contractor. More puzzling was that later Kilgore covered for him when Brand fell into a conflict with the Mexican Cartel. Most recently, when Dehra was taken into custody, Kilgore had left him behind, choosing not to cover all his bases.

Brand concluded that this new development must have been a recent change – possibly days or hours old. The uncertainty of the source of this danger concerned Brand to the point he felt a burning desire to systematically begin an elimination of those who might be allied with the unseen forces committed to destroy him.

He lifted the pistol, unsure how to proceed.

"Brand," Spencer pleaded, suspecting the worst was about to occur. "You have very few options. Killing a federal agent is not one of them – at least if you want to have any chance to live through this thing."

"Oh yeah?" Brand returned with interest. "What are they then?"

"I don't know, but I do know that murdering a federal cop will make things worse."

Brand studied the floor as his mind worked. Finally, he focused on Spencer.

"Where does Kilgore live?" he asked with a new energy generated from deciding on a plan of action.

"You don't want to do that," Spencer warned.

"Answer me without any more warnings or advice and I won't kill you, Agent Spencer."

38

BRAND PARKED IN FRONT OF A MOTEL in San Antonio. He spared no further concern for Spencer, bound, and gagged on the living room floor of the mobile home outside of Uvalde. The next hit team would find him. What they did with the agent was of no concern to him. The man deserved whatever ends he received.

He had to get to Kilgore before Spencer was found.

Brand felt exhaustion dulling his senses, beckoning him towards comforting darkness. He teetered dangerously on a precipice. He was seduced by the safety of the dark rented room where he could hide and heal. He only wanted to sleep; to let everything pass by. Adrenalin roused him as he reminded himself that these moments might well be his last. His decisions and subsequent actions would determine whether he lived or died. If he lived, he might be able to contribute to how much longer that would last.

He put the car in gear and headed for a neighborhood on the near north central side of the city. He would confront Kilgore.

As he had so often in the past few hours, he experienced a heart-wrenching pain. Dehra had been killed in jail. He wasn't certain if Spencer's reference to a "pink haired dyke" was accurate or if he was engaged in some sort of cruel hyperbole. What was certain was that Dehra Duncan was not in witness protection. She was dead. Kilgore was responsible for her death, as far as Brand was concerned. That would weigh heavily against Kilgore in the coming confrontation. Spencer's claim that he and the team had been sent to kill him by Kilgore was astounding in how it clarified his relationship with the agent.

It hadn't been more than two days since he saw the DEA man at his office. It seemed ridiculous that they talked payroll and about the Tel Gong mission like everything was good between them. It occurred to Brand that Kilgore was putting his plan in motion, knowing its goal was to eliminate Brand.

How brazen Kilgore was, Brand thought with a disbelieving shake of his head.

Brand believed up until this moment that he could see through lies and subterfuge, especially amongst those he knew personally. He now doubted everything he believed before. What he still believed – what he chose to cling to – was his ability to deal with those who opposed him. Kilgore was on that list now.

Brand cranked the engine and drove the gray sedan out of the motel parking lot. Rest would have to wait. He reminded himself that these might be his last hours on earth. He would not go alone.

Paramount to Brand was an accounting for Dehra. She deserved none of what happened to her. He knew instinctively that she blamed him for all of this. He knew that he had nothing to do with the wet teams that pursued her and Leon, but he felt that it was his responsibility to her memory and what she meant to him to make those responsible pay.

He keyed Kilgore's address into his GPS. With luck, Kilgore would not learn of Spencer's capture and subsequent betrayal.

39

KILGORE LOCKED THE DESK drawer and gathered his attaché case. The initial report from Tel Gong was bad. Local law enforcement was processing the crime scene at the plant after an early arriving employee reported dead bodies in a stairwell.

Further reports had confirmed that Spencer was not among the casualties. Notably, neither was Carson Brand. The DEA agent locked his office door, nodding to a lone analyst, working late at his desk.

The man ignored him, his fingers striking a rough staccato on his keyboard with much more strength than necessary to type on the networked machine. Late night work was not for everyone, Kilgore observed.

Kilgore forgot the man as his conflicted feelings pressed to the forefront of his attention. Carson Brand was the first for which he had ever received an NSA level 6 suppress order. Known as an S-6, the measure was no more commonly used than the Logan Act. Both were official policy edicts, but neither was ever used. Authorization for the S-6 came from above the agency director level. The director was not even allowed to amend or retract an S-6 edict.

Kilgore scanned his badge at the security kiosk in the lobby. He left the building, locating his sedan where it waited in the front row of the parking lot. He looked around him suspiciously. He felt exposed and vulnerable. He was unaccustomed to feeling the need to watch over his shoulder.

As it had since he last saw Brand, a nagging twinge of guilt rose in him. Brand was not a friend, but Kilgore liked him. The young guy was kind of a superhero around the office. Despite Spencer despising him, Kilgore believed that even that sworn foe recognized the singularly heroic nature of the man. Probably, it was this very nature that elicited Spencer's hatred. One could not help but feel threatened by the hapless courage of the man. Being similar in age, maybe Spencer saw his own weaknesses in bold relief when near Brand.

Kilgore never signed up to become a murderer. He served his country in the tritest terms: right hand on heart, tearful eye towards the flag, heart swelling with national pride. None of that made him feel any less guilty for what he had done. He was no better than the cartel thugs he investigated.

He could not assign the mantle of cartel to the American government, but he couldn't deny the similarities in how it was dealing with an American citizen. He had his suspicions, but it seemed the most ludicrous conspiracy theory to believe in a secret plot amongst officials so high in the ranks of the Justice Department. What would motivate it? Who was behind it? It occurred to Kilgore that he wasn't privy to important details. Brand must pose a threat in a way he was not aware.

Putting a hit out on Carson Brand was his greatest shame. Although the director had briefed Kilgore, then followed that meeting with friendly council, Kilgore knew what they did was wrong. They were charged with bringing evildoers to justice, not killing those who served the cause.

He understood that his superiors believed the good of the country was at risk here. Obviously, there was more to this than even the director knew. What other reason could there be to issue the S-6?

Kilgore unlocked the car door, tossing his briefcase in the back seat.

Where were Spencer and Brand? Why had the team failed? Unless Spencer had gone completely rogue and captured Brand for his selfish ends, he would have contacted Kilgore with a report. What if Brand, unbelievably, had gotten the drop on Spencer and captured him?

Kilgore backed the car out of the parking space. He drove to the street entrance. He waited there for a long moment, his mind filled with foreboding. He knew Brand well enough to know his next stop would be to see Kilgore himself.

Kilgore's hand dropped to his service weapon, the hard grip providing some comfort against his growing doubts.

Since that day, some six months before, when Carson Brand first appeared on the DEA radar, Kilgore had followed his remarkable exploits with a secret admiration. It had been his idea to recruit him as a clandestine contractor. Since then, Brand had been a great source of tall tales, and unbelievable survivability in the direst circumstances thrown at him by the cartel and other shady characters.

His admiration had always been one of wonder and support for the man. Now that he faced the unpleasant possibility that he would have to face Brand as an adversary, he was frightened. He hated to admit it, but he feared the younger man. What he knew of him assured Kilgore that Brand would bring the full weight of his rage against him. He considered calling in back-up, but the directive from above on the S-6 edict was clear that no one outside of the directive channel be knowledgeable nor involved with events to or peripheral to the edict. He was alone unless he could reach Spencer. His instincts told him Spencer was beyond helping him.

A spurt of adrenalin fired his insides as he realized that he was a target in one of the man's crusades rather than an interested observer. He took some succor from confidence in his training and experience as a federal agent. He hoped he would have the chance to reason with Brand. If not, the chips would fall where they may.

Kilgore stepped on the gas, entering the roadway as the ebb and flow of the traffic allowed. His concern focused on what Spencer knew about him and what Brand might be able to extract of that knowledge. If Spencer was placed under enough duress, Brand would learn that Kilgore was behind the team sent for him. Spencer knew a lot about Kilgore, and it was likely that Brand would learn this info.

Spencer had never been to Kilgore's house. Did he know the address by some other means? Kilgore had to risk it. It made more sense that Brand would wait for him outside DEA headquarters and follow him to a place where he held the advantage. Involuntarily, Kilgore searched his mirrors, for a conspicuous vehicle that might exhibit signs it was driven by someone following him.

Calling upon his reason, Kilgore reviewed the timeline he could assemble from the police reports and what he knew about Brand.

It had been nearly 24 hours since Brand and Spencer disappeared. Kilgore accepted that one or both were probably back in San Antonio. He knew the make and model of Brand's car. Unfortunately, that information scarcely helped. Almost every car on the road looked the same. Most were smaller sedans and silver or gray in color. In the econobox world, cars were difficult to distinguish at a distance.

He again scanned his six carefully. Brand had no training in tailing and should be easy to spot if he followed.

Kilgore saw nothing suspicious.

He turned onto his street. As always, cars were crowded along the curbs on both sides.

Kilgore frowned.

The HOA rules clearly stated that there was to be no curb parking and all cars must be kept in a garage. He had received a nastygram from the HOA for keeping his trash and recycle bins out too long, but they never made a move on the curb parking issue.

I guess you can't win a fight when the entire neighborhood chooses to disregard a bi-law, Kilgore lamented.

His house was on the left. There was no car in the drive and his curb was clear of parked cars.

40

BRAND WAITED OUTSIDE KILGORE'S HOME. He hid inside a tall cedar fenced side yard of an empty house across the street. He could see Kilgore's home clearly between the fence boards. His vantage point was good, but his cover was bad. Twice he had spotted SAPD cruisers pass by. He didn't know if they were sentries for Kilgore, or if they were merely doing their job. He left the car two blocks away parked behind the community center and pool for the sub-division. His car was nondescript, but it had been obtained from a DEA lot. Kilgore could have easily spotted the car.

Brand leaned against the fence. Kilgore was a federal agent with training. It was certain that Spencer was missed by now. He would deal with Kilgore's defenses as they presented themselves.

He knew his plan was not safe nor was it wise. He also knew that he had the element of surprise on his side. Further questions to Spencer about the particulars of Kilgore's home led him to believe that Spencer had never been to the house. It was possible that Kilgore had no idea that Brand would find out his address. That theory was still to be tested.

It was nearly dark when a blue sedan with government plates approached slowly then turned into Kilgore's driveway. Brand moved to the gate, his hand on the latch. He peered through a gap in the fencing. The driver was without question Agent Kilgore.

He would approach from an angle where he would not be visible in Kilgore's mirrors until he was upon him. There were several cars parked on the curb. He could use them for additional cover as he approached.

He waited until Kilgore stopped the car.

Brand pushed through the gate, sprinting across the lawn. He adjusted his angle of approach to place a parked car between him and Kilgore's view. He crossed the street. He was in Kilgore's yard before the agent opened his car door. Brand put his hand behind his back where he gripped the handle of the automatic in his belt line.

Kilgore opened the car door, reacting to Brand's sudden appearance with a startled look and a grunt.

"Don't do anything stupid," Brand warned, shrugging his right shoulder to indicate the gun in his grasp.

Kilgore considered Brand for a moment before he stepped from the car. Brand stiffened as the agent retrieved his attaché from the back seat.

Kilgore closed the back door carefully and faced Brand, raising his hands slightly to demonstrate his submission.

"I'll follow you inside," Brand directed. "Lower your hands, Agent."

Kilgore obeyed, keeping an eye on Brand as he led the way to his front door.

"This is unnecessary…" Kilgore began.

"Save it until we get inside," Brand commanded with little patience in his tone.

Brand followed Kilgore inside the front door, closing the door behind them, and twisting the deadbolt lock.

"Do you want a drink?" Kilgore asked, trying to force an amiable tone. "You hooked me on Bourbon."

"Yeah," Brand admitted. "I could use a drink."

Kilgore moved to a richly finished wooden liquor cabinet and poured two generous drinks in crystal high ball glasses.

"Ice?"

"Not this time."

Kilgore handed one of the glasses to Brand, taking a seat on the leather love seat before a stone fireplace. Although the fading dusk was still providing a pink glow outside, landscape lighting accented the view through large windows overlooking a grotto-like swimming pool surrounded by perfectly manicured landscaping.

Brand took a seat across from Kilgore on the edge of a stiff-backed side chair. He downed the contents of the glass in a single draught.

"Thirsty?" Kilgore asked trying to lighten the mood.

"Why did you lie to me about Dehra?" Brand asked pointedly.

"There are greater forces at work here than just you and me," Kilgore replied. "I presumed I could protect you from what you are facing now."

"You are lying, Kilgore. You tried to have me killed. That is not a good start considering what I have been dealing with lately."

"I…," Kilgore stammered. Something in Brand's expression stopped him before he could manufacture a justification for his lie.

"You're right," he admitted in weary surrender. "I guess I owe you the truth. I regret sending those men after you. I am sure you don't want to hear me say I was only following orders, but it is true. I have no say in the matter.

Kilgore drank from the glass, making a face at the bitter heat of the bourbon.

"I'm sorry for lying to you about Dehra and I am very sorry she died in jail. We believe it was orchestrated by the Chinese."

"Is all of this about the fucking Chinese?" Brand snarled, his anger freshened by the talk of Dehra's murder. "Dehra eavesdrops on a conversation about a Chinese telecom company spying on Americans. Next a hit team is dispatched and nearly kills us all. The NSA sends me into the same telecom company to handle some bullshit spy thing. I conveniently end up where I need to be, and a hit team is waiting for me. At least two of the goons in masks are federal agents."

Kilgore wanted to ask about Spencer, but he hesitated, unsure how to ask.

Brand nodded grimly.

"That asshole is still alive, if another hit team hasn't killed him by mistake, thinking it is me. Either way, he is lucky I didn't finish him after he stabbed me in the back."

Kilgore looked at his feet to cover his relief.

"Figuratively?"

"Want to see the wound, Kilgore?"

Kilgore shook his head in return.

"I understand."

"How do we stop this force that seems to want me dead?" Brand asked with a candor that hurt Kilgore. At some level Brand still trusted him and wanted his help.

Both knew Kilgore had dispatched the hit team himself. The paradox was immense.

The agent grappled with his feelings of guilt and betrayal. An S-6 was inviolate. This was the first one Kilgore had ever been involved in, but he had attended several briefings and familiarization training sessions. The overarching truth was that there was no escape from the edict. No one knew from where the edict was generated. That meant no one knew how to identify who needed to be contacted to countermand it.

"This thing has taken on a life of its own," Kilgore began.

Brand was about to interrupt him when Kilgore continued with an impatience that confirmed the truth of what he shared.

"You are screwed. It would do you no good even to turn yourself in. I don't know who you have pissed off at the top of the food chain, but they want you dead and there is nothing anyone can do to change that."

It was Brand's turn to consider his next words.

"Why did you send Spencer after me?"

Kilgore saw the blunder in his honesty. Brand knew he was a dead man and that gave him no option other than to follow his baser instincts – to exact vengeance from those responsible.

Checkmate.

"I only conveyed the orders given me, Brand. Spencer volunteered. I approved him joining the team. My personal feelings haven't changed. This is not personal, nor is it something I agree with. I simply don't have a say in it."

"You seem pretty cool for a man who is about to die for following orders."

"You're not going to kill me, Brand." Kilgore observed with little confidence. "I can help you."

"You said you were not in control. How can you stop it?"

"I said I had no say in it. That is a lot different than having no control."

Kilgore sipped from the glass once more, considering his next words. Night had fallen and the lone lamp on the side table provided the only light in the room, but Kilgore saw Brand's frustration growing in the dark intensity of his gaze and the square set to his shoulders. He felt none of the confidence of his words. He knew that he was in grave peril.

"I'm going to share with you a theory I have. I believe the kill order on you comes directly from the Chinese government. Tel Gong appeared on federal task forces' radar some five years ago. Threat assessment mechanisms across all thirteen federal intelligence agencies issued warnings about the company and its likely intentions. In less than 48 hours a complete standdown was issued, killing the spin-up of interdiction actions against the company.

"Department heads were debriefed, and it was as if the entire alert was a false alarm. Our intel apparatus does not have false alarms. When intel triggers all monitors in all bureaus, that is not a false alarm. Someone is covering for Tel Gong, someone way up in the government."

A splat and a tinkle of shattered glass caused Brand to jump from his seat. Kilgore's head snapped back, and a thin geyser of blood spewed from his temple as a bullet passed through his skull. Another shot struck the chair where Brand had been. The large dark windows overlooking the backyard cracked as the heavy panes sagged against the holes where bullets had passed through.

Brand peered over the top of the coffee table. Two men in black tactical gear shot out the knobs of the French doors and kicked them inward. A fresh volley from the sniper covered their entry.

Brand pulled the pistol from his waistband, looking for an escape route. Chambering a round, he shot the nearest of the two assailants before he was pinned behind the coffee table by the fire of the second.

The second man leaped for cover behind the kitchen wall.

Brand was pinned down by the sniper outside. He was alive only because of the bad light in the living room. With a self-critical curse Brand shot out the lamp bulb, casting the room in complete darkness. His eyes adjusted quickly to the dark conditions. He made out the dim silhouette of the sniper a few yards from the house in the open in the back yard. Brand sent two rounds through the window. He wasn't certain of the hit, but the sniper fell to the ground in a heap. The gunman in the kitchen rounded the corner, weapon in firing position, as Brand leaped towards the kitchen, over Kilgore's motionless body.

The gunman was forced to expose himself fully as he cleared the wall to create a shot at Brand. Brand shot the man as he fired. He heard the whine of a bullet, like a singing hornet, take a lock of his hair. A nine mil round from his pistol smacked soddenly center mass on the gunman. The gunman attempted to gather himself for another shot. Brand double tapped him. The gunman fell hard to the smooth floor tiles.

Brand returned to Kilgore. He checked the agent for vitals. He was not surprised there were none. He ran through the broken French doors where the sniper lay on the pool surround, groaning in a spreading puddle of blood. Brand finished him with a shot.

He surveyed the darkness around him for any sign of additional assailants before climbing the cedar fence and escaping through the rear neighbor's yard.

The sound of police sirens grew in the distance as he secreted his pistol and walked calmly along the street until he returned to his car. He pulled away from the community center, turning onto a side street as the blue glow of flashing lights preceded approaching police cars.

41

BRAND FLOPPED ON THE DOUBLE BED in the dark motel room. On his way back to the motel he had disposed of the DEA car in a low-income neighborhood of San Antonio's east side. The excitement and the adrenalin he felt during the conflict at Kilgore's had served as a temporary anesthetic, warming him, and making him mindless of his pain and discomfort. The inactivity of the long drive stiffened the leg. He felt the sting of the wound in his back. After leaving the car, the short walk to the nearest bus stop extracted groans and sheets of sweat from him, as the pain from the knife wounds and his growing fatigue crippled him. Three bus changes, and another painful walk, brought him back to his motel.

Exhausted, he dropped onto the stiff bedspread. He didn't bother to turn on a light. His mood was as dark as the cold room. The discomfort of his wounds and to-the-core fatigue were a light-hearted preview of what he knew lay in wait ahead. Dread and irresistible foreboding convinced him that he would not be able to sleep. The stress of a dangerously shrinking world dominated his future and his outlook upon that future.

Dehra was dead. Kilgore was dead. He was one mistake from joining them. His instincts and his training had kept him alive so far. He knew that would not be enough to sustain him. He needed help. He knew of no one who could or would help him. All that remained was to figure a way to reverse the S-6, as Kilgore called it. Someone started this. That same person could stop it. At least, that made sense to him.

One name came to the front of his imaginings, Ha Wang, COO of Tel Gong. Childs might have manufactured the circumstance of Wang's arrival to the Uvalde location to lure him on. What if Wang was actually present at the Uvalde facility – or would be? Brand had to risk it. He had no other option. Despite appearing desperate and risky, it was his only move. He sensed that in strategic planning, making the only move available inherently meant that others probably knew what he would do. He would work it out as he went: another bad plan to add to his list.

Brand awoke with a groan. He had dreamt that a swat team was banging on his motel door. He lay motionless, bathed in sweat, listening, with every fiber of his being strung tight as a bow over violin strings. He heard nothing outside his door.

With an effort he talked himself into a weak version of calm, but he could not convince himself to move from the bed for some moments. Much of the delay stemmed from the throbbing of his wounded leg and back. The previous night's walk followed by hours of stillness had stiffened the leg particularly. To move was an agony.

He finally raised himself from the bed with a groan. He limped with difficulty, going to the window beside the door. He parted the curtain a crack. The same cars were in the same places in the lot outside. He looked at the clock next to his bed. 3:03AM.

Brand stretched and shook the leg as he moved to the long vanity where he splashed water on his face. His habitual stubbornly dogged attitude drove away any residual clouds of doubt from his resolve.

In his teens, when he jumped out of the top of the 30-foot-tall tree on the bank of the Comal River at Hinman Island, into only fourteen feet deep clear water, he had used the same strength of resolve to remove his fearful doubt.

He had fought and defeated many foes in his life. He had prevailed to a large degree because he never doubted that he could win. He never had facts nor physical advantages to support his faith. He had won on faith in himself alone. He did not believe he would succeed today. He only knew that he had to. That had always been enough.

Brand left the motel room for the warm humid San Antonio early morning murk. He walked with a listing gait beyond the quartz vapor lights of the motel parking lot.

In the darkness he lifted his pace, ignoring the pain with difficulty. He would need to be mobile and on the highway before light. As he moved, the leg loosened, but he felt a warm flow of blood leaking past his hurriedly applied bandage. He spotted a small dark stain soaking through his jeans. The pattern was narrow, indicating to him that the bandage was holding well enough. At least he hoped it was.

He hailed a lone cab, stalking the dark morning streets, and soon arrived at the downtown bus station. He purchased a ticket to Del Rio. The route map showed that the bus would make a stop in Uvalde along the way.

Two hours later he stepped onto the corner where the two major highways crossed in the center of Uvalde.

He enjoyed the cooling quiet of the early morning. Traffic was light, mainly trucks and service industry tradesmen, moving purposefully towards their appointed destinations. Brand walked along Highway 90, headed east. His destination was Tel Gong but he had no real plan for entering and gaining access to the company's COO.

A fast-food burger joint drew his attention. He was hungry and he needed time to compose a plan. He crossed the road and entered the A frame building. He ordered a double meat cheeseburger, fries, and a root beer. He waited in one of the front facing window booths with an orange and white numbered table tree on the table.

There were no guarantees that Wang would be at the Tel Gong facility. The answer to the question, or at least a solution to discovering the answer, presented itself as a payphone just outside the side doors of the restaurant. Brand was surprised that payphones still existing.

Brand stepped outside and dialed 411. To his dismay information was still a thing. It cost him 50 cents, but he learned the number for Tel Gong in Uvalde. He pressed the number one on the dial and he was connected to the main switchboard for the telecom company. He asked for Ha Wang and was told the COO was unavailable but if he left a name and number, he would return the call as he was able.

"Is Mr. Wang on the premises?" Brand asked.

"He is here but away from his office currently," was the answer.

"Would you tell him that Carson Brand is calling please?"

"Spell that for me."

Brand hung up.

He returned to his table where his food waited.

He finished his meal in less than fifteen minutes. He had not realized he was so hungry. As he left the restaurant, he asked a cowboy in an old pick-up truck if he would give him a ride to Tel Gong.

The cowboy shrugged and agreed to help.

Brand enjoyed the breeze buffeting him through the open window of the truck. The driver dropped him at the front door of the facility, wishing him good luck.

Brand thanked him as he pulled away.

Brand attached his old employee badge and entered the double glass front doors. A security guard surveyed him critically from head to foot as he approached.

"Can I help you?" the burly guard asked.

"I'm late for work and my badge didn't work on the back door. Can you buzz me in? I don't want to lose my job."

"Let me see your badge." The guard ordered.

Brand raised it to eye level.

"New hire," the guard observed from the date on the badge.

"Yeah," Brand admitted. "I know. It's a bad start. Can you help me out please?"

"Alright," the guard agreed. "This is a one-time thing, brother. Uvalde strong."

"You got that right."

Brand passed through the security doors and into the corporate offices and meeting rooms of the administrative wing. He knew precisely how to find Wang's office, so he would suffer no wasted time searching for the man. Brand took the elevator to the third floor and made his way to Wang's office. He frowned at his memory of the last time he was there. This time, the hallway was empty. He would soon see if he received a similar welcome when he arrived at Wang's office.

The tall double doors were directly before him. He paused just outside Wang's office, his hand on the large door handle. He pushed the door open. The heavy door swung outward silently on well-oiled sturdy hinges.

Brand stepped into the office as the big door closed behind him. Wang's large desk was vacant. Behind the desk, wall to wall windows looked out upon the warming Southwest Texas morning. Brand's scan took in the office on each side of the desk. On the right was a ceiling height complex of bookcases, wet bar, and curio shelves, built in an unmistakably east Asian motif. Left of the desk was a small conference table surrounded by cushioned seating. Beyond the table was a door to an adjacent room. Brand moved to explore what was behind the door when he heard a toilet flush. He hurried forward, taking concealment against the wall beside the door.

Wang emerged from the opened door, headed to his desk. He saw Brand move from the corner of his eye. With impressive deftness and quick reactions, he turned towards Brand, intercepting his move to grab him from behind. Brand felt Wang move below his reaching arms, striking with an arcing kick. Brand turned slightly to absorb the blow with his hip. The power of the blow threw Brand off balance for a moment. Wang moved in with unexpected aggression, pressing his attack. He struck Brand twice in the face with alternating blows from each fist.

Brand was surprised at the COO's ability. He had underestimated the slight executive. Judging from the power of the three blows delivered, he would be in trouble if he didn't gain the advantage. He felt like he had a good idea of Wang's strength. He doubted the man could topple him with a single blow, making his response decision easier. He had received vast training in hand-to-hand combat, but this time he drew from his deeper street fighting experience.

Wang set himself in a defensive stance in preparation for his attacker's next move. His eyes widened in surprise as the man moved directly towards him with little effort towards defending against an attack from Wang. The COO lowered his body a fraction as he rolled into a stiff legged round house kick.

With unbelievably quick reactions, Brand stepped into the kick, taking the blow to his lowered left arm. He folded his left arm, capturing the leg, then struck with two quick but hard punches with his right into Wang's groin. The COO folded up like a lawn chair in a strong wind.

Wang lay on the carpet groaning for several minutes.

Brand waited patiently, squatting nearby as he watched the man slowly regain his composure.

Wang raised himself onto his elbows, looking searchingly at Brand.

"So, you are the one who tried to break into my office."

Brand nodded. He was not, as Wang perceived, agreeing with the accusation. He was confirming that he would punish the man for Dehra's and Leon's deaths.

"Let me help you up," Brand offered as he stood.

Wang moved a hand until it was outstretched towards Brand.

Brand reached towards the hand. Just before he took Wang's hand, he kicked the COO hard in the ribcage.

Wang folded in pain once more.

"You think about tricking me again and you won't be able to rise on your own – ever."

Wang suspected that at least one of his ribs was broken. The pain was sharp, and his breathing came at a price.

"You are a dead man," Wang groaned through set teeth. "You will not leave this building alive."

"Maybe," Brand agreed. "But neither will you."

Brand produced the pistol he had secreted in his belt line.

Wang looked at the weapon with wide eyes.

"You are going to tell me how you managed to turn the federal government against me."

"I'm telling you nothing."

Brand grasped Wang's thick shiny hair and dragged him across the office floor to one of the chairs before his desk.

"Wrong fucking answer. I am sick of people telling me what they can't or won't do when I'm holding the gun."

Brand lifted Wang into one of the two seats as the large doors to the office opened and a half dozen security men stormed in, guns at the ready.

Brand put the gun to Wang's head.

"Another step and Wang dies."

The security detail didn't even slow their approach. They were on Brand in an instant. He resisted as best he could, but soon he was disarmed and cuffed.

"Kill him," Wang ordered, smoothing his hair and clothing.

"We can't do that," one of the guards refused nervously.

"Do as I say," Wang screamed with unfettered rage.

"We already called the police," the guard explained. "I'm not going to murder someone in front of the FBI."

Wang stepped forward, delivering a vicious punch to Brand's face. The blow turned his head and blood trickled from his nose.

"You punch like a bitch," Brand sneered at the smaller man. "Looks like I don't die today, Cato."

Wang stepped close to Brand. Two security men freshened their hold on the prisoner as he struggled to get at the COO.

"We'll see about that," Wang growled in a low dangerous tone. "I turned everyone on you. I will keep my word, just not immediately."

Wang stepped back, taking a deep cleansing breath.

"Take him out of my office."

The security detail dragged Brand to the front doors of the Tel Gong facility where sheriff's deputies and FBI vehicles were sliding to a halt.

Brand stood silently as FBI agents closed on him. Each held pistols at the ready. One of the security guards removed his cuffs. For an instant he considered the odds against him. He didn't doubt what Wang had said in his office. That split second was his only hesitation.

Unbidden, he walked towards the agents, his hands above his head. To his surprise he wasn't shot. Instead, the cordon of agents moved in as one. He felt hands and the weight of trained men as they moved to take hold of him. The man to his right received an elbow to the throat for his efforts. Another man dropped to the dirt as his ankle was shattered from a hard right foot.

Brand leaped left into the fewer numbers on that side of the group's combined forces around him. His *Sombo* training and quick reflexes helped as he used the weight of the attacking men against them.

An elbow grasp around the neck of the nearest man anchored him as Brand whipped the man around and below him, wrenching the man's neck badly. The falling agent's legs tripped two other agents. The larger group behind Brand fell heavily upon him. He felt his limbs in vice-like grips, then the weight of several agents atop him as they bound his wrists and ankles with plastic pull ties. His limbs were bound tightly enough to cut off circulation. He was restrained with attached ties, pulled until his limbs ached from the contortion.

One agent punched him hard in the face.

"Motherfucker," the agent growled in anger.

"Let me up and say that," Brand muttered through ground teeth, his fury at full flame.

"Transport this piece of shit," another agent commanded. Brand turned his head enough to see the speaker as the man he had grabbed by the neck.

Several men lifted Brand to his feet.

"Which one of you numb nuts took off his cuffs?" This again was the agent with the strained neck.

42

WANG WAS FURIOUS. He slammed an impotent fist onto his desk. His arrival at the Uvalde plant had solved nothing, it seemed. Carson Brand was in FBI custody, booked and printed. Now there was a paper trail that could not be covered up. Local papers were already running the story of the San Antonio man who had come to the aid of two Uvalde residents then was attacked himself, finally apprehended at the Tel Gong plant outside of Uvalde.

Carson Brand looked like a fucking hero to anyone who read the story. Heroes generate followers. Wang did not want the American to be known – famous or notorious.

He could think of no clandestine means by which to dispose of Carson Brand. He might arrange to have him killed inside the prison, as he had the girl. The girl had been risky. He allowed that a certain amount of luck had aided him then.

Despite his training with the MSS, Wang was a touch superstitious. That instinct warned caution now. The American seemed to possess a quantity of lucky fortune. He had miraculously escaped several tight spots with apparent ease. Wang reflected upon his younger days when he had learned that fortune favors only one side at a time. That does not mean that the favored side was right or just, but only that the favored side held the advantage.

Wang believed that Brand wielded the advantage at present. It was possible, even likely, that that balance would shift. Until it did, Wang would have to weigh his efforts against the advantage arrayed on the American's side.

More on his mind these days was the response beyond the Chinese government officials. Even at their highest levels, Chinese officials feared the power of the Lexicon. Wang had learned early during his time serving the will of the Chinese Communist Party that there was indeed a higher power – one to which even the mighty Chinese nation bowed.

The Lexicon was a conglomeration of the wealthiest oligarchs on the planet. Assembled decades ago, the Lexicon represented an authority which no nation dared oppose. Even the posturing United States of America deferred authority to this wealthiest block of humanity ever assembled since the pathetic human species slithered out of the slimy ponds from which they were spawned.

If he failed, Wang would face a reckoning from the mightiest authority on earth.

He picked up his desk phone and dialed his contact at the state department. His man answered with no greeting, only a single word.

"What?"

"You failed," Wang accused him with matching brevity. "Fix this."

"He is in FBI custody. I can't help much, but I have an idea. Let me work."

"Let you work? I haven't stopped you. I would like to see a positive result from the work you have allegedly done so far."

The man on the other end of the call made no reply. Wang could almost feel the effort of his restraint. He was certain the other's appearance of restraint struggled under the possibilities of the danger Wang represented to him and his career; and the unmentionable wealth from which he was benefiting as a result of their affiliation. Wang hoped there was also a small measure of shame at selling out his country for those things.

The phone went dead.

Wang dialed another number, this time an internal extension.

"Come to my office – now."

43

CHIEF OF THE UVALDE POLICE, Austin Hilbet, drove his police car slowly. His low-profile bar lights lighted the early evening around him with strobing blue and red flares. Drivers ahead pulled over to allow him right of way. He drove in the left lane of the curved highway bridge against oncoming traffic.

He followed a slowly moving older sedan.

The car must have been manufactured in the early seventies, long before he was born, the Chief mused.

The car ahead of him was known to him. His following speed was ten miles per hour. The driver sat straight up in the driver seat. He could see the driver's hands on the steering wheel, the driver's head hardly reached over the front seat head rest - silver, curly, wispy hair, perfectly coifed.

Hilbet rolled down his driver side window, waving at those drivers who pulled over to make room for him and the slow-moving pursued auto.

He nodded at a man in an older red pick-up truck, pulled over onto the road's shoulder.

"Hey Chief," the driver called with a grin. "Careful now."

Hilbet grinned good-naturedly and waved in return at the sally.

He followed the old car over the bridge. A short distance further, the driver turned onto a side street into a tidy neighborhood of turn of the century houses with well cared for lawns and gardens. The car turned into one of the driveways, narrowly avoiding a leaning mailbox teetering next to the street apron.

Hilbet halted his squad car at the drive entrance, watching as the driver carefully parked the car in the single space carport beside a neat white frame house.

The driver door opened, and a diminutive elderly woman eased herself from the car, carrying her large purse on her forearm. She closed the car door and looked at the police car with the whirling light bars as if she hadn't noticed the car before. She moved fraily towards the police car.

Hilbet quickly turned off the lights and stepped out of the car. He didn't want her to make the journey to the end of the driveway. He held up his hands to halt her progress.

"Mrs. Ellet," he called with an apologetic smile. "Just checking on you. No need to come over."

He approached the bent elderly woman as he spoke.

"How are you doing, Ma'am?"

Mrs. Ellet smiled, raising her hand to ward off his concern.

"I am just fine, Austin. I just had my hair fixed. Will you come in for an iced tea or maybe a cup of coffee?"

"I wish I could," he replied with genuine regret. "I have a concern at the station I need to attend to."

"Oh, for Gordon's seed," she exclaimed. "Is someone up to some orneriness this evening?"

"They certainly are, Mrs. Ellet, but not anything that should worry you."

"Well, Austin, you be careful. Since the school shootings, you never know what people are going to do."

"That's true. Do you need help inside, ma'am?"

Mrs. Ellet smiled knowingly at the Chief.

"I'm still getting around as well as I always have, Austin. You go on. I'm just fine."

"Yes ma'am," Hilbet agreed as he turned with a wave. He returned to his car and drove away with a last look after Mrs. Ellet.

44

BRAND WAS TO SPEND THE NIGHT in the only jail cell in the Uvalde police station. He awaited a federal official who would drive him to a federal holding cell, probably in San Antonio.

The cell was carpeted, and the bed was a folding camping cot. He had never seen a carpeted cell before, and lately, he had seen the inside of a lot of holding cells. Almost as an afterthought, a narrow steel cage had been erected in the corner of the small police station. Brand was certain that with enough impetus, he could drive his weight against the cell wall and dislodge it from the anchors holding it to the wall of the frame building. Escape did not occupy him currently. His mind was busy with the unusual details surrounding his incarceration.

He had overheard a couple of the local officers complaining that the prisoner should have been transported to the county lockup just outside of town. The federal agents had prevailed with the promise of a short stay until the prisoner transport arrived. Brand had also overheard them mention their concern for his safety in general population, even in a holding cell.

Within an hour of his confinement, a reporter with the local San Antonio newspaper, *The Express News,* had talked her way inside the station. She asked him questions about his background, Dehra and Leon, and his affiliation with Tel Gong. He had offered no comment. He had covered his face as she pointed her iPhone at him, snapping photos of him through the bars. Finally, the police chief arrived to see the melee and had the reporter escorted outside. The expulsion preceded the chief's excoriating one of the officers for the breach of security.

The officer explained that the reporter was from the San Antonio newspaper, and he hadn't seen any danger in it.

Brand glanced at the officer siting at the duty desk. It was late afternoon with no sign of the fed transport. The local cops had begun to display their impatience with watching the fed prisoner.

"If you were our perp," one of the cops complained. "You would already be in county by now. We aren't manned to babysit prisoners."

Brand read his nametag. Officer Pierce was only doing his job. Brand replied with a moderated tone.

"It wasn't my idea, Officer Pierce. I'm not sure why I am here or in custody."

Pierce shook his head.

"If I had a dime…," he began.

"You wouldn't be here wasting your time on me, am I right?"

Pierce grinned.

"Yeah, you're right."

As the sun set on the little police station, Brand grew more concerned. He was exposed in the little jail, with inexperienced guards on duty. He felt the slow pull of worry like a small itch in his mind. The morning's interview with the news reporter troubled him. As always, Brand was mindful that the Cartel was probably still looking for him. The news article would lead them directly to him. He doubted the two local cops would present much of a deterrent if a strong-willed force of Sicarios were dispatched to collect him. The threat of being killed by the feds was as troubling as the cartel, both outcomes were equally dire. If he fell into the hands of the drug cartel he would be lost for certain. He held to the hope that he might find a way out of his trouble with the federal government. The potential of a new danger struck him with an almost physical blow. What if he was being held in a low security location by design?

The police chief arrived just after the eight o'clock hour. He paused at the front door. His surprise was obvious when he saw that his prisoner had not been collected by the FBI.

"Why are you still here?" he asked Brand directly although Brand doubted that he expected him to answer.

"We called," Pierce replied in a bored voice. "They said someone was en route."

"When was that?"

"About three hours ago."

Chief Hilbet gave the officer a long look of dismay.

"I know, Chief," the officer agreed. "I don't know what else to do here."

Hilbet walked to the cell. His jaw muscles worked as he surveyed Brand through his tumultuous doubts.

"What's your story prisoner?" he asked with conviction.

Brand said nothing as he considered the question. He was surprised that the Chief was talking to him. The feds who brought him there gave clear instructions to have no contact with the prisoner unless it was to feed him or let him use the restroom.

Hilbet straightened in preparation to move away. He stopped short at the sound of Brand's voice.

"I'm from San Antonio originally. The DEA recruited me to work as a contractor for them. They loaned me to the NSA and here I am. This whole thing has something to do with that Chinese owned plant just outside of your town. I don't know anything else that you don't already know."

"Thanks. You appear to be in some pretty hot water. I'm just a small-town police chief. We don't get this kind of action here. After the news zoo around the school shootings, we have been a ghost town on the criminal front. Don't get me wrong, we like it that way. This just seems strange to me."

"I agree with you Chief. Maybe you can just let me go and I'll take the action with me."

Hilbet laughed with genuine mirth.

"Don't think I haven't thought about it. You just cool your heels until morning. If you are still here, we'll pick this up again after breakfast."

Brand settled back onto the cot. His head sank into the mealy pillow. He molded the pillow into a solid mass under his head.

He doubted he had that kind of time.

"Pierce," Hilbet continued. "You guys take off. I'll stick around for the feds. There's no point in all of us losing sleep tonight."

Pierce frowned at his feet.

"I would rather wait it out with you, Austin."

Hilbet considered the officer with a warm look of thanks.

"I appreciate you, Justin. Go on, Git," he ordered with a playful grin. "I'll be okay with our desperado here."

Pierce and the other officer departed reluctantly.

Hilbet took a chair at the nearest desk to the jail cell. He leaned back in the steel chair, stretching his arms to the ceiling. He looked the desktop over, inspecting the strewn papers and notes. Finding nothing to hold his attention his gaze took in his prisoner.

"Dinner should be here soon," he announced brightly. "You hungry?"

Brand looked at the Police Chief critically.

"You don't have to stick around here."

Hilbet took this in with obvious interest.

"No? Why not?" he asked with a grin.

"This has nothing to do with you," Brand explained. "There is a lot here that isn't apparent on the surface."

"I'm starting to get a feel for that," Hilbet agreed. "Why don't you fill me in?"

"It's better that you don't know any more than you do."

Hilbet frowned, his grin fading like the setting Sun.

"I'm not real patient with word games, Mr. Brand."

"Brand. Call me Brand."

"Whatever. Why don't you speak plainly, you know, like I am a cop?"

Brand considered it for a moment. He could plainly see that the officer did not take him or his warnings seriously. He didn't find a reason to fault him either. He was just getting used to the peculiar situation he was in. No one would believe that the federal government had a kill order against him. Further, no one would believe that he was also targeted for death by a drug cartel. He decided on a different tact.

"Are you from Uvalde originally?" Brand asked.

Hilbet considered Brand and his effort to change the subject for a long moment before he replied. Finally, his demeaner relaxed. Despite being a small-town cop, he was trained as a cop, and knew how to be patient in the pursuit of information in an interview.

"Yeah. Born and raised."

"I used to come here with my dad when I was a kid, came through really, on our way to the Frio."

"Concan?"

"We rented a river cabin off 127."

"Nice. The crowds can be bad at Garner."

"We fished more than tubed."

"Where are you from originally?" Hilbet asked.

"San Antonio, born and raised. I went to Churchill."

"Silver spoon crowd," Hilbet observed.

"Right," Brand scoffed at the observation.

"I grew up in the construction business. My dad was a GC. I had a little framing business for a while."

"Not anymore?"

"All that is in the past."

Hilbet looked significantly at the cell bars.

"That's how it looks."

Brand grimaced as the memories of his old life flooded back once more.

"How did a Churchill boy go from carpenter to outlaw?"

Brand chuckled without mirth.

"A long string of bad decisions."

Hilbet nodded. Despite his misgivings about the prisoner, he liked him.

"I'm sorry for you, Brand," he said with sincere feeling. "I see a lot of this sort of thing. The straight and narrow can sure seem difficult to some. It's tough for everyone, but real difficult for some."

Brand made no reply. The loss of those he loved and the strange circumstances that had brought him to that cell were not things he was inclined to share.

"You mentioned that the DEA recruited you. Tell me about that part."

I had a friend who got involved with the drug cartel. My association with him introduced me to the DEA. They figured out that I had no part in his dealings, but they thought my friendship with him might be used to their advantage in their drug war."

Brand shook his head as he emphasized the term 'Drug War.'

"Were you able to help?"

"Not really. I don't think the drug war can be won."

"No?"

"Based on what I have seen, you cut off the head and two more take its place. I think the risk reward is too attractive to the bad guys. I'm no expert, but I think you take the profit out of it and the cartels will lose interest."

"Legalize drugs?"

"I ran a business. High demand and low availability of a product equals high profits. I don't see another way."

Brand shifted his position on the cot.

"But I'm not a cop. What do I know?"

"Above my pay grade," Hilbet admitted.

There was a knock at the front door.

Hilbet stood as a lean woman in jeans and a Uvalde Strong tee entered with two boxes of food.

Brand's mouth began to water. He realized he was ravenously hungry.

"You are an angel, Kathy," Hilbet said to the woman.

She glanced at Brand as she placed the boxes on the desk.

"Are you going to be all night?" she asked of Hilbet.

"Yeah," Hilbet replied regretfully. "Sorry sweetie. The job."

"Just check in with me when you can. I don't like you here alone."

She glanced at Brand once again.

Hilbet squeezed her arm.

"I'll be fine. Where's Caleb?"

"He's with your mom. I'm going by to get him now."

"Tuck him in for me. I'll see you in the morning."

"Okay. Call me."

"I will. Goodnight."

Kathy left as Hilbet opened the boxes, passing one to Brand.

"Eat up. I can't promise you breakfast."

45

CERVANTES WAS NOT DEAD. He was not mutilated. He was not on the run. None of those things were off the table unless he succeeded. He had returned to Texas only a couple of days before. He had no team to call upon. Castillo had placed the burden of correcting his failures squarely upon his shoulders. Returning to San Antonio and the bar where he had last seen Carson Brand had yielded no results so far. He had not appeared there, and no one knew where to find him. Cervantes watched the waning sunset light from across the street from Rod Dog's Saloon. He closed his eyes, listening to the laboring engine of his rental car. The little car struggled in its lone task – to keep the air conditioner blowing cold air onto the driver's face.

Michael Cervantes prided himself in his inexhaustible patience. He considered himself a man of reason and tactical ability. So it was with grim surprise that he found he had indeed reached the limit of all of these traits. He was frustrated. He was angry at the unfamiliar discomfort the frustration visited upon him. He ground his teeth with an audible crunch. He craved an outlet for his ire.

His gaze once more rested upon the filling parking lot outside the bar. The place was packed. He was in the seventh hour of his vigil. He had seen the dark-headed bartender arrive on a motorcycle. He had noted each car and its occupants as they arrived up to this point. He had seen no sign of Carson Brand or the tattooed blonde woman he had seen him with during their last meeting. He struck the steering wheel at the memory. The DEA had placed him in mortal danger with the cartel.

He glanced aside at the chain Mexican restaurant nearby. An empty cup and discarded food wrappers from his earlier meal lay crumpled in a heap on the passenger side floor. He killed the motor, stepped from the car, and made his way to the restaurant. He was hungry and he predicted a long night of waiting and watching. He navigated around and through the cars circling the restaurant in search of the drive through, soon arriving at the front door of the restaurant. With a hand on the door handle he paused. The front page of a newspaper inside a large, square, glass-fronted, red metal dispenser caught his eye. At the bottom right, just above the fold, he read the headline, *San Antonio Man Thwarts Hit Squad – Chinese Company Implicated.*

Cervantes purchased a copy and scanned the article. The article read that Carson Brand of San Antonio was in Uvalde, in the city jail. The man in the photo held his hands aloft to cover his face, but Cervantes recognized him anyway. It was him. It was Carson Brand. In a wave his self-possession returned. He was no longer frustrated. In fact, he felt sheepish embarrassment that he had doubted himself at all. He dropped the paper in the waste basket and ordered a meal and a large drink. He had a drive ahead of him.

He had only one task left to complete before departing.

It was just after 1am when Michael Cervantes entered the rental car and started the engine. He looked across the street at Rod Dog's Saloon as he shifted the car into drive. Smoke and flames billowed out the back of the building. Patrons scurried out the front door in a panicked mass. He could just make out growing flames inside the bar through the tinted front windows.

He stepped on the gas, leaving the fiery ruin behind.

46

BRAND CALLED OUT IN AN URGENT whisper, waking the Chief with a snort. Hilbet rubbed his eyes before leveling a bloodshot stare at his prisoner.

"What?"

"Someone is outside the station."

"So? We are in a city. People walk around at night."

"Do they normally peek in the windows at the back side of the building?"

The chief righted his chair, taking a deep breath to clear his head.

"No," he agreed. "Not normally."

He strapped on his gun belt and grabbed his hat.

"I'll check it out."

"I wouldn't go out there if I were you," Brand warned. "There may be cartel hit men waiting for you out there."

"What are you talking about?" the Chief asked in disbelief.

"In an unassociated matter, a Mexican drug cartel is gunning for me."

"You told me that I know everything you know."

"It didn't seem relevant at the time. The cartel has nothing to do with my problems with the feds."

Hilbet considered his next move for a moment. Finally, he moved to the front door.

"Chief," Brand warned. "You can't go out there."

"You don't understand," Hilbet disagreed in a voice tight with fearful resolve. "I have to go. It's my job."

Brand understood the sense of duty he saw in the Chief. He had often felt it himself. He also knew that, like himself, no one could change what he had to do.

Hilbet unlocked the front door and stepped into the early morning darkness.

Brand listened intently, his nerves as tightly strung as piano wire. He waited with his hands on the bars of the door of his cell. He applied pressure to the door, testing its strength. He froze at the sound of something banging against the back wall of the station. He heard two shots fired closely together. It had to have ben two guns fired almost simultaneously.

With renewed urgency Brand shook the door of the cell. It rattled but held. He backed to the rear of the cell before launching himself against the cell bars opposite the wall anchors. He imagined he felt some give, but further inspection revealed no weakening of the wall anchors.

Cervantes kicked the officer's inert body. The man did not move. The cartel man's aim had been accurate and lethal. The officer's eyes had not yet adjusted to the dim conditions and his shot had flown wide in the dark. Cervantes had held the advantage.

Cervantes looked around him. He saw no sign of a reaction to the gunshots in surprised noises or curious lights in windows. He moved into the shadows against the building and worked his way around to the front of the police station. He checked his pistol. It was ready for the grim work ahead. He came to the front corner of the building.

A car's headlights turned onto the unlighted street a block away. The vehicle approached slowly, as if it were being driven on patrol.

Cervantes hid behind the corner until it passed him.

He expelled his held breath. It was a garbage truck beginning its rounds. He moved along the front of the building until he came to the front door. He peered inside through the glass door. The room was dark.

He tried the door. It was locked. He moved to the curb, collecting a broken piece of concrete. He threw the concrete fragment through the door glass. It shattered the glass with an alarmingly loud crash. Cervantes reached in and unlocked the bolt on the door, stepping into the air-conditioned darkness of the police station. His eyes adjusted to the deeper darkness inside. He quickly located the dim outline of a lone jail cell. A barely distinguishable dark figure stood inside at the cell door.

"This is the end, asshole," he muttered as he brought his pistol on line for the kill shot. The man in the cell did not move, nor did he cower from the danger bearing down upon him.

"Hero," Cervantes noted sadly before pulling the trigger.

The shot was deafening, illuminating the room like a flash bulb. The dark figure appeared briefly in the light. It was an overall work suit on a hanger, hung from the cell door frame.

Too late, Cervantes pivoted to locate the American.

Brand struck his gun hand with a police baton. The weapon clattered onto the vinyl flooring as Brand tackled Cervantes.

Cervantes was squat but strong. He struck down upon Brand's shoulders with both hard elbows.

Brand collapsed under the blow.

Cervantes followed him to the ground with a flurry of rights to Brand's head.

Brand shielded his face with his left arm as he brought the nightstick up with his right. It caught Cervantes in the neck just below his jawline.

Cervantes fell back.

The small weakness was all Brand needed. He rolled to his feet and pursued Cervantes as the latter tried to roll away from the attack. Brand collapsed his windpipe with another blow from the baton.

Cervantes grabbed his throat with both hands, trying to regain his breath. Brand hit him again with the baton, crushing his eye socket. He moved to the gun Cervantes had dropped. He picked up the pistol and returned to Cervantes.

Cervantes gurgled a plea for his life, one hand on his throat, the other outstretched as if to ward off the inevitable shot.

Brand shot the outstretched hand then placed a bullet between his eyes. He went to the front door, flipping the light switch on.

Cervantes lay in a growing pool of blood. The cell cage was bent and askew where it had twisted from the force where Brand had unfastened it from the wall. A janitor's coverall suit with a hole in the breast hung by a wooden hanger from the front door of the cell.

Brand rushed outside, quickly locating the Chief, prostrate on the ground behind the station. He checked him for vitals. He detected a faint pulse. Brand lifted him in his arms and returned him to the police station.

He placed the Chief on the threadbare sofa at the far side of the room. He wrapped the bullet wound with a bandage from the station first aid kit as he dialed 911. He conveyed the details of the wounded Chief and the cartel thug who shot him.

The operator spoke with impersonal efficiency.

"I have notified the sheriff's department. Officers are on their way. Stay with me on the phone until they arrive."

Brand hung up the phone.

Hilbet's face was a pale gray. Brand checked his pulse once more. He felt nothing. He leaned near the Chief's face, listening for breathing. The man was not breathing. Brand looked around him. The officers would be there soon. The opportunity to be free of all of this spun like a wheel in his head. To stay there was to die.

He had to act quickly.

Officers arrived before the station in multiple cars, lights, and sirens at full settings. Officer Pierce opened his cruiser's driver door as the sheriff's deputies arrived. He jumped out of his car, shotgun in hand.

"We have a federal prisoner in the cell. I don't know what the situation is inside. I believe the guy may have escaped and may be armed and dangerous."

"We have to breach now," one of the deputies said. "We will not wait and see."

"Alright," Pierce agreed. "I'll lead."

Pierce was handed a ballistic shield and an eight-man team stormed the front door en masse.

The dead cartel thug's body in a pool of blood caught their attention first.

"Secure the area," was the shouted command as the group rose to maximum alert.

Across the room, on the floor near the threadbare sofa, Brand was on his knees over the prostrate chief, administering CPR. He blew in the man's mouth then administered four compressions.

"He stopped breathing," Brand explained between compressions. "Help me."

One of the deputies called into his shoulder mic for EMS.

Another rushed to the chief, pulling Brand aside.

"I've got this," the deputy announced. "Get this guy into a real jail cell."

Brand was lifted to his feet and cuffed. Two deputies ushered him outside into an awaiting sheriff's cruiser. He was taken away to the county lock up where he was confined to a private cell.

He found a position which caused him the least discomfort from his wounds as he lay alone on the hard bunk, his mind busy with the events of the last few days.

The door to his cell opened, disturbing his thoughts. He was taken to the infirmary where his wounds and injuries were attended to. The medical care and mild pain killers administered provided him welcome relief after days of discomfort and make-shift bandages.

He was returned to his cell in relative comfort, allowing him to doze during those brief intervals when he wasn't disturbed by jail noises or guards making their rounds. Throughout the morning he caught the curious gazes of several guards and jail personnel as they spied on him through the cell door's narrow view port. His reputation preceded him.

The morning wore on until he heard the mounting noises of the jail house waking. Loud voices rang out as inmates moved to the chow hall. From that moment and throughout the rest of the day he was beset upon by the continuous din of confined humanity, filling his small cell with white noise.

A tray was left on the floor of his cell with no preamble nor instructions. He was certain that to the jailers he was a special case. It was likely that the sheriff's department had no idea what to do with him. He ate with the perfunctory motions of an automaton. Uncertainty clouded his reason. Solitude slowed time. His tortured imagination forestalled the anesthetic of sleep. He abided in a region of languid doubt, unanswered questions tormenting him with the frustration of unknown consequences – unseen plans for him.

Some hours later he was roused from his blank reverie by the bang and grind of the cell door opening.

Two deputies entered.

"Hands on the wall," was the command.

He was cuffed and shackled. The jailers held each arm, pushing him forward along a green doored, vinyl tiled hallway, then through a motorized steel riveted door into the central booking area. His escort guided him into a private room near the fingerprinting machine. They sat him in a chair and left the room, slamming and locking the door behind them.

Brand estimated another half an hour before the door opened once more and three suited feds entered. Two waited by the door, the third sat across the small steel topped table from Brand.

"Carson Brand," the seated fed said. "Is that your name?"

Brand eyed the man silently. What kind of game was the FBI man playing?

"You know who I am," Brand said mildly. "Why do you people have to continuously try to mind fuck me?"

"Answer the question."

Brand sighed in frustration.

"Answer me!"

"Yes! My name is Carson Brand. What's yours?"

"We are here to take you away from here."

"Well, you're a little late," Brand remarked with dark anger. "Your slow rolling this thing cost the life of a good cop. It nearly got me killed too."

"The cop didn't die. He is in critical condition. You probably saved his life. Why didn't you run when you had the chance?"

"What is this?" Brand asked uncertainly. "Are you being serious? You really don't know who I am? You're not stringing me along?"

"Mr. Brand, stand up please."

Brand obeyed.

The feds removed his restraints and replaced them with their own.

They led him past a crowded holding cell, down a hallway and into a closed sallyport. They helped him into a black SUV where he sat in the back seat between the two feds who hadn't spoken to him in the room. The man who had questioned him sat behind the wheel. He honked the horn, waiting for the tall steel rolling door to open before driving out of the sallyport and into the late afternoon heat.

The feds on either side pressed him down low in his seat until he was face down over his knees. They held him in that position until they left town and entered open country. They released him and he sat up, looking in turn at each agent with silent curiosity.

Brand was surprised again when the SUV pulled into the driveway of his mobile home just outside of Uvalde. They pulled him from the vehicle and dragged him inside. He was convinced that something bad was about to happen. Would they try to make his death look like an accident in the home? Would it look like a suicide? Were they going to burn down the mobile home around him?

Inside, Brand looked askance towards where he had beaten Spencer. He was relieved that the agent's rotting corpse was not leaning against the wall where he had left him. The federal agents uncuffed him and shoved him onto the sofa. The man who had interviewed him produced his service weapon, training it on him.

"Don't move," he warned in a low menacing tone.

Brand obeyed. His memory somehow went to his dead friend Bert. How did his best friend meet his death? Brand hoped to meet it like a man. He resolved to die silently, no pleas, no begging for his life, no empty negotiations.

He heard a voice behind him.

"I told you being a contractor was a bad idea."

Brand dared not move. The voice was familiar.

A red-headed man came around the sofa and faced Brand, shaking his head.

Brand recognized Dennis Moore, the FBI agent with whom he had gone through training at *Camp Bravura*, near Houston; the agent for whom he had handed a terrorist cell on a silver platter.

"Don't look so surprised," Moore said with a grin. "Your face may stick that way."

Brand looked towards the armed agent before once more surveying his old friend. Moore looked no different, perhaps a bit harder around the eyes.

Moore nodded and the agent holstered his weapon.

Brand stood, embracing Moore in a welcoming bearhug.

Moore pointed at the men in the room one at a time as he introduced them.

"These three men and I are the only federal agents you can trust for now. The man with the gun is Special Agent Danny Wallis. This is Special Agent Ian Nadworny, and Special Agent Al King."

"Pleased to meet you," Brand said, nodding at each man in turn. "I thought I was dead, Dennis."

"Brother, you are dead. At least you are if I can't fix this thing for you. Who the hell did you piss off, Brand? An S-6? I've never seen one before you. The word is that you are on a killing rampage. They say you killed DEA Agent Kilgore in his home."

"I didn't kill him." Brand denied with heat. "We were hit by a team. A sniper took him out."

"Calm down," Moore said with a hands down gesture. "This whole thing stinks like a setup. I have done some research, but I can't find who put the S-6 on you. I suspect it is the Chinese."

"That is what I have learned," Brand admitted. "Since when do the Chinese put American federal agency hits on American citizens?"

Moore shrugged.

"I'm not quite the conspiracy nut you believed I was, huh?"

"I'm a believer now. I won't doubt you again."

During their training at *Camp Bravura*, Brand had discounted many of Agent Moore's theories as right-wing B.S. Brand slowly allowed increasing credence for Moore's theories, especially when his information about the middle eastern ties to a political campaign with which Brand had worked had been proven valid. This new wrinkle with the Chinese Communist Party seemed to have legs of its own.

"So how did you find me?" Brand asked as it dawned on him that old acquaintances were popping up out of the woodwork.

"The same way your Mexican friend did," Moore explained blandly. "That news article put you on the map. You can bet that's how the cartel located you."

"That was some bad luck," Brand observed. "I would have been just fine without that reporter showing up when she did."

Moore made no comment, but his expression gave Brand a bad feeling.

"What am I missing?"

"I don't see how you have stayed alive this long," Moore exclaimed with wonder. "You were set up, my friend. Someone sent that reporter to get your story and publish your identity and whereabouts."

Brand was struck silent. His instincts had warned him about being held for too long in that weak jail cell with ineffective protection. He had even experienced misgivings about the reporter. He vowed to take his hunches more seriously in the future.

"Since I am doubting my instincts right now, I have another question for you."

Moore put his hands in his pockets.

"Yes?"

"Why should I trust you and your three amigos if everyone in the FBI is gunning for me?"

"I'm glad you asked me that because it means you are starting to use your head for something other than your hat. However, I can't tell you that. We are in a precarious position ourselves, under orders from a concerned party within the government who has to remain anonymous until we root out this Chinese insider playing hell with our process."

"Then it won't surprise you that I am a little doubtful," Brand said with alacrity he did not feel.

"We didn't take you into the woods and drop one behind your ear, did we?"

Brand shrugged at the reasonable observation.

"Good enough for me."

"Good. Let's talk about how we get you out of here. Do you have a car?"

"It was parked at Tel Gong when I saw it last. Gray sedan. Keys are in it."

"We'll pick it up if it hasn't been towed. We'll claim we need it for evidence."

"It's a DEA drug car."

"That makes it easier. I'll call you with details. Do you have a phone?"

Brand looked at Moore skeptically.

"I'll have the car dropped off here. We'll put a burner with my direct number in the glove box. Did you bring your dick, or do I need to issue you one of those too?"

"I'm covered there."

"We'll see," Moore said, the humor of their back-and-forth dissipating as he struggled to formulate a plan. "I'm not certain what to do with you. You are wanted for the murder of Kilgore and an agent found here in your home."

"Spencer is dead?"

"Yeah. He is. Are you saying you didn't do that one either?"

"Shit, Moore. I wanted to after what happened to the girl, Dehra. I roughed him up a bit to get Kilgore's address, but he was alive right there when I left him."

Brand pointed to the place against the wall where he had last seen Spencer.

"Who killed him?" Brand continued with a dark look on his face. "I thought the feds were on my trail and would free him when they got here."

Brand looked at Moore with a frown.

"The feds wouldn't kill one of their own, would they?"

Moore and his men looked at one another uncomfortably.

"You don't believe me?" Brand asked emphatically.

Moore considered Brand for a long silent moment, judgement plain on his face.

"The only reason I am here is because my instincts tell me that you are a good man at your core. You have pulled the trigger on several cartel goons and a couple of mercenary types. You waited around and saved that Uvalde Chief of Police knowing you would be returned to a cell. The only thing stopping me from trusting you completely is your unpredictable temper."

Brand swallowed hard at the truth he heard.

"Dennis…fellas. I am not a murderer. Spencer and Kilgore were a pain in my ass: Spencer particularly. I am in hell right now. I don't know how I got to this place in my life, but I am not in control of things. My one aim is to survive each day. That has included neutralizing bad guys who were trying to kill me. I have to live with those. Kilgore was telling me what you are telling me about the Chinese when he was killed.

"Spencer led a hit team that tried to kill me at Tel Gong. I knocked him around a little to get information from him, but I did not kill him."

Brand looked at the men around him. They seemed doubtful.

"If I had killed federal agents, would I have stuck around to face the consequences at the Uvalde police station? I already knew about this S-6 bullshit. That would have been enough reason for most people to run. If I had murdered two federal agents on top of that, don't you think it would have been sufficient cause for me to de-ass the A.O?"

"So how do you square yourself with the fact that your first action after you figured a lot of this out was going to Tel Gong and attacking the COO in his office?"

Brand frowned at the mention of Wang.

"Like I said," Moore continued. "I'm here now. I pulled you out of county lock up where you would not have seen evening chow. We'll see where this thing goes. I can't make any promises. One way or the other, you owe me, Brand."

"Yeah," Brand agreed in a low voice. "I guess I do."

"Don't make such a big a deal of it. I hate it when you get weepy. By the way, you look like shit."

"Thanks. I've been short on sleep and long on trouble. I'm also a little sore around the edges."

Brand flexed his stiff leg demonstratively.

"I'm not talking about your physical appearance, although you could use a shower from where I'm standing."

Moore looked at his men as if to ensure their continued commitment. His gaze returned to Brand. He looked him over slowly before he spoke.

"I knew this guy, "Moore continued pointedly. "We used to train at the same gym. A few months after we met, he went to work as a dancer at a strip joint, some male review something or other. Anyway, I remember seeing him a couple years later. I don't know if it was the drugs, the women, the late hours, or the job, but he looked like someone had climbed up inside of him and whipped his ass from the inside. He had a dead look in the eyes and a darkness about his personality. His injuries were all internal and self-inflicted. You have that same look, friend. If you get out of this shit storm, you might want to consider a change of vocation."

Brand made no rejoinder. He wanted to disagree with his old friend's criticisms but could find no argument with Moore's observations.

He was weary deep inside, where sleep couldn't reach. Maybe Moore was right.

"Let me tell you what we think is going on here," Moore said taking a seat across from the sofa.

Brand sat on the sofa.

"You are caught up in a trashy novel type of international espionage story. I've done a little poking around the bureau with no significant results. Someone high up is throwing a blanket over this whole thing. The internet is alive with rumors that the *World Monetary Fund* is under the control of some outfit called *The Lexicon*. The Lexicon is an elite club made up of the wealthiest international oligarchs in the world. They are working with the Chinese to create a new world order. You might have heard it referred to as *The Great Reset*.

"Anyway, they want to do away with national currencies, property ownership, and they want to Lo-jack everyone on the planet so they can control them. I believe this Tel Gong has developed a way to track phones and gather intel about their travel, social and buying habits. Everyone carries a phone. A cell phone is a more acceptable form of tracking than mandating that everyone accept a chip planted under their skin.

"The Chinese are already doing it. A large number of elected and unelected U.S. officials support the program here. The word is that there is already secret nationwide testing of the retail market for conversion to this new global economy model. It is being done by the big internet giants and paid for by the Chinese and The Lexicon. We are talking billions if not trillions in potential profits for those funding it."

Brand sat slack jawed and silent. He remembered his promise of belief in the man, but doubt caused him to suspect that Moore was a crackpot and a loose cannon. For all he knew, Moore might no longer be an FBI agent.

"Brand, don't look at me like that," Moore warned. "If anyone should place credence in this theory it should be you. Aren't you being pursued by hit squads, federal agents with kill orders, and a Chinese company seems to be behind it all?"

Brand saw the sense of what he heard but it was too much to believe.

Moore rose from his chair, annoyed at Brand's disbelief.

"Think about it – or don't! I don't give a shit. I've done my part here. So much for never doubting me again"

"Hold on Dennis," Brand said as he stood. "You were right before, and you may be right now. I need a little time to get my head around all of this. Why can't you take this to someone higher up who may not be involved – like this private party you are talking about?"

"I have no proof and no evidence. It would sound just as crazy to anyone I went to - that is if I could find someone who is not involved in it. There used to be a thumb drive, but it has been either misplaced according to some, or never existed in the first place according to others."

"What do you want me to do?"

Moore opened the door, and the other three agents left the mobile home. The agent paused. He controlled his temper with difficulty.

"This is some serious Orwellian shit."

Mastering his fit of anger, he said, "I don't want to believe it, but I have to be open to the facts. I believe the two most powerful nations on the planet and a group of the wealthiest people on the planet want you dead. I can't do much about it with what I have. I'll get you a car and a phone. Do you have any cash?"

Brand moved to the kitchen. He opened the cabinet door under the sink and felt around. He touched NSA Agent Child's pistol where he had taped it tightly to the bottom side of the countertop. His searching fingers passed the hidden weapon and moved until he felt another taped package. He withdrew a plastic bag containing a stack of bills.

"Yeah," Brand replied, tucking the money in his pocket. "I guess they didn't find it when they collected the body."

"Call me when you are on the road," Moore ordered. "Stay alive."

47

THE EASY WAY WAS NO LONGER on the table. Carson Brand was off the grid. He was spirited away from the county jail by FBI agents, at least they had proper ID and made the right calls to take custody of him.

Wang for the first time felt doubt creep into his faith in his well buttressed plan. He was out of ideas. The American's fortune was unending. The news article pinpointing the man's location had seemed a sure victory. Wang's intel was vast. He knew of Carson Brand's grim relations with the Mexican drug cartel. If the cartel had succeeded in killing Brand, Wang would have been invisible in the plot. His connection in the FBI had created the scheme. It was fool proof as far as anyone could see.

Yet it failed.

The county lock up was plan B. If allowed to proceed to fruition, forces had been arrayed to handle him inside the jail. The backup plan was infallible.

Yet it failed.

Wang's superstitious instincts were in full force. Was this man going to be the end of his ambitions? Could one man thwart a global operation?

The obvious answer was absolutely not! One man could not nullify the will of a nation. One man could not stand against the might of billions of well-placed dollars. One man could not prevail against the will of fate.

The men who freed Carson Brand troubled him. His contact assured him that the agents at the jail had moved the prisoner without official orders. They had been identified as FBI agents, but they had not acted on orders from the bureau.

Wang fumed at the troubling unknowns. Who controlled the actions of these men? The FBI was under his control, or it was supposed to be. That control was demonstrably untrue. Someone with power of office moved against him within the Bureau.

His people within the state department and all associated agencies wielded the authority he required to manipulate the events necessary to achieve his goals.

Wang believed fully that there was no one filling any position who could not be purchased. If money was not part of the price, he had at his disposal anything that would be.

Wang again struck the top of his expensive desk. His continued leadership in this matter was limited by his ability to succeed. The meeting in the hotel overlooking the *Gan Chiang River* had been no more than a wrist slap compared to what would happen if he failed again. Too much was at risk. Too much had gone wrong to allow this mission to continue as it had lately.

He knew he was under heavy scrutiny from those counting upon him in his home country and others in The Lexicon. He knew without a doubt that the latter secret organization would not warn him before taking matters into their own hands.

Despite the memory stick being quickly recovered, the loose end Carson Brand represented was not allowed to remain. The American had to die for Wang to abide once more in safe climes where he could peacefully complete his task as assigned.

He struggled with the unknown variables in his plans. Had he already exhausted the patience of those involved parties within The Lexicon? Would the next wet team arrive at his doorstep? Was he too late? He had no way of knowing where he stood with the Oligarchy.

As he had so many times in the past few days, he shook his head sadly, melancholy memories of his family and his homeland beckoning him. He reminded himself that he had volunteered to head the American mission. He had committed himself through training and grueling preparation for his role here.

With operational authority, he berated himself, came responsibility. With responsibility came risk.

His desk phone rang, startling him out of his reverie.

"Yes," he said into the handset. "Send the information directly to my cell."

Ha listened to the speaker on the other side of the call for a long moment. He drummed the top of the desk with the fingers of his left hand. The right held the handset at a distance from his ear. The speaker was nearly yelling into the phone.

"I understand. I was just now considering the implications. Send the information over the VTP app."

Wang hung up the phone. He rubbed his hands together like a miser trapped in a vault full of gold and precious gems. Was he fortunate or was he trapped?

Whichever turned out to be true, he would have the names of the agents who had spirited the American from his jail cell.

His cell vibrated announcing the arrival of the awaited information.

Wang opened the app and viewed the message.

"Dennis Moore," Wang read thoughtfully. "Al King, Danny Wallis, Ian Nadworny."

None of the names were familiar.

Wang committed the agents' names to memory then called his man in the bureau.

48

DENNIS MOORE ARRIVED AT THE downtown San Antonio bureau office two hours after leaving Brand at his mobile home. The other agents dropped him at the front lobby then drove away. The trip from Uvalde had been tense with doubt and fear. His associates believed as he believed, but their resolve lacked his strength of commitment.

Moore was used to it by now. He had always been the outlier when it came to following his instincts. His gut was fully engaged in confirming his suspicions. Training was worthless if not wielded with respect for those natural tendencies the Bureau looked for in its agents. Agency recruiters depended solely upon an astringent profile and specific requirements regarding what they called the appropriate *Mental and Physical Array* of the candidate.

No one entered service without a perfect match with the appropriate MPA. Moore noticed too often that once recruited, the candidates tended to abandon any reliance upon those innate gifts in favor of straight procedural and rote process when conducting their day to days. Moore believed the agency would be a far better place and the work would bear greater fruit if reliance upon the God given were encouraged as much as the tactics of process and training.

Moore was a bureau man to the bone. He loved his organization. What he saw screamed of a debilitating cancer which threatened to cripple the once great Federal detective branch. Couple with that a growing taint of a foreign enemy infiltrating her ranks, the danger was palpable.

Every fact pointed to a breach in the organization. That breach had manifested a will of its own, growing rapidly to the point that Moore was unsure if he could succeed. He felt despair that he could trust not one of his brothers in arms. From what he knew, even they had no clue they were being manipulated. Those God given traits would be sufficient to alert anyone of their perfidy.

He knew the trite justification. He heard it daily over morning coffee uttered in flippant dismissive tones.

> *Theirs not to reason why,*
> *Theirs but to do and die.*
> *Into the valley of Death*
> *Rode the six hundred.*

They were not Alfred, Lord Tennyson's Light Brigade. This was not a "Cheerio, King and Country, onward into the breach" moment.

Even in the service of a nation, he thought, we are still Americans. We are still required to think. We are still a free nation.

Moore's phone rang. He pulled it from his pocket.

After a moment of listening he replied, "On my way, sir."

He pocketed his phone as his gait increased. The Station Deputy Chief sounded furious.

Despite experiencing a deepening dread at the call to the meeting, Moore believed he would learn much from the next few minutes with his highers up.

Moore arrived at the SDC's office. A stern-faced secretary buzzed him in.

Behind a large, cluttered desk sat SDC Holland. He was bald and looked harried. His shiny bowed head bore testament to the hard life of a Deputy Chief. To his responsibility fell a continuous flow of unpleasant tasks. The only thing that kept him going was the knowledge that someday he would be Director and some other poor dick would have this thankless job.

"Sit down, Moore," he ordered the out of breath agent.

Moore took the proffered seat and waited in silence.

The phone rang on the SDC's desk. He answered on the first ting.

"Yeah, he's here," he said after a brief word from the caller.

Holland hung up the phone and glared at Moore from over the paperwork piled atop his desk.

"Did I miss the memo where you were promoted to my job?" Holland asked with no appreciation for the sarcasm in his words.

"No sir," Moore replied with the economy of words appropriate to his station.

"Are you experiencing some kind of mental break?"

"No sir."

"Did someone play a joke on you and give you erroneous orders which you followed like a green jackass recruit?"

Holland's color reddened as he spoke to the point that Moore feared the SDC would explode if he continued to anger at this rate.

"No sir."

"I see," Holland concluded with over-dramatic emphasis. "Then how am I to understand that one of my best agents – strike that – my top agent took it upon himself to enlist the aid of three other agents, travel to jerkwater, Texas, and retrieve a dangerous suspect from a lockup where he was under our custody and control?"

The door opened behind Moore.

He looked over his shoulder.

Closing the door was the tallest and most striking looking female FBI agent he had ever seen. She ignored his gaping stare as she moved fluidly towards the SDC's desk.

"Deputy Holland," she said in a voice which Moore felt was perfect for a woman who looked like that. "Please continue."

Holland reddened even more as he struggled to regain his tirade momentum.

"Moore," he demanded with renewed ire. "Tell me how I am to understand this behavior."

Moore crossed his leg over his knee. He took a moment to survey the newcomer before he spoke.

"Deputy Holland, I don't know this person and I can't read her badge from here. Does she have situational authority here?"

"Agent Moore," Holland said, gesturing to each person as he spoke. "This is Lisa Womack of the Justice Department. She has been tasked to vet or condemn your actions in Uvalde."

Moore's eyebrows arched in interest.

"So, the administration has an interest in a local suspect accused of state level crimes?"

"I suggest you mind your tone, Mister," Holland warned.

Womack merely smiled with an economical stretching of her lips, as if she was assessing the tough act of the seated agent. She did not seem put off or challenged by the question.

"It's okay Holland," she said lightly. "I'm certain Agent Moore realizes the precarious position he is in."

She moved to the second seat before Holland's desk. She sat next to Moore. He could smell her perfume and something else.

No way, Moore thought. He sat back deeper into his chair.

"Dude looks like a lady?" Womack asked pointedly but nonplussed. "Do we have a problem, Mr. Moore?"

"It's Agent Moore, and your problem is the only one here."

"Clever," Womack observed sarcastically. "I am here under the direct authority of the President. I suggest you remember that as we move forward."

49

HIS DEA CAR WAS DROPPED OFF in the driveway before his rented mobile home. The delivery was made without preamble. Two men arrived in two cars. One parked the car while the other waited in the second one idling at the curb. The driver of Brand's car moved to the other car, got into the passenger seat, and they were gone in a cloud of dust.

Brand had long since gathered his scant belongings. He dropped the door key on the kitchen counter and left the little mobile home for good. He fired up the car and pulled away. He knew he was being predictable, but he headed east on Hwy 90, back to San Antonio.

He could almost hear Moore berate him for doing something so predictable – so stupid.

Fuck Dennis Moore. Fuck the FBI. And fuck that Chinese asshole at Tel Gong. This was not his fight. He had narrowly escaped death by torture at the hands of Rabino and the cartel. Because he had met a girl at a bar, suddenly he was sucked into an international incident that had resulted in his own government putting out a hit on him. This was some shit. This was some unfair bullshit.

He had around $8,000.00 in cash, a car full of gas, and no ties. What did that mean in opportunity terms? There were three things that bothered him right now. The most pressing was figuring out how to stay alive against the will of the US and Chinese governments and an international group of billionaires with a hard-on for him. The second was to put the hurt on Haoran Wang for killing Dehra and Leon. The third was to check on Karen. His luck with women lately was all bad. He had to be certain she was not seen as an associate for the growing number of forces arrayed against him.

With dread, Brand glanced at the burner phone, next to the loaded nine mil in the seat beside him. He didn't want to call Moore, primarily because he would have to answer pointed questions as to his plans and face a certain ass chewing for the answers.

He watched the road for a long time, ignoring the phone. The heat of the Sun through the car windows comforted him. The tawny grass and ramshackle buildings along the road took him back to the days before his mind was troubled by violent and powerful foes bent upon his destruction.

Man, he could use a reset, he fantasized helplessly.

There didn't seem to be any way out of this for him. He was as screwed as anyone could be. These quiet moments alone, driving along familiar roads towards his hometown, would likely be his last. As before, in his rented mobile home, surrounded by armed agents, Brand considered how he would handle his last moments. Doubtlessly he was in his last days. Moore had seemed to be his salvation, but even he admitted his inability to affect any solution. His advice was to go to ground and wait things out. That was no plan of action. That was the opposite of a plan of action.

Unexplainably, his mind returned to his late best friend Bert. He may have seemed carefree, focused only upon beautiful women, but the man had a love for life that presented itself as an indominable nature of optimism and possibility. Other than that moment in the cluttered alley in Piedras Negras, where Bert's confidence had cracked, his last day was spent in quintessential Bert Gotardi style.

Brand yearned for a moment more with Bert. Alone in the car, Brand had no sounding board; no snappy repartee; no opposing and unreasonable argument with which to frame his beliefs and his subsequent actions. They rarely agreed on matters of principle or morals, but Bert always represented a perspective open to the wants and needs of the human animal. He embraced the primitive desires and aims of the creature others clothed in courteous restraint and walked around like awkward marionettes manipulated by the hands of children.

Brand grinned unconsciously at the metaphor. That was something Bert would have said. It surprised Brand that he came up with the imagery on his own. Maybe they hadn't been so different.

The sedan jogged him as he drove over a railroad crossing.

His smile faded into a tight thin line. The smallest circumstance could end him. A blowout leaving him on the side of the road, or a speeding ticket would find him back in the hands of the law, a certain death sentence. Those odds were not the basis for long term survival. If he was to die within days – maybe hours – he had to handle those few issues he could manage. He would have to reverse his order of march, so to speak. He would see Karen then work back to Wang and the cartel.

Work to the crescendo, he vowed, for that is the end of the road for him. The one positive in it was that he need not worry about jail time or punishment for what he would do. He had a free hand to do what he had to do. Freedom from consequence was liberating.

"Damn, Bert," he muttered aloud. "I guess you were right all along."

He had no choice but to release the animal. Brand called it his Black Dog, the rage that hid below the surface, aching for escape. Kilgore told him when they met that he suffered from a condition called *Blind Rage Syndrome*. Apparently, the Vikings considered it a gift from the gods bestowed upon their fiercest warriors. Even this amusing fantasy gave Brand little comfort. His fate was sealed.

Brand watched his speed. Doing so got him past a county cop near Brackettville, hiding in wait for speeders.

He passed the entrance to the film location where had been shot the John Wayne movie *The Alamo*. Beyond that, as he drew nearer San Antonio, the terrain changed to a more rolling greener clime. He entered the outskirts of the bustling south Texas city around mid-afternoon. He made his way towards the northeast side of town. He still hadn't called Moore.

When he arrived before Rod Dog Saloon, the parking lot was cordoned off with yellow caution tape. The roof above the bar was a black collapsed hole. The animated dog logo was a melted sagging ooze, and the insides of the glass doors and windows were sooty black.

Brand headed for Karen's house.

She met him at the door.

"Where have you been," she asked frantically, pulling him inside and closing the door.

She bolted and chain locked the door, then led him into the living room. He joined her on the sofa.

"The Dog burned down?" he asked pointlessly.

"It was burned to the ground," she corrected him. "Someone started a fire in the kitchen while the place was packed. We were able to clear the bar without anyone dying. Someone outside said they saw a tough looking Mexican man leaving the scene, walking too slowly for someone scared by a fire. I think he was one of your friends from the cartel."

Brand nodded his sad agreement. So, he thought regretfully. His actions were responsible for another disaster for his friends.

"Where have you been?" Karen repeated. "The news is reporting that you killed two federal agents then escaped jail in Uvalde County. There is a statewide manhunt looking for you."

"I didn't see any roadblocks or increased police presence," Brand replied more to himself than her question.

"The cops who talked to me said they believed you would head for Mexico or west towards El Paso."

"You talked to the cops about me?"

"They took me in for questioning," she explained in irritation. "They tried to accuse me of aiding and abetting a fugitive from justice."

"Shit."

"Shit is right. I didn't say anything in spite of their threats to put me in prison for the rest of my life. My attorney got me out of there without any charges filed."

"You have an attorney?"

"A customer from the bar."

"Of course. Can I help with the fees?"

"He didn't charge me anything."

"That place was like our family home," Brand observed with regret. "Is Rod going to rebuild?"

"No, he's retiring," she said. "Stop talking about the damn bar. Did you do what they say you did?"

"Of course not," he replied flatly. "I've got the Feds, the Chinese, and every billionaire on the planet gunning for me. They killed the two agents while trying to get to me, I think."

Karen made no response as she struggled to catch up.

"Wait here a second," she said finally. She rose and disappeared down the hall towards her bedroom. She returned with a padded shipping envelope. She sat once more, handing the envelope over.

"This arrived at the Dog a few days before the bar burned down. It was hidden in our mail. I found it while I was throwing away the junk mail the day of the fire. It's addressed to you with no return address."

Brand took the envelope. There was no stamp or address, only his name hand printed on the envelope.

"Someone dropped it off?" he asked as he searched for a tear tab to open it.

"Must have," she agreed. "It wasn't mailed. I haven't had time to ask any of the other bartenders since the fire."

Brand finally tore open the top. Inside was only a memory stick. It was not the same color or type as the drive with which Dehra had recorded Wang's conversation. This one was a cartoon character with a thumb slide USB connector. He searched the inside of the envelope and extracted a hand-written note. The handwriting matched the writing on the envelope. He read the signature before reading the message. It was signed M.K. - Matthew Kilgore.

Brand read the message on the steno paper.

Brand,

I made a copy of the drive Dehra gave me. I don't know who to trust with this information. I listened to the contents. The conversation on the drive along with the mass effort to get you out of the way indicates to me that there are highly placed US government officials in on whatever these people are planning to do.

I arrested Dehra and have arranged for her to have her own cell. I plan to get her moved as soon as I can.

I'm sorry for keeping you out of the loop but I don't know what we are up against. There is a kill order on you. I apologize for what I have to do, but I see no other way to keep me and my family safe other than to go along.

Since I have known you, I have seen you get out of some pretty tight spots. I hope you are able to survive this one. If you are reading this, you have survived again – so far.

I don't know who to get this to in the government. Everyone can't be involved. There has to be someone who can make things right.

Brand, I am not your ally. I can't be. I can't advise you what to do about any of this. I can't help you. I have to continue to act against you. I am sorry, Brand. I am counting on your tenacity and toughness to do what needs to be done. Maybe someday you can forgive me.

MK

Brand looked at Karen blankly.

Karen pulled the letter from him and read the contents.

"So, it's true," she said as she returned the letter to Brand.

Brand shrugged.

"It's true," he confirmed.

He stood from the sofa, folding the letter, and stuffing it in his pocket. He hid the cartoon figure in the opposite pants pocket. He dropped a stack of hundreds onto the coffee table.

"What's that for?" Karen asked.

"You are out of a job for a while. This will help. I'm not sure if I will have a chance to spend it."

"What are you going to do?"

Brand looked at her as if he was seeing her for the first time.

"Karen," he said with an odd ring to his voice. "I'm going to take this to the newspaper and leak the whole thing. I'm going there tomorrow morning at nine in the morning."

"I'll go with you."

"I need to do this alone. You are too deeply involved. I know you have nothing to do with this and you know it. I don't believe the police believe that. Stay clear of me and all of this. Forget about me. I am not coming back here. I can't see you again. I'm sorry."

Karen was shocked by his words.

"You don't mean that, Brand," she stammered as tears filled her eyes. "We can fix this together."

"Do what I say," Brand muttered with a severity she had never heard from him.

"Why are you doing this?" she asked in a quavering voice.

"Because I don't want what happens to everyone I love in my life to happen to you."

Karen stood mutely, her hands frozen in a gesture of supplication.

Brand moved to the bar near the kitchen, extracting Kilgore's letter from his pocket. He grabbed a pen and wrote rapidly on the page. He showed the writing to Karen.

Your house might be bugged.

She nodded.

He went to her, kissed her, then left out the front door.

50

MOORE HEARD ABOUT THE STAKEOUT at the *San Antonio Express Newspaper Office* too late to intervene. Newly acquired intel indicated that Carson Brand was going to the press with some type of sensitive national security information.

It was a quarter till nine and Moore was half an hour from downtown. Brand was not answering his calls on the burner phone.

"Dumb shit," Moore muttered for the tenth time.

Why would Brand return to San Antonio? Admittedly, it probably was the only reason he was still at large. A dragnet had been stretched south and west thinking he would flee. The personality profiles never fit when it came to Brand. He was unpredictable, unless you knew him, Moore thought grimly.

Going to the press with his story about hit teams and government conspiracies with no proof would do little to protect him or to save his life. He was a minor celebrity with the Uvalde stories of his fighting off bad guys to save two Uvalde natives. The additional news of his killing two federal officers all but nullified any sympathy he might have gained.

Moore arrived on scene at twenty minutes after nine. He parked his sedan two blocks over then entered the operational area. He spotted no fewer than three sniper nests on buildings overlooking the newspaper office. Suspiciously fed looking passersby and loiterers appeared at random intervals on the street and sidewalks out front.

He located the disguised command post van at the end of the block. The sliding door of the panel truck opened, and DOJ agent Womack pulled him inside.

Two tactical techs sat before video screens and a large bank of technical equipment, monitoring surveillance equipment and radio communications.

"Are you trying to blow my op?" Womack asked Moore pointedly.

"I wanted to make sure you don't kill him during your op."

Womack eyed Moore suspiciously for a moment.

"We plan to take him without incident if we are able," she assured him unconvincingly.

"Everyone knows about the S-6 edict," Moore said.

"And your point is?"

"This looks more like a hit than an apprehension."

"The outcome is strictly up to the perp," Womack said firmly. "Besides, why are you here? I could have you hauled in for obstruction or in the least dereliction."

"You asked for my help in our last meeting. I am here to help. How is that a violation?"

"Just stay out of the way, Agent Moore. We have a job to do."

"Do you want me to leave?"

"Just shut up and stay put."

Moore, Womack, and her team stayed in place until just before noon. Womack ordered a stand down.

"I guess your boy got cold feet," Womack told Moore.

"My boy?" Moore responded with annoyance. "He is not my boy any more than you are my girl, or anyone's girl for that matter."

Moore saw the techs smirk out of the corner of his eye as Womack faced him fully, anger building in her tall frame.

"Do you have a problem with my gender or any part of my appearance?"

"As a federal agent," Moore replied evenly. "I respect your rank and position. As far as your personal life: you can do what you want to. But understand that if you are going to suck a dick or take it up the ass, you had better expect to catch some shit for it – even biological women do."

"You are screwed now, Moore," Womack announced. "I have witnesses to your hate speech, your transphobic hate speech. I hope you enjoy the few days you have left with the FBI."

Womack indicated the two techs.

"I didn't hear anything," one of the techs informed the tall agent.

"Hear what?" the other asked innocently.

Moore opened the sliding door.

"Well, it's a relief that I am not going to be screwed by you Agent Womack."

He left the van and slammed the door closed behind him.

51

BRAND WATCHED AS MOORE MOVED along the sidewalk headed back to his car. Moore passed within a few feet of him as he sat at a table in a small deli and coffee shop on the ground floor of a high-rise building, sipping at a cup of coffee.

Moore moved along until he came to his sedan. He unlocked the car and drove into traffic.

Brand called Moore a few minutes later.

"Sorry for not calling sooner," Brand said into the phone.

"I take it you are nearby," Moore guessed sardonically.

"What makes you say that?"

"Save it. What is your game, Brand? Why set all of this up?"

"Just confirming that a friend's house was bugged by the feds. While I was at her house, she gave me an envelope left at the bar where she works. The bar burned down a few days ago but she still had the envelope. I told her that I was taking the thumb drive to the press. You know the rest."

Moore pulled over his car.

"So, what is on the drive?" he asked.

"Kilgore sent me the envelope with a copy of the lost thumb drive. On it is a recording of a conversation where Ha Wang is talking with a tech guy named Bill where he admits to being involved in a plot with the Chinese and a group of investors to overthrow our country and enslave our citizens. Kilgore included a note apologizing for sending the hit team after me. He said he did it only because he was worried for his safety and the safety of his family."

"Do you have the drive with you?" Moore asked.

"Yeah," Brand replied. "You said you needed proof to take to your contact. I've got it. What is your plan?"

"We need to meet."

"When?"

"You are close, so how about now?"

"Okay," Brand agreed. "I'm at the Downtown Deli and Coffee Bar. I'll wait for you here."

"Good," Moore said. "I'll be there in a couple minutes. I'm right around the corner."

Moore got back on the road.

Brand tossed his trash into the waste basket as he left through the front door of the deli. He crossed the street and entered a comic book store. He stretched his wounded leg and thumbed through the pages of a magazine as he watched the deli.

He waited nearly half an hour before Moore arrived at the deli. Brand surmised he left his car some distance away, continuing on foot. Brand was concerned how long it had taken his friend to arrive after being only a few blocks away.

Moore entered the deli and looked around. Brand could easily see him through the glass panes comprising the entire facing side of the restaurant. Moore ordered at the counter, paid in cash, then moved aside to await his order.

Brand scanned the street as well as he could through the front windows of the bookstore. He saw no suspicious characters lying in wait.

He racked the magazine and moved towards the front door. He stopped short as a white panel van slid to a halt in front of the deli. Armed men leapt from the van and rushed towards the deli, guns drawn.

Brand ducked behind the wall near the front door. He heard screams and shouting as the team stormed the front door of the restaurant. Brand could just make out Moore over the hood of the van. He backed against the wall as the men converged upon him. Brand couldn't make out what he said, but Moore appeared to be identifying himself as a federal agent.

His assailants were not listening.

The four men shoved Moore onto the floor and bound his wrists with double ringed slip ties.

To Brand's eye, the team didn't seem like federal agents. Each had long hair, beards, and tattoos covering their arms. They wore dark pants and tight black tee shirts.

Brand felt the compunction of an irresistible impulse and went with it. With a last stretch of his leg, he rushed out of the bookstore, picking up speed and impetus as he passed around the front of the van. He ignored the pain in his protesting leg. He snatched a stainless table knife from one of the tables outside. He struck the team as they dragged Moore through the narrow front door. Brand hit the group at full speed. They fell back into the deli as Brand broke through them like a bowling ball through pins.

He struck the first man in the throat with a fist and the next he kicked in the nuts.

The others reacted quickly, exhibiting advanced training. The nearest man swung the barrel of his pistol in a wide arc.

Brand raised his left arm and the barrel glanced off his shoulder, tweaking the wound in his back. With his right hand he buried the knife in the man's neck. Brand twisted his position to catch the man's weapon as it fell from his senseless hand.

The move opened him to a blow to the back of the head from a large man with a ponytail. The strike angered Brand. He rolled forward, spinning at the last moment and fired a shot, striking the ponytail man. He shot into the group to discourage another sneak attack. He was lucky not to hit Moore with the snapshot. Instead, he hit one of the team, center mass. He saw it was the man he had encountered first and hit in the throat.

A shot sounded immediately after his fire. The bullet pulled his shirt as it passed through before shattering white ceramic tile on the wall behind him.

The patrons screamed and fled for cover, knocking down tables and chairs. One of the tables struck another one of the team who held Moore. The table hit the man behind his knee. He fell to his knees, dragging Moore with him.

Brand rose to a crouching posture as the fallen man brought his pistol on line for a shot. Brand shot him just above his collar line. He spat blood and fell on his face. The last member of the team took cover behind a pregnant woman, pulling her near to shield himself.

Brand hesitated only a split second before opening a round hole in his forehead. The woman fell from his grasp with a cry.

Brand checked himself for injury before moving forward and helping Moore to his feet. A waitress watched him, frozen in place by the violence she had witnessed.

"Give me that knife," Brand ordered, pointing at a carving knife behind her on a cutting block in the food prep area on the back wall of the deli.

The waitress only stared at him.

"Give me that knife," he yelled at her. "Now!"

She jerked to life and looked around to locate the knife he wanted. She saw it and quickly passed it over.

Brand cut Moore's cuffs and led him from the store. Moore seemed as stunned as the waitress. He followed Brand silently for some half a block before he seemed to regain his senses.

"What the hell just happened?" were his first words.

"Welcome to my world Agent Moore," Brand replied in a tight voice. "Those guys were not feds. They were merc's and they were after you, not me."

Brand pulled Moore around the corner and pointed at the passenger door of the little gray sedan. He took the driver seat and started the car. Moore entered and sat in the seat next to him.

Brand spun the tires as he pulled away from the curb.

Moore looked at his hands, rubbing his red wrists as he reviewed the last few minutes in silent anger.

"You know the city?" Moore asked finally.

Brand nodded as he ran a red light then turned right on the next street.

"Head towards Interstate Ten and Martin Luther King."

Brand made his way to the freeway and the area Moore indicated.

"Do you trust me?" Moore asked pointedly.

"I don't have the luxury of trusting anyone, Dennis. Don't take it personally."

Brand glanced at Moore as he weaved through traffic on the expressway, gauging his reaction to his answer.

Moore nodded.

"In the final analysis," he observed. "It's better that you didn't trust me. I would be in a much more serious situation, and you might be in the same."

"We have to rely on each other for now," Brand said with pathos. "It looks like you have ventured outside of whatever invisible boundary you crossed to get a hit team on your ass."

"Turn here," Moore instructed as Brand entered an older neighborhood of white clapboard houses shaded with large sycamore and elm trees.

"This is a pretty rough part of town," Brand noted as he turned on the indicated street. "We are a bit too white for safety here."

"In the fifties," Moore explained. "When this was a vibrant neighborhood filled with working middle class families, the FBI created a safe house in this neighborhood. The intent was for agents to blend in with the residents. The house is no longer used but is still available."

Brand pulled his car into a narrow driveway on the left side of the yard of a single-story white frame house with a green asphalt roof, surrounded by a dilapidated white picket fence. Brand turned off the car and waited for Moore to lead. Large trees shaded the front yard and the drive from the heat of the day.

"Let's get settled in," Moore said. "Then we'll go to the grocery for a few items to see us through the next few days we may have to hide here."

Brand nodded then stepped out of the car.

Moore followed suit, looking around him cautiously.

Brand gathered his bag from the back seat then followed Moore to the front door.

"Are you wounded?" Moore asked after noticing his limp.

"A couple of knife wounds," Brand replied as casually as he could. His leg was very sore after the burst of strenuous activity in the deli.

"Do you need a doctor?"

"Probably. We'll deal with it later. I'm well enough to pull you out of the shit."

"Up to you," Moore said with a grateful smile.

Brand followed Moore onto the front porch. As Moore searched for a key Brand looked around him.

Cicadas buzzed in the trees. The sound of children playing came from somewhere down the block. A light wind blew, rustling the leaves in the tall trees. Brand took in the moment with a melancholy ache. He once again was reminded of the days before all of this.

Moore opened the front door. Brand's serene wish for the impossible stayed behind as he followed Moore into the little house. Inside, the house was dusty and dank but in good condition. He saw no broken windows or refuse as one might suspect of a long vacant house in that neighborhood.

Moore noticed the same things.

"Tempered glass," he explained. "Doorknob reinforcement plates, and steel enforced framing. The house was built by a flat earther conspiracy nut back in the day. He was convinced he would need to hide out from the anarchy of a post-apocalyptic society. The bureau acquired the house after his death. It was perfect for the FBI because of the building enhancements and the location."

Brand flipped a light switch. A bare bulb in the center of the living room ceiling glowed yellow.

"The fed has been paying the light bill," he observed.

He looked around the house. It had three small bedrooms, fully furnished with period appointments, and a single bathroom with a white clawfoot tub. He saw no ceiling registers and no AC units in the windows.

He returned to the living room where Moore was checking his phone.

"No air conditioning," he told the agent. "It's going to get hot in here."

"My guys aren't answering my texts," Moore announced with worry plain in his tone. "I need to call them."

Brand shrugged as he inspected the kitchen. The fridge was old but the freon compressor rattled and hummed when he plugged it in. The interior of the old icebox was clean with only a slightly smelly aroma from disuse. The cabinets were empty of canned food. Only dusty dishes and cookware occupied the papered shelves.

"No one is answering their phone," Moore finally said after dialing the three agents he had introduced to Brand in Uvalde. "This isn't good."

Brand returned to the living room and stood before Moore.

"You think they are dead?" he asked seriously.

"They didn't have you to save them," Moore replied significantly.

"Whoever is running this operation is taking no chances," Brand concluded decisively. "How can you cover up something like this? This conspiracy is so big and so solidly entrenched that someone is willing to risk killing agents openly – on the street. What are we up against Dennis?"

Moore swallowed. It was plain he was having trouble getting past the plight of his missing men. He considered Brand for another moment before he answered.

"Have you noticed a familiar theme with this situation and that terrorist cell I told you about a few months ago? Both times set off alarm bells within every intelligence agency in the country. Both were quelled with the same story, that it was all a false alarm. Also, both events involve known enemies of the U.S. government. In both cases there seemed to be large amounts of money supporting them. Finally, that money was based offshore and seemed to be known to the higher-ups in government.

"It seems reasonable to me that there are forces embedded in the highest levels of power in our government who support these endeavors and don't seem to like America very much.

"The assault upon me and my men could only come from an authority too high ranking to be frightened by the consequences of killing American agents. The stakes have to be so high and the time frame for success so short that extreme actions are an acceptable risk for their desired ends."

Brand sat on the arm of the threadbare sofa, unconsciously rubbing around the wound in his leg as he listened.

"The president? Congress? Some high-ranking head of the military or a secret spy organization?" he asked.

"The answer isn't ever that cut and dried," Moore explained. "In the FBI we deal with a lot of organized crime. Although different in many ways than this, the M.O. is the same. Those who call the shots always keep to cover as lower-level operatives do the dirty work and make things happen. Kilgore put the hit team on you at Tel Gong, but he didn't make the decision to do so. He was following orders. This team today was a contract job. Anyone could have been behind it. This was the same job you were supposed to be doing for the DEA."

Brand crossed his arms, uncomfortable talking about his time with the DEA.

"Washington sent down a Tranny DOJ agent to oversee your capture, or elimination, at the newspaper office. That rules out the station chief here. Our culprit is upper DOJ staff or above."

"Why a Transvestite?"

"Not a feature of the situation, just odd. Sending down a DOJ official to oversee an FBI op is unusual yes, but it also points to how high this goes. If DOJ agent Womack was also involved in the team sent after me, then the dirty boss is even higher than DOJ level."

"Why do you say that?"

"Killing or capturing FBI agents is extremely risky, not to mention dangerous. Like any other law enforcement organization, we protect our own. To risk alienating the Bureau indicates very high stakes indeed."

"You said you are working with someone."

Moore nodded seriously.

"I can't really talk about it right now."

"Trust huh?"

"I'm an FBI agent. You are a civilian. There is still a line I can't allow you to cross."

"Have it your way," Brand said with surprising amity. "What is the plan?"

"I'll keep trying the agents. If they miss their end of the day check in, I know they are either incapacitated or in custody."

"And if that happens?" Brand pressed.

"I don't have a backup plan for any of this," Moore admitted. "I didn't consider actions against FBI agents as a possibility. Let me have your burner. I need to make a couple of calls and we don't want any of it traced to you or me."

Brand tossed Moore his burner phone then collected his gym bag containing his few possessions.

"Any preference on bedrooms?" he asked Moore. "I'm going to get a nap in before it gets too hot in here to sleep."

"Your choice," Moore replied vacantly as he keyed in a number from his contacts list on his FBI phone.

Brand took the bedroom on the southeast corner of the house. With effort, he opened the windows. As he hoped, the prevailing southeasterly breeze billowed the curtains slightly. He removed his shoes and shirt, removed the dusty bedspread, then flopped on the bed. He looked to his new dressings on his wounds. They seemed fine. The surrounding areas were no longer red and inflamed. His leg still ached as badly in repose as it had under his weight, but the pain seemed lessened since the infirmary care. He bore the discomfort for a few moments as he waited for the leg to relax. Soon the pain subsided to a manageable level.

As he settled into his pillow, his thoughts paraded unbeckoned before his mind's eye, delaying sleep. The recurring image of Dehra occupied most of the time he lay there awaiting the healing balm of sleep. He gave some mental effort to who might be behind the attacks upon Moore and himself. Of the dark musings he entertained, Dehra's murder was by far the most prevalent. Kilgore had all but confirmed that Wang was behind all of this, including Dehra's death. No matter who was complicit with him inside the government law enforcement bureaucracy, Brand vowed to have one last go at Wang.

Brand woke some hours later. The bedroom was dark. Outside the trembling curtains the outside was colored in dusky hue. A cool breeze glowed gently through the window.

Brand sat up, listening for noises from outside or within the house. He swung his feet onto the floor, moistening his dry lips with the tip of his tongue. His skin tasted salty. He had slept through the hottest part of the afternoon, likely soaked in sweat while he slept.

Getting to his feet, Brand was pleased that his leg seemed better after the break. He left the bedroom in search of Moore. A careful inspection of the house turned up no one. Moore was not there. Brand's phone was gone. He returned to the bedroom. He inventoried his gym bag. Spencer's pistol, the thumb drive and his money were still there. Moore had not gone through his things, at least he had not removed anything.

Brand returned to the living room and peeked out the front window curtains. The car was missing from the driveway. Moore was mobile. He had left no note and hadn't awakened him before leaving. Brand guessed Moore was not planning to be gone long.

Brand retrieved the gun and took a seat on the sofa in the dark living room. He waited for Moore another two hours before the front windows were illuminated by the DEA car's headlamps.

Moore entered moments later with a full bag of groceries.

Brand helped with the bag, stowing the items as Moore filled him in on the latest news.

"My boys are in custody. No one knows what they are charged with. There is an all points on you and a full court press search going on for me. I spoke with my contact I told you about. She has learned quite a bit more about how deep this conspiracy goes. Apparently, every head of every major federal law enforcement agency is involved. It appears that anyone appointed to administrative office by the president's team are involved.

"FBI Director Chris Rayburn is knowledgeable about the entire operation if not actually working as a part of it. CIA Director Burnett seems to be handing out the marching orders to the domestic agencies. Someone in his employ has been commissioning the hit teams sent against you, and more recently, me.

"We don't have a provable connection to the Chinese Communist party, but the results so far benefit them more than any one of our other international enemies. Wang's involvement and the rumors circulating as to what he is doing at Tel Gong is very strong circumstantial evidence proving Chinese involvement."

Brand leaned on the countertop with his arms crossed over his chest. The pistol stuck out of his beltline. Moore seemed for the first time to notice Brand was armed.

"Expecting trouble?"

"I wasn't sure. Is the gun bothering you?"

Moore considered Brand for a moment as he decided how he felt about everything he had learned.

"Naw," he finally replied, turning towards the sofa. "I need to sleep. Do you mind cooking something up for us?"

"No problem." Brand said. "I'll wake you up in an hour to eat."

Moore fell onto the sofa, shifting his body until he found a comfortable position. He was instantly asleep.

Brand cooked dinner, then breakfast the next morning.

Moore was most impressed with his biscuits and gravy.

"You made these from scratch," he observed.

"While you slept it off this morning. I had to go to the store for more ingredients and some peanut butter and jelly, but yeah, they are from scratch."

"I was expecting fried bologna and cheese sandwiches."

"I don't know of any Texas man worth his salt who can't cook, or who would eat fried bologna and cheese for breakfast."

They ate in silence, wolfing down biscuits covered in sausage gravy, fried eggs, fried bacon, and coffee.

After the meal Brand poured the remainder of the coffee into their cups. He eyeballed Moore as he slurped from his coffee cup.

Moore wiped bacon grease from his lips and sat back, sipping hot coffee.

"We need to provide my contact with evidence linking Wang and possibly the moles he controls in the federal government. Any ideas?"

Brand nodded.

"We have the memory stick. What else can we get our hands on?"

"I have an idea I think you are going to get behind one hundred percent."

52

HA WANG WAS ON THE PHONE as he entered the back door of his limo. The driver closed the door behind him then moved to the front driver side door. He didn't notice that the driver took longer than necessary to open the door and take his seat behind the wheel.

"I am headed to the airport now. I will be in D.C. by close of business today," Wang said into the phone. "You have my itinerary. Send a car for me on the tarmac. I'll come to you."

Wang ended the call as the driver put the car in gear.

"Get a move on," Wang ordered the sluggish driver. "I've got a plane waiting."

"Yes sir," the driver replied with a friendly tone. I need to unlock the doors for a moment. I hope you don't mind."

"I do mind," Wang complained as the door lock snapped up and the left side door opened.

Brand entered the limo back seat with a gun trained on Wang.

"Sit still, Wang," Brand said in a steady voice. "Give me your phone, please."

Wang hesitated as he struggled to grasp the significance of Brand's appearance.

Brand helped him by batting him in the face with the barrel assembly of the 9mm Glock pistol.

Wang clutched his nose and held the phone out to Brand. Brand took the phone and pocketed it, careful not to accidentally make a call.

The driver, Dennis Moore, drove away from the Tel Gong facility, headed towards the small airfield just outside of Uvalde. He parked the car in one of the parking slots near the private hangar owned by Tel Gong. The three walked together to the awaiting private jet. They climbed the steps to the plane.

A well coifed female flight attendant welcomed them.

"Hello Mr. Wang," she said with a wide smile. "We weren't expecting your two guests. We'll note the change on the manifest. Please take your seats gentlemen. We will be departing shortly."

The flight to Washington DC took nearly four hours. After dismissing the flight attendant under the guise of conducting an important secret meeting, Brand and Moore spent that time looking through Wang's phone and briefing him on his duties when they landed.

At first Wang was resistant, but he finally agreed to meet their requests rather than suffer amputation of three of the fingers on his right hand. After releasing the digits from the adjustable vice grips, they assured him he would regain the use of those fingers in a few days.

A car met them when they landed at Ronald Reagan. Moore overcame the driver's objections with his FBI badge and sat in the front seat. Brand accompanied Wang in the back, tapping him with the Glock when he seemed to be occupied with planning his escape rather than focusing on what they required of him.

Moore waited until they had crossed into D.C. proper to give the driver an additional stop on the way to FBI headquarters.

"We need to make a quick stop at 601 4th street."

"My instructions are clear Special Agent Moore, directly to the Hoover Building with no stops."

Moore frowned at the driver.

"You are new here," Moore observed. "This won't take long, only a minute or two. You won't be missed."

Moore, Brand and Wang left the car idling at the curb before the Washington FBI Field Office in downtown DC. They entered the side door of a converted blood drive bus.

Inside, they unlocked Wang's phone with his facial recognition app, then handed his phone and the memory stick over to Sandy Kincaid, a reporter for the Washington Post. She took the phone through a narrow corridor to a back room in the bus.

Wang protested weakly until she returned the phone to him.

She handed the memory stick to Moore.

"Please get a copy to Homeland Security Chief of Homeland Security Niel," Moore instructed the reporter. "She will take it from here."

"Will do, Dennis," she agreed. "I'm going to press immediately with this."

"That's our deal," Moore confirmed.

They returned to the idling car.

In minutes, the car stopped before the J Edgar Hoover Building. The driver was silent as he figured out that he had been used and was likely to be taken into custody for his part.

Brand left Moore and Wang on the sidewalk. He disappeared into the busy pedestrian traffic before the building.

Moore escorted Wang inside the lobby of the large FBI headquarters building where he placed him under arrest for espionage.

Within ten minutes he was on the 11th floor, standing before FBI Director Rayburn himself. Moore had never seen him in person. He had seen him only on TV where he testified before congress. He lacked the polished persona he presented before the committee in the capital chambers.

"What kind of stunt are you trying to pull Special Agent Moore?" Rayburn asked with easily conjured self-righteous indignation.

"I'm calling for your resignation, Director Rayburn. I am also placing you under arrest for treason."

"Moore," Rayburn said with impressive calm. "You are known for your conspiracy theories and your right leaning flights of fancy, but you have taken it too far this time. Your career is over."

"I know that you and your counterpart in Langley are complicit in a plot with the Chinese Communist Party to undermine the American government and the American people."

"Strictly to humor your ridiculous claims, Agent Moore, there is a huge difference between claiming to know something and being able to prove the claim."

Rayburn motioned to men standing outside the door to his office.

Three agents entered the office and arrayed themselves behind Moore.

"Place Special Agent Moore under arrest. He and his co-conspirators will face charges of sedition and treason."

Moore glanced at the three agents then looked once more at Rayburn.

"We have the thumb drive with Wang's conversation on it and we have your cell number in his phone and phone records accounting several phone calls made between the two of you during specific times intersecting violent actions against American citizens and federal agents."

Rayburn's desk phone rang.

Rayburn ignored the call as he considered Moore and his claims.

"You should answer the call," Moore advised him.

The phone rang three more times before he picked up.

"Director Rayburn here," he said into the phone.

He was silent for a long moment as he listened to the caller. Finally, he handed the phone to Moore with a frown.

"She wants to speak to you."

Moore took the phone. Homeland Security Director Niel was on the call.

"Hold your position, Agent Moore. DOJ officials are en route to take Rayburn into custody. Good work. I am in possession of the drive and the contents of Ha Wang's phone data. I'll catch up with you later."

The phone went dead. Moore heard a commotion outside the office as alarming rumors about their boss went the rounds of the building.

Finally, the door burst open, and half a dozen DOJ officials and federal officers entered the office. Moore watched as Rayburn was cuffed and taken away, complaining about the indignity he was suffering.

53

BRAND SAT OUTSIDE THE Smithsonian Museum in the shade of a grove of old trees on the Ellipse. He had wanted to visit the museum all his life. He recalled his father promising that they would go to Washington together and tour the nation's capital. That promise would not be kept.

Brand was here, now, under the strangest of circumstances. He was alone in the home of every federal policing agency looking for him. His last call before disposing of the burner phone Moore loaned him was to contact the agent one last time. He and Moore set this place for a meeting.

Brand was in possession of a bus ticket back to Texas and a pocketful of cartel cash. He had no identification and no belongings. His gym bag of personal things was still in the bedroom in the FBI safehouse in San Antonio.

"Hey cowboy," Moore said from behind Brand.

Brand started at Moore's sudden appearance.

"Drop back to Defcon five my man, It's only me."

Brand rose and accepted Moore's hand.

"Have a seat and I'll catch you up."

They sat on the bench. Both were silent for a moment in their thoughts. Brand listened to the birds. The troubles of man seemed far away indeed in the songs of the birds as they fretted about their own troubles and needs.

"First off," Moore began. "You are cleared of any wrongdoing. The gunplay with the mercenaries will be dismissed as self-defense. The two DEA agents are being investigated. The caliber of the rounds that killed the agents don't match your gun. The one that killed Kilgore was obviously from the sniper rifle belonging to the shooter they found near the pool.

"There is an investigation into the county lockup where Dehra Duncan was murdered. They have a suspect, an Audrey Pyle in custody. She has freely confessed to the crime. Rayburn is in custody as is the director of the CIA. They are reportedly singing like the birds here, giving details on their confederates and the details of the conspiracy. It seems to go deep into the Administration and touches every federal agency including the DOJ."

"Did you find your men?" Brand asked.

"All three are safe and sound. They were detained in office until I was 'handled' when I went 'rogue.' These were the words of FBI higher ups."

What about Wang?" Brand asked.

Moore frowned and shook his head.

"With the strained relations with China, Wang is being handled with kid gloves. He is claiming diplomatic immunity. My sense is that he will not qualify because of the charges pending against him and his company. Tel Gong is under scrutiny from the FCC and Federal Trade Commission for antitrust violations. I doubt the company will continue to operate in the U.S. I wouldn't be surprised if Wang ultimately claims asylum. The CCP does not handle failure very well."

Brand studied his hands for a long moment as he grappled with the anger struggling to rise to the surface. The idea of Wang not only getting off without punishment, but becoming a U.S. citizen, was galling in light of his part in Dehra's murder.

"What are your plans now that you are a free man?"

Brand shrugged.

"I guess I'll head back to Texas. I don't have any other play."

"I've got an idea if you are open to something new."

Brand looked curiously at Moore who grinned good-naturedly in return.

"Well?" Brand urged.

"I have a friend, a former Navy Seal baddass type. I told him about you and how well you did at Camp Bravura. I gave him some general bullet points about your field application of those skills. He normally only accepts prior service special operators in his company, but he says he is interested in chatting with you."

"Is this like Blackwater or something?"

"Blackwater is a relic of the past, Brand. The corporate security business is far more sophisticated than it was then. He runs a company called Sovereign Services, Limited. He provides personal and corporate security for the wealthy and for officials in developing countries. He has different levels of personnel required for his operation. He is willing to start you in entry level corporate security, you know, C Suite folks. Plenty of upside potential and the money is good. What do you think?"

"I'm not interested in being a security guard in a lobby or tooling around a shopping center in a truck with a blue light."

"That is not what he does. You won't find many Navy Seal types working as security guards in malls. The gig comes with inherent dangers and risks. I think it is right up your alley."

"I'm interested. How do I meet this guy, what's his name?"

"Dick Riser. He headquarters in Maryland, not far from here. I can set up a meet for you for tomorrow if you want."

"That's really his name?"

"Don't be an ass. It's Richard, and he is a highly decorated war hero."

"I'm grateful for his service."

"So does tomorrow work with your busy schedule?"

"Let's make the meeting next week and I am good."

"Brand don't jerk me around on this one. I'm going out on a limb vouching for you."

"I've got one last thing to do then I am completely available. Moore, I still have stuff in the safe house."

You have some shitty clothes and travel size toiletries in that bag."

"So, you did go through my bag while I was asleep."

"I'm a cop. Of course, I went through your stuff while you were asleep."

"I've got to say goodbye to some folks. Look, Moore. Don't make me explain it. This war hero and his company have been operating just fine without me, surely, they can wait a couple more days for me to swoop in and save them from ruin and bankruptcy."

"Alright smartass. I'll let him know Monday week. I'll tell him by close of business. Does that suit your busy travel schedule?"

"Perfectly."

They stood from the bench. Moore stuck out his hand.

Brand took it.

Moore looked keenly into Brand's eyes.

"Thank you for saving my ass back there. I owe you, friend. I won't forget it."

"Don't make a bid deal of it," Brand said, repeating Moore's words. "I hate it when you cry."

"Smartass," Moore muttered.

"I hear you Dennis," Brand said soberly. "You don't owe me a thing. You are my only friend now. That means a lot to me. Stay in touch."

"You too."

Brand walked towards the Lincoln Memorial, leaving Moore behind.

Epilogue

WANG LANDED AT HOUSTON Intercontinental Airport. From there he boarded a thirty-minute hop to San Antonio International Airport. After much to do he was able to hire a car at transportation. He had been lucky to escape Washington. He was released on diplomatic immunity, but the Chinese consulate counselor advised him to leave the country as soon as possible. He doubted the diplomatic immunity would hold up long-term with the ongoing investigations. Wang's negotiations for asylum with the U.S. State Department were not public yet, but it would not be long before that changed. He had one last errand to accomplish before he cut ties with China.

He had a back-up plan for just this eventuality. He had to get access to the safe in his office. Tel Gong was controlled by someone new. The American based operations were being closed and moved to Baumholder, Germany.

With a little luck he could sneak into his old office, secure the cash, stock certificates, and bearer bonds he had accumulated during his years in America, then get out again undetected.

The corporate relocation wasn't surprising to him. He had always believed America was too big a bite, even for China. Starting smaller with a splintering Europe was a more reasonable goal. Of late the EU was in a constant state of turmoil and upheaval. Covert operations on an international scale would be easier in that environment. No matter. Wang was no longer a part of it.

He could not return to China. He would be jailed in the best-case scenario or killed in a more likely scenario. America provided a pleasant choice in which to live out his days. With his nest egg, he could carve out a very comfortable life for himself. Maybe he would even end up with a beautiful wife and a family.

He arrived at the Uvalde plant. He instructed the driver to wait in the parking lot for him. He made his way in silence to his office. As anticipated, the place was in a state of rushed chaos. Security was nearly non-existent. Those who recognized him had no idea what his status was within the company. He arrived at the double doors to his office. He pulled one of the doors open. He was surprised that the office was unlocked but not worried. His safe was a floor safe under the area rug under his desk. He was the only one who knew of it.

Despite the darkness in the office, Wang didn't bother to turn on the lights. He knew his old office intimately and he would be quick at his task. He shoved his desk forward towards the entry doors, exposing a large enough portion of the large rug to fold it out of the way. Once clear, the bare tiled floor contained the dark square face of the floor safe in bold relief, even in the dim conditions.

He spun the dial tumbler deftly, pulling open the safe door. He collected a canvas bag, preloaded with what he came for. He closed the door and pulled the rug back over the safe. He didn't bother moving the desk. He would be gone long before someone checked the room.

Slinging the heavy canvas bag over his shoulder, he made his way towards the doors. He heard two chirps of a silenced pistol. His chest burned where the two bullets passed through. Wang fell to the floor. A masked gunman approached from a corner of the darkened room. He placed a final round between the COO's eyes then collected the canvas bag. He shouldered the bag and left the room.

Brand sat across the bar from Karen. As usual, she was busy with thirsty bar patrons. Brand spun the highball glass in his fingers, watching the ice and bourbon swirl with the motion. He lifted the glass and emptied its contents in a single swallow.

Karen refilled his glass with a smile.

"What do you think of the new place?" she asked with shining eyes.

"You weren't out of work for long," Brand commented as he looked around. "I see a lot of familiar faces from the Dog. I could drink here."

"We are so lucky to get your seal of approval," Karen said sarcastically with a smile that took the edge off it.

"I'm just not sure about the name," Brand continued. "Barflies? Not very pretty."

"You'll get used to it. Everyone else has."

Brand made no rejoinder. He sipped the fresh Bourbon with an appropriately squinted reaction to the familiar burn of the booze.

Brand entered a large modern building through towering glass entry doors. He checked in with security before he was allowed into the offices of Sovereign Services, Limited. A well-dressed receptionist greeted hm with learned proficiency.

"Mr. Riser is expecting you," she said. "Please take a seat and I'll notify you when he is ready to receive you. May I offer you something to drink?"

"No thank you," Brand replied as he moved to the waiting area where he took a seat in one of the expensive leather chairs. He had hardly found a comfortable position when the receptionist informed him that Mr. Riser would see him now.

Brand took an elevator to the fifth floor where the doors opened to a large glass walled office overlooking downtown Bethesda. He took in the huge office in a quick survey.

Riser stood behind his desk. He was every bit of six inches over six feet tall. His build showed fitness and power. His jaw was covered by a well-trimmed dark beard. His piercing blue eyes cut into his guest as he made his initial appraisal of the new man.

He came around the desk and grasped Brand's hand in a muscular grip.

"Carson Brand," he said with real warmth. "I'm Richard Riser. Dennis tells me you are quite the operator. It's good to meet you in the flesh. Join me at the bar."

Riser led the way to a long glass and steel bar as fully stocked as any night club in town. He poured two bourbons, handing one to Brand.

Brand followed the big man's lead, sitting at one of the sturdy bar stools. They sipped their cocktails for a full minute before Riser broke the silence.

"Have you just arrived in town or are you settled in yet?"

"I just got here."

"Excellent. I'll have Courtney get you settled in. How are you set for cash, transportation, or personal effects?"

"Aren't we moving ahead of ourselves? I was expecting an interview – maybe a couple of probing questions."

Riser laughed good-naturedly.

"I interviewed you when you stepped off of that elevator. We've already done an extensive background on you. I know more about you than you know about yourself. I know the real thing when I see it. What about you, Brand? Did you do your homework on us?"

"Only what is on your web site and available to search."

"It's obvious that you will not fill one of our analyst roles. That is a good thing. I prefer hard blunt objects on my teams. I, of course, require intellect, but applied to situational awareness, reaction to threats, and problem solving in the field."

Brand drained his bourbon. He watched the big former SEAL appraisingly. He felt unmistakably that the man watched his every move, down to the minutiae level.

"You're right," Riser agreed to whatever he thought was going through Brand's mind. "You have a lot to learn. It won't take long. You have good bones, as is so popular to say. I have to warn you. We are a cliquish bunch, mostly SEAL's. Acceptance will not come easy or soon. Are you in?"

Brand smiled at the strange interview he was enduring.

"Yeah," he replied, extending his hand. "I'm in."

ABOUT THE AUTHOR

CRAIG RAINEY (1962 -) WAS BORN IN SAN ANGELO, TEXAS, AND LIVES IN AUSTIN. HE IS AN AWARD-WINNING FILM ACTOR, AUTHOR, SCREENWRITER, AND MUSICIAN. HE COWBOYED PROFESSIONALLY, IS A MILITARY VETERAN, AND HAS APPEARED ON SCREEN IN MORE THAN 60 FILMS.